A KILLER RETREAT

A Downward Dog Mystery

TRACY WEBER

D0188485

MIDNIGHT INK
WOODBURY, MINNESOTA

FIRST EDITION
First Printing, 2015

Book design by Donna Burch-Brown
Cover design by Kevin R. Brown
Cover illustration: Nicole Alesi/Deborah Wolfe Ltd
Edited by Connie Hill

Midnight Ink, an imprint of Llewellyn Worldwide Ltd.

This is a work of fiction. Names, characters, places, and incidents are either the product of the author's imagination or are used fictitiously, and any resemblance to actual persons, living or dead, business establishments, events, or locales is entirely coincidental.

Library of Congress Cataloging-in-Publication Data

Weber, Tracy.
    A killer retreat : a downward dog mystery / Tracy Weber. — First edition.
        pages cm. — (A downward dog mystery ; 2)
    ISBN 978-0-7387-4209-0
    I. Title.
    PS3623.E3953K55   2015
    813'.6—dc23   2014032995

Midnight Ink
Llewellyn Worldwide Ltd.
2143 Wooddale Drive
Woodbury, MN 55125-2989
www.midnightinkbooks.com

Printed in the United States of America

"Fun characters, a gorgeous German Shepherd dog, and a murder with more suspects than you can shake a stick at. *Killer Retreat* is a must read for cozy fans!"

—Sparkle Abbey, author of the
Pampered Pet Mystery series

Murder Strikes a Pose

"Cozy fans will eagerly await the next installment."

—*Publishers Weekly*

"*Murder Strikes a Pose* by Tracy Weber is a delightful debut novel featuring Kate Davidson, a caring but feist yoga teacher…Namaste to Weber and her fresh, new heroine!"

—Penny Warner, author of
How to Dine on Killer Wine

"[T]his charming debut mystery…pieces together a skillful collage of mystery, yoga, and plenty of dog stories against the unique backdrop of Seattle characters and neighborhoods. The delightful start of a promising new series. I couldn't put it down!"

—Waverly Fitzgerald, author of
Dial C for Chihuahua

"Three woofs for Tracy Weber's first Downward Dog Mystery, *Murder Strikes a Pose*. Great characters, keep-you-guessing plot, plenty of laughs, and dogs—what more could we want? Ah, yes—the next book!"

—Sheila Webster Boneham, award-winning author of
Drop Dead on Recall

A KILLER RETREAT

DEDICATION

To my husband Marc. Without your support
my writing wouldn't be possible.

ACKNOWLEDGMENTS

I always assumed writing would be a lonely endeavor. I couldn't have been more wrong. Thank you to the readers who have contacted me to tell me that they've enjoyed my work and to the writers who've encouraged me to keep persevering. Your support means the world to me.

For *A Killer Retreat*, I have so many people to thank that I don't even know where to begin.

My mom Marcia's enthusiastic support of the series has touched me, and I'm pretty sure she has single-handedly kept the Billings Barnes and Noble in business since my first book was released. My yoga students have attended events, read my work, and given me encouragement even when I've struggled. My wonderful agent, Margaret Bail, editors Terri Bischoff and Connie Hill at Midnight Ink, and freelance editor Marta Tanrikulu have all given me invaluable help and feedback.

Special thanks to D.P. Lyle MD, who helped me work out the technical details of the crimes in this book. He is kind, generous with his time, and an invaluable resource to all of us in the crime writing community. Of course if there are any errors in this work, they are completely mine.

My husband, Marc, supports me in all of my crazy endeavors but chooses to work in the background, designing and maintaining my website, creating marketing materials, helping me brainstorm plot points, and putting up with the angst, heartache, joy, frustration, and excitement that are all part of being a writer. Thank you, honey.

Finally, I have to acknowledge my own personal Bella, German shepherd Tasha. You're getting older, sweetie, so we don't have as many adventures as we used to, but rest assured that you are woven into the fabric of my stories and branded on my heart. I hope we have many more years together. You will always be my inspiration and the greatest joy of my life.

ONE

"THIS IS BAD, MICHAEL. She's not responding. I think she might be dead."

Queasy unease tugged at my belly; anxiety shortened my breath. What if my plan had been reckless? What if the universe was cautioning me—warning me to abort? I turned to Michael for guidance.

"What was I thinking? I can't be away from the yoga studio for ten days. Maybe this is a sign."

"Of mental illness, maybe," he grumbled.

I ignored the world's grumpiest boyfriend and continued shaking my shiny new cell phone, like an exasperated mother trying to rouse a slumbering teenager. The screen remained dark. I turned the device sideways and tapped it against the dashboard. Nothing. Frustrated, I pounded on the phone's back with the heel of my hand. Maybe a high-tech Heimlich maneuver would convince it to cough up my messages.

"Would you *please* stop messing with that thing?" Michael snapped. "That's the twelfth time you've checked messages since we left Seattle. And calling it 'she' is just plain creepy. It's not female."

"Of course she is." I pointed to the cartoon chicken on the cover. "It says right here: Yoga Chick. Besides, she's wearing a pink headband. If she were the Yoga Dude, she'd wear blue."

Michael closed his eyes and rubbed the center of his forehead. "Fine. Have it your way. It's a girl. Either way, we're on vacation. Now put that damned thing away."

I grumped right back at him. "*You're* on vacation. I'm working." I tossed the traitorous device on the dashboard. "Which is more than I can say for this piece of garbage." I sighed. "I miss Old Reliable. He may not have had a camera or Internet access, but he was a lot easier to use."

Against my better judgment, I'd let my best friend Rene talk me into buying a smart phone for my ten-day working vacation on Orcas Island. She promised me that I'd love my new technological wonder child—that it would make staying connected with my yoga studio a breeze, even from a remote retreat center. She swore the only thing I'd regret was that I hadn't purchased it earlier. Now, parked at the Anacortes ferry terminal waiting to board the three-fifty ferry, I realized there was one fatal flaw in her argument: I was a certified techno-klutz. I'd never figure out how to use the blasted thing.

Michael shook his head. "Kate, you have major control issues. We've been gone for three hours. I promise you, the yoga studio hasn't burned down yet."

"How do you know? What if I forgot to blow out the candles? The whole place may have gone up in flames." I retrieved the phone from the dashboard and pressed random places on the screen, hoping it would magically come back to life. "I wonder if I accidentally turned it off again."

Michael looked up at the ceiling and mumbled. "Please don't let there be cell phone reception on Orcas."

My mouth felt suddenly dry. "Honey, please. Don't even joke about that. I'm freaked out enough as it is. Remember, you only have one employee to worry about. I have eight."

Michael seemed surprisingly blasé about leaving his pet supply store, Pete's Pets, while we went on our first vacation together, especially since he was leaving it in the hands of my nemesis, Tiffany. As much as I envied his confidence, I couldn't quite replicate it.

I hadn't gone on vacation since opening Serenity Yoga over two years ago. I'd barely gotten used to leaving the other instructors in charge while I worked from home a few afternoons a week. Agreeing to travel 120 miles to an island only accessible by ferry? I must have been crazy.

Michael grabbed the phone from my hands and pressed his index finger against the screen—in the exact same place I'd touched only seconds before. The phone immediately came to life. "Oh, for God's sake, Kate. The phone's fine." He pointed at the missed calls indicator. Zero. "Nobody's called. They probably haven't even noticed that you're gone yet." He leaned across the seat, stuffed the Yoga Chick in the glove box, and locked it.

"What the he—"

"Your phone privileges have officially been revoked. The studio can live without you for the next half hour." He tucked the key into his front pants pocket.

I considered reaching inside his trousers to retrieve it, but the elderly couple parked next to us might not have appreciated the show. I gave him a sultry pout instead, hoping to make him feel guilty.

"Stop sulking, Kate. It won't work. The phone's mine now." He smiled at me mischievously. "If you're really good, I'll teach you how to check e-mail on the ferry." He opened the driver's side door. "Let's take Bella for a walk."

At the sound of the w-word, Bella, my hundred-pound German shepherd, woke up from her nap, pressed her nose against the SUV's window, and whined, clearly agreeing with Michael's plan.

That made one of us.

I scanned the parking lot. "I don't know, Michael. That doesn't seem like such a great idea. There are a lot of dogs out there. I'd rather wait until we get to Elysian Springs. At least we know leashes are required there."

The center's leash policy was the first question I asked when Alicia, my studio's landlord, talked me into taking the week-long teaching position at the newly reopened retreat center. Bella's reactivity toward other dogs had improved significantly in the six months I'd owned her, but her training wasn't yet foolproof. I had no desire to spend Michael's and my time together running frantically away from off-leash dogs and their oblivious owners.

Michael looked at his watch. "It's only two-thirty, Kate. We've got over an hour until we can board the ferry. Who wants to spend it sitting in the car?" He pointed to the edge of the parking lot. "Besides, look at the sign."

I read it out loud. "Leash laws strictly enforced. All animals must be under restraint."

Michael wrinkled his brow, feigning concern. "On second thought, you'd better stay in the car. I forgot your muzzle." I playfully slugged him on the shoulder. His grin spread from his lips to his sparkling blue-green eyes. "Besides, look at Bella. She's literally drooling for a chance to play on that beach."

He was right—about the drooling dog, that is. Wet saliva droplets fell from Bella's lower lip and landed in an ever-expanding puddle at the edge of her seat. She whined and pressed her nose against the window, clearly willing the door to open.

And who could blame her?

The backdrop surrounding us was gorgeous—almost a study in color. Bright yellow wind socks fluttered aimlessly toward Puget Sound's purple-blue water, as if pointing to the emerald-green hills of the San Juan Islands. Seagulls cawed overhead, begging for handouts.

There wasn't a raindrop in sight.

Thirty-two Puget Sound winters had taught me that mid-October sunshine was a treasure, not to be wasted. Any day now, nature's paintbrush would gray-wash the area with ten straight months of rain. This might be our last sunny afternoon until August.

"All right, you two, you win. But give me a minute to get ready."

I double-checked the contents of my fanny pack. Dog waste bags, check. Disgusting, freeze-dried lamb lung, check. Emergency bottle of Spot Stop, check. I hadn't been forced to use the citronella dog-stopping spray yet, but like any self respecting Boy Scouts wannabe, I figured it paid to be prepared.

I tossed in some kissably fresh breath mints and attached Bella's leash to the front of her harness. Only one more item to double check before I could fully relax. I climbed out of the passenger side door, inhaled the cool, brackish breeze, and popped open the back of the SUV. I moved Michael's suitcase to the side and opened the cooler. Bella's medicine was still there, right underneath the packs of Blue Ice.

"For God's sake, Kate. Now you're checking for Bella's enzymes again? Do I have to throw them in the glove box with your phone?"

I ignored his teasing barb and closed the trunk. Checking the cooler for the third time since leaving Seattle might seem a tad neurotic, but I had good reason. Feeding a dog with EPI—Exocrine Pancreatic Insufficiency—was no trivial matter. The autoimmune disease had destroyed Bella's pancreas, leaving her unable to digest food without special prescription enzymes. When I adopted Bella after her owner's murder six months ago, she was literally starving to death. She'd gained over twenty-five pounds since then, but I couldn't afford to be complacent. Bella could lose that weight in a heartbeat.

Our comfortable—if complicated—feeding routine involved grinding Bella's grain-free kibble to a powder, adding three separate types of powdered medicine, mixing it all in warm—never hot—water, and allowing the disgusting-looking concoction to sit and "incubate" for at least twenty minutes. Dogs with EPI need to eat multiple small meals, so I fed Bella three times a day. Mealtime was tough enough to get right at home. When traveling, it could easily become a nightmare.

I brought along two duffel bags filled with Bella's feeding supplies, but even I had to draw the line at lugging along my industrial-strength grinder. So I prepared all thirty of Bella's meals in advance—except for adding water and the most important of the powdered ingredients, the enzymes. Since they had to remain cool, I'd packed them on ice. Michael could complain about my obsessive-compulsive tendencies all he wanted. Bella would starve without that medicine, and I wasn't willing to risk leaving it behind.

I walked to the driver's side door, leaned through the open window, and planted a kiss on his still-grumbling lips. "You're right. The medicine's in the cooler, right where I packed it." I paused. "But I still think we should have brought Bella's crate."

Michael shrugged. "I already told you. The crate didn't fit. We could bring Bella, or we could bring her crate. Not both."

I frowned. "Being without it makes me nervous. Maybe we should have driven both vehicles..." I looked back toward Seattle, which was over ninety minutes away.

Michael must have read my thoughts. "We're not going back, Kate."

"But—"

"Look around. We're already boxed in. We couldn't get out of the parking lot if we tried." He opened the door. "Bella and I are going to the beach. Are you coming?"

I didn't generally respond well to edicts, but in this case, Michael was right. The only way to get the Explorer out of this parking lot was to drive it onto the ferry. We might as well enjoy ourselves until then. I grabbed Bella's leash. "Come on, girl, let's go."

Bella leaped from the car and glued her nose to the ground, pausing only long enough to cover up the scent of another dog's urine with her own. The three of us walked across the holding area through several lines of densely parked cars until we reached the edge of the asphalt. I peered down the steep, football field-sized embankment that led to the beach, but I couldn't make out a clear trail. A jungle of blooming brown cattails, tall grasses, and thorny blackberry bushes obscured my view past the first several yards.

I pointed toward a man-made path that paralleled the beach, about twenty feet above it. "I don't know, Michael. Maybe we should stay up here on the walkway. I'd rather go to the beach, but if we stick to the paved trail, at least we can see more than five feet in front of us."

Bella sensed my reticence, but she clearly didn't share it. She sniffed the air, whined impatiently, and lunged forward, dragging me down the hill toward the brackish water.

"Kate, wait!" Michael yelled at my back.

"Bella, stop!" I yelled at Bella's.

The hundred-pound, beach-seeking missile didn't even slow down. I held on tight and ran full speed behind her. One quick turn right and Bella skidded to a stop, blocked by a dense, thorny blackberry bush. She paused long enough to sniff the air again, then reversed course and zoomed past Michael. Michael had quick reflexes—he owned a pet store, after all. He dealt with out-of-control canines every day. He dove for her leash.

Bella was quicker.

She zigged under his outstretched arms and zagged past his legs, dragging me through an ankle-deep mud puddle. My shoes made a disgusting thwok as they pulled from the muck.

I stumbled behind Bella past two more dead ends, until she finally found an opening. She jumped over a tree root, soared over one final crest, and agilely landed mere feet from the water. I tripped over the same obstacles and splatted face-first into the dirt.

An annoyed-looking, out-of-breath Michael grabbed Bella's leash and pulled me to my feet. "Why'd you two take off without me?"

I'm fine, Michael, really. Thanks for asking.

I wiped at the caked mud on my pants and looked toward the water. This was what all of the fuss was about?

The vista before me consisted of a muddy, fishy-smelling expanse of muck strewn with dead seaweed, discarded logs, and the occasional seagull's corpse. By human standards, it wasn't exactly postcard material. But to Bella and her cavorting canine friends, it was a veritable doggie Disneyland.

Bella whined, danced, and pulled at the end of her leash, begging to frolic in the water. I was tempted to unhook her leash and let her run, but it was too risky. Bella loved most people, but dogs were a different story. Given a choice, she was more likely to eat a pugnacious pug than invite it for dinner.

Fortunately, Bella didn't seem to mind her six-foot tether. She was too busy waging war on a piece of driftwood half-buried in the muck. She gripped the exposed end between her molars and planted her rear paws. A series of sharp, growl-ridden tugs later, the waterlogged wood flew through the air, spraying my shirt with a rainbow of algae and decomposing seaweed. Bella the Conqueror shook her head vigorously, play-killing her new favorite stick and splattering me in even more slime.

I took Michael's hand as we headed south along the beach and away from the ferry terminal. Bella alternated between dragging me along the shore and playing "tug the disgusting, slimy stick" with Michael. I mourned my muck-covered shoes, wiped algae off my shirt, and gazed longingly up at the walking trail Bella had vetoed. The asphalt path was liberally dotted with scenic outlooks, wooden benches, and strategically placed garbage cans. It was obviously where the sane people walked.

There wasn't a dog person among them.

All of us crazy dog people tiptoed through goose droppings while lugging around plastic bags filled with dog waste.

Michael didn't seem to notice. He let go of my hand, picked up a rock, and tossed it deep out into the water. He pointed to a preschool-aged boy scavenging treasures along the shoreline.

"He's cute, isn't he?" Michael's eyes held a faraway look. "Think we'll have kids someday?"

I felt the blood drain from my face. Children? Did he just ask me about children?

Michael and I had been dating for six months, and until now, he'd never mentioned wanting a family. Kids were fine—great even—as long as they were someone else's. But one of my own? The only experience I had with children was in the Mommy and Me yoga class, and even then, I chose to remain on the sidelines. From what I could tell as an observer, the teacher of those exhausted-looking moms and their cute-but-often-screaming progeny should be nominated for sainthood.

"Kate? You OK? You look a little pale."

I cleared the tightness out of my throat. "I'm fine." Time to change the subject. I pointed across the water at the Elwha, slowly chugging its way toward us. "Looks like the ferry's almost here. We should start heading back."

I silently chided myself as we walked back toward the car. Maybe picking this particular working vacation for Michael's and my first trip together hadn't been such a good idea. When I asked Michael to come with me, ten days away seemed exciting—romantic, even. But I hadn't considered the week's main event: the marriage ceremony of Elysian Springs' two caretakers, Emmy and Josh.

Michael had recently started to give me *the look*. I'd read about that look. I'd seen it in movies. I'd even daydreamed about it. But I'd never had *the look* flashed my way. I bolted long before I allowed any relationship to get that far. When it came to men, Rene said it best: I was a serial dumper.

But Michael was different. I didn't *want* to bolt from Michael. I adored him. Next to Bella, he was the best thing that had happened to me in a very long time.

Still, every time he gave me *the look*, I felt an almost irresistible urge to grab Bella, tuck her hundred-pound body under my arm, and run. Cohabiting for ten days might already strain our fledgling relationship. Attending a wedding? That was just asking for trouble.

Michael interrupted my musing. "Heads up, Kate. Trouble ahead."

My heart skipped a beat, and not in the titillating, romantic way Michael's look might imply. Several yards away, a small, yapping, black and white Jack Russell terrier bounded along the beach—by himself. He was almost completely white, with black ears and a single black spot that covered his right eye. Cute, in an incorrigible pirate sort of way.

At least 100 feet behind him walked, or more accurately teetered, a thin, blonde woman wearing spiky red heels, a leopard print miniskirt, and a disgusted frown. She held a cigarette in one hand and a cell phone in the other. I watched her pick her way through the seaweed, rocks, and other beach debris. My first thought was *take a look at that woman's outfit. She's obviously not from Seattle.* My second was *and her dog's about to get slaughtered.*

I waved to get her attention, but she didn't respond. I cupped my hands around my mouth and yelled, "Please call your dog!" Nothing. Maybe she couldn't hear me.

Unfortunately, the same couldn't be said for her canine companion. He turned toward my voice and quivered with excitement. I could even have sworn that he smiled.

Uh oh.

I commanded Bella in what I hoped was an enticing, yet authoritative, tone. "Bella, sit."

As trained, Bella turned her back to the off-leash dog, faced me, and plopped her rear on the ground, fully expecting the treat she was due. I pulled several pieces of dried lamb from my fanny pack, gave her one, and held the rest in reserve.

The terrier sniffed the air. His brown eyes glinted with interest.

My pretend authority morphed into all-too-real terror. I vigorously gesticulated at the phone-engrossed woman. "Hey!" I yelled, pointing at Bella. "This one doesn't like other dogs!" The oblivious owner looked up from her phone, frowned, and turned away.

The pup took one last glance at Bella, then made his decision.

Target acquired.

He bounded toward Bella, wearing a huge doggie grin. I swore I could read that crazy pup's mind. *This is going to be so much fun! First I'm going to eat all of those treats. Then I'm going to grab that big shepherd by her scruff, and we're going to wrestle and roll around on the ground. I'll jump on her back, and pull on her ears, and—*

Bella glared at the approaching menace, furrowed her brow, and sent me her own silent message. *I know it upsets you when I get angry. Therefore I will allow the annoying mosquito-dog to live. As long as it doesn't touch me or my food.*

This was not going to end well.

I grabbed Bella's harness, held on tight, and fed her a rapid-fire stream of treats. Michael stepped in front of us, pointed his index finger at the misfired rocket-dog, and yelled. "Go home! Now!"

That crazy dog never even slowed down. It ducked underneath Michael's outstretched arm, jumped straight up like pogo stick, and snatched Bella's treats from my hand.

Michael soared through the air like an unpadded football player. He reflexively grabbed the tiny creature midair then ran off in the opposite direction, putting as much distance between the two dogs as possible. The clearly unhappy pooch wiggled, squirmed, scratched, and yelped, trying to get away.

Bella made no attempt to hide her opinion of the rude stranger-dog. Her muscles tensed; her hair stood on end; she almost decapitated my treat hand and growled under her breath between swallows. But even though her eyes gleamed with malice, her body didn't move.

The overdressed dog walker finally reached us. She ended her phone call with a well-placed poke from a razor-sharp, burgundy-painted fingernail. Up close, I could tell that my first impression had been correct. This woman couldn't possibly be from Seattle. Pacific Northwesterners are notorious for wearing down-to-earth, casual attire. The heavily made-up woman before me wore a huge diamond ring on her fourth finger, matching full-carat studs in her earlobes, and a soft, buttery leather jacket that cost more than the average yoga teacher made in a month. I pasted on a warm smile, hoping to soften her brittle expression.

"I'm sorry about all of the fuss. Would you please hang on to your dog for a minute so we can get by?"

She ignored me and stomped up to Michael.

"Don't. Ever. Touch. My. Dog."

She snatched the wiggling pup from his hands and gave me a look that would have frozen a Popsicle. "There's nothing wrong with *my* dog." She pointed a sharp talon at Bella. "If you can't control *that* disgusting creature, you shouldn't take it out in public."

Prickly defensiveness needled the back of my neck. Who was she calling disgusting? *Her* dog was the one with the problem. Bella hadn't so much as twitched during the entire incident.

The burgundy-nailed socialite dropped her cigarette and stubbed it out underneath her stiletto. She tottered about ten feet away, then turned back to give one final comment.

"Bandit can run wherever he wants. Control your own damned dog!"

She dropped the still-off-leash terriorist back on the ground, pulled out her cell phone, and resumed walking. Bandit bolted toward Bella again.

I had no choice; the only way out of this predicament was up. "Bella, come!" I yelled. I pulled on her leash and ran toward the elevated trail as fast as my stubby five-foot-three-inch body could take me. Bella and I scurried up the rock wall to the path above, claws and shoes slipping on the steep incline. Michael played goalie, fending off the fifteen-pound fur ball. Once Bella and I were safely out of range, he scaled the rock wall after us.

I leaned on a picnic bench and gasped for air, reeling from a tornado-like storm of conflicting emotions: heart-stopping panic, growly defensiveness, righteous indignation—and more than a little leftover twitchiness from Michael's comment about children. In the midst of the chaos, my rattled mind grasped the familiar.

Rage.

"Stay here with Bella," I said through clenched teeth. My entire body was hot—ready to burst into flames. I felt like a fire breathing dragon covered in gasoline.

Michael blocked me and grabbed my arm. I tried to duck around him.

"What was that woman's problem?" I tried to pull my arm away, but Michael held on tight. "Let me go. I'm going after her. She can't let her dog charge Bella like that!"

Michael spoke in the tone used by parents of recalcitrant toddlers. "Leave it, Kate."

Leave it? Did he just say leave it?

"Leave it" was a common dog command, one I'd been trying to teach Bella for weeks. When I said "leave it," Bella was supposed to ignore whatever she was going after and pay attention to me.

Unfortunately for Michael, I wasn't yet trained.

I was about to tell Michael *what* he could leave and precisely *where* he could leave it, when a voice sounded over the loudspeaker. "Now boarding walk-on passengers for the three-fifty sailing to Orcas Island. Drivers, please return to your vehicles."

The prospect of missing the ferry quashed my inner inferno. If we missed this sailing, we were in for a long wait. The next ferry didn't leave until eight. I took several deep breaths, trying to rein in my Mount Vesuvius-like temper.

Michael's voice softened. "Kate, honey, let it go. Not everyone understands how dangerous it is to let their dogs run out of control like that. You won't change her mind, anyway. We need to head back to the car." He released my arm. "Besides, we'll probably never see her again. She doesn't seem like the roughing-it type."

My spine still tingled with electric annoyance, but deep down inside, I knew Michael was right. Nobody wore an expensive leather jacket and diamond studs to a vegan retreat center. I'd gain nothing by creating a scene. Nothing but embarrassment and a four-hour wait for the next ferry.

The sound of starting car engines rumbled from the holding area.

I frowned toward the beach; Bella whined and pulled toward the parking lot.

"Kate?"

"OK. Let's head back."

Michael admonished me as we hurried back to the ferry. "That temper of yours is going to get you into real trouble some day."

TWO

"I STILL CAN'T BELIEVE the nerve of that stupid b—"

Michael gave me a stern look.

"Of that stupid *beach witch*."

"Don't call her a witch, either. Ease off on the mean nicknames. There's no need to be snide."

"But she *was* a witch! How could she call Bella disgusting? Bella was an angel! Her dog, on the other hand..."

Michael gripped the Explorer's steering wheel so hard his knuckles turned white. I'd managed to complain for three hours straight about our ill-fated dog encounter. I fumed during the sixty-five minute ferry ride, griped the entire drive to Eastsound, Orcas Island's largest city, and grumbled through every bite of our otherwise delicious Mexican dinner. My irritated complaints burned hotter than the jalapeño margaritas I slurped between sentences.

No doubt about it, I was still angry. But I was also practicing a skill never taught in *The Yoga Sutras*: active avoidance. After listening to me rant for 180 minutes straight, Michael would be in no mood to discuss our future progeny or daydream about weddings. I glanced at my watch. Three hours down, 237 more to go. If I didn't come up with a new way to distract him soon, it could be a very long trip.

"I'm telling you, Michael, that woman—"

"For goodness sake, Kate. Don't you need to check your voice mail or something?"

I continued grumbling, but I pulled out my cell phone—which Michael had returned to me on the ferry—and poked at it repeatedly with my index finger until it finally turned on.

Michael reached over and turned up the radio.

Twenty music-filled, conversation-free minutes later, we arrived at Elysian Springs. Michael drove down a long gravel driveway and parked next to a multi-acre field dotted with picnic tables, fire pits, and volleyball nets. A large, six-sided yurt stood on one end; children's playground equipment occupied the other.

I opened the car door and took a deep breath of nature's finest air freshener—a mixture of salt, pine, and a scent I could only describe as pure, unadulterated oxygen. The sky had turned blue-black, but the moon glowed pale yellow, illuminating the area around me.

I stretched the stiffness out of my back and slowly turned a full circle to take in my surroundings. The property was huge—much larger than I'd imagined. An eclectic variety of ancient log cabins, small painted sheds, and multilevel houses dotted the horizon. Signs pointed the way to the beach, several hiking trails, the center's campgrounds, and an organic garden. A newer-looking group of buildings housed some of the facility's recently added amenities, including a library, restaurant, hot tubs, and sauna. Michael and I would have no trouble occupying our free time.

Michael took Bella for a brief walk to explore her new territory while I followed a dimly lit path to a building marked "Office." Each crunch of my shoes against the bark-covered trail released more of my tension. According to MapQuest, Michael and I had only travelled 120 miles from Seattle, but I felt like I'd disembarked on an entirely different planet.

As a yoga teacher, I made a living—albeit one barely above poverty level—helping others find inner peace. But I could never fully escape the noise of the city. The rumble of cars trapped on traffic-snarled highways, the pounding barrage of construction, the ever-present buzz of ambient electricity. Sound waves battered my eardrums 24/7, pummeling my nervous system with energetic dissonance.

But not here.

Here, my nervous system unwound in a soothing vacation from mechanized sound. All I could hear were the soft, breath-like sounds of the ocean punctuated by the hollow clunking of bamboo wind chimes. I'd been at Elysian Springs less than ten minutes, but I had already fallen in love. Someday I might have to move here.

A "Closed" sign hung from the office's door, but a large manila envelope with my name on it was taped to the front. The envelope contained two sets of keys to our cabin, a map of the grounds, and an invitation to attend an open house the following evening. A second, smaller envelope contained a key to Shanti House—the yurt I'd seen earlier—and a list of the classes I was scheduled to teach in exchange for my stay. I smiled. *Shanti* was the Sanskrit word for peace, the perfect name for a yoga and meditation space.

I returned the contents to the envelope, turned to walk back to the car—and froze.

What was that smell?

I took three quick sniffs, like Bella scenting a cat near her territory. Acrid cigarette smoke stung my nostrils.

A female voice whispered from around the corner. "I can't talk long. Bruce will get suspicious."

My shoulders crept up to my earlobes. My teeth ground together. That voice sounded familiar. Frighteningly, annoyingly familiar.

It couldn't be...

I tiptoed toward the sound, praying that my suspicions were wrong.

"I know. I'd rather be there with you, too." No reply. I assumed she was talking on a cell phone. "I told you. I *had* to come. Bruce would have blown a gasket if I missed the wedding."

I didn't want to eavesdrop—or at least that's what I told myself. No self-respecting yoga teacher would engage in such boorish behavior. But I had to confirm the speaker's identity, if not for myself, then for Bella. I flattened my body against the building, leaned to the side in a poorly executed Crescent Moon Pose, and peeked around the corner. All I could make out was the orange glow of her cigarette.

"Don't be stupid," she whispered. "You know I can't risk being seen with you here. Besides, this place is perfectly awful. You wouldn't like it at all." She took a long drag from her cigarette. "It's bad enough that we had to fly all the way across the country to meet Emilee's countrified boyfriend and his hillbilly family.

Couldn't she at least have had the common courtesy to get married some place decent, like Canlis?"

Emilee? Does she mean Emmy?

The name screeched through my psyche like two pieces of Styrofoam rubbed together. Emmy was one of the center's two caretakers. Canlis, one of Seattle's fanciest restaurants. The type of restaurant a diamond-encrusted beach walker might like to frequent.

I sagged against the cool wood siding and continued listening.

"Well, Bruce certainly shouldn't have to pay for it. That old battle axe got plenty of money in the divorce settlement. Surely, she could spring for something better than this rat trap."

Deep in my core, I already knew the speaker's identity. I didn't want to believe it, but I knew. Still, a girl can dream can't she? There was only one way to find out for sure. I held my breath and silently counted.

One, two …

At three, I flew forward, quickly glanced around the corner, and jumped back again.

Suspicions confirmed.

It was the Beach Witch. And she was here for the wedding.

Her whispers grew louder and more agitated. "Helen will get more money out of Bruce over my dead body."

Now *there* was a thought …

"Don't you *dare* threaten me."

I flinched. Had I said that out loud?

I peeked around the corner again, half-expecting to find myself nose-to-agitated-nose with a stiletto-heeled blonde. I saw the back of her jacket instead. She faced away from me, phone still firmly glued to her ear.

"I told you, I'm working on it. First I have to get those interminable alimony payments stopped." She took a final drag from her cigarette and dropped the butt on the ground. "Yeah, well, we'll see how guilty Bruce feels when I tell him her little secret."

Michael yelled from the parking lot. "Kate? Are you coming?"

She glanced furtively toward the sound. "Someone's coming. I have to go." She hung up the phone with an audible click, shoved it into her jacket pocket, and scurried away.

I emerged from my hiding place, stomped out her still smoldering cigarette, and shook my entire body, like Bella did when she forced water from her deep black coat.

I tried to reassure myself that my discovery wasn't all bad. True, the Beach Witch and I would have to coexist on the same ninety acres for the next several days. But on the plus side, she didn't seem like the yoga type. She'd probably kick a down dog before she'd practice one.

I chose to ignore the quiet voice in my head urging me to grab Bella and race back to Seattle, while we could still escape.

———

Michael and I followed the map to our cabin and parked directly outside of it.

"I'll bring the bags inside in a minute," Michael said. "Let's go check out the space." He led me to the tiny deck and opened the door with a flourish. "After you, Madame."

I stepped into the living room and flipped on the lights. One of the two remaining bulbs in the overhead fixture flickered, sizzled, and went out, plunging the room into dingy grayness.

This is it? Seriously?

Our cabin was, to put it mildly, a dump. It looked nothing like the opulent, eco-sensitive, fair-trade-decorated accommodations bragged about on Elysian Springs' website. Nothing at all.

The accommodations online featured gleaming bamboo floors, brightly colored area rugs, and soothing indoor water fountains. Our cabin boasted scuffed pine flooring, an ancient, filthy welcome mat, and water dripping from a leaky kitchen faucet.

At first I felt profound disappointment, but after a few moments I let go of my expectations and tapped into the energy of the space. The energy felt deep. Quaint. Peaceful. To my surprise, I *liked* Michael's and my new dumpy digs, even if they would never grace the cover of *House Beautiful*.

Bella didn't share my initial dumpy-digs disappointment. She charged gleefully through the door and explored her new surroundings, completely ignoring the "Please Keep Dogs Off Furniture" signs. First she ran into the kitchen and placed her paws on the counter, hoping to find pot roast, I assumed. Then she jumped on the couch and furiously dug, as if searching for buried treasure. Finding nothing of interest there, she leaped onto the room's only guest chair, sat, and regally stared across the room at Michael and me. A German shepherd queen commanding her subjects.

"Bella, off," I said uselessly.

Bella atypically complied. Living room secured, she galloped off to the bedroom, where she jumped on the sagging, headboard-free mattress, turned a quick circle, and flopped on her belly. The ancient box spring groaned in metallic complaint; Bella moaned in pure canine pleasure. She rolled to her side, spread her body diagonally across the mattress, and claimed it as her own. Evidently, Michael and I could sleep on the floor.

While Bella took a well-earned nap and Michael brought in the luggage, I did some exploring of my own. A little cleaning was definitely in order. A fine layer of dust covered the windowsill; intricate cobwebs decorated the corners; dust bunnies peeked out from under the sofa. The chipped porcelain sink in the kitchen was bare, except for a single threadbare towel draped over the faucet. I opened the cupboards and discovered several mismatched plates, four plastic glasses, and an assortment of chipped coffee mugs.

I vowed to take a dust rag to the place the next morning and brighten the living room with a bouquet of fresh-cut flowers. In the meantime, I grabbed the first two duffle bags off the floor and started unpacking the myriad of treats, toys, food, and medicines that I had packed for Bella. I opened one of the plastic containers of Bella's food and admired my handiwork. A small pile of powdered medicines sat at the top. I laid its twenty-nine identical friends out on the table and lined them up like soldiers in formation.

Michael set the final two bags on the floor. "Didn't you say we were staying in a cabin for four?"

"I thought so. When I agreed to take lodging as part of my fee, they said I could bring up to three friends." I gestured around the room. "But where would the other two sleep?"

Michael tugged at the edge of the couch. It flopped open in an undignified a flurry of dust, fur, animal dander, and debris.

Bella charged from the bedroom and skidded to a stop. An exposed, uninaugurated surface would never do. She jumped onto the middle of the sofa bed, flipped on her back, and proceeded to roll back and forth, waving her paws in the air. Michael sneezed.

I laughed. "It's a good thing Rene and Sam didn't come, after all. Can you imagine Rene sleeping on that hide-a-bed?" Rene was my best friend, my touchstone. During the tough months after my father's death, she had even been the source of my sanity. But her idea of *roughing it* was staying in a suite without in-room Jacuzzis. I'd never live it down if she had to sleep in the middle of this dust bowl.

"Have you heard from her since we left?" Michael asked.

I pulled the Yoga Chick out of my purse and pressed on the screen. For once she magically came to life. Still no missed calls. "No, she hasn't called once."

"That's not like her."

"No, it's not. Neither is cancelling at the last minute." I bit my lower lip. "Do you think I should be worried?"

"Anyone can get the stomach flu, Kate. You'd just be stressing out over nothing." He paused a beat. "But then again, when has that ever stopped you?" He grinned and scooted away before I could hit him with one of the couch's throw pillows.

Michael meant well, but he didn't know Rene—not the way I did. Rene's stomach was tougher than mummified shoe leather. In the eighteen years she and I had been friends, Rene had never missed a meal. And she lived for the opportunity to make my life miserable. Forgoing a week-long vacation with nothing better to do than torture me? She'd have to be terminal.

"I don't know, Michael. Rene never gets sick. I hope she doesn't have something serious."

"Don't worry. She'll be back on her feet in no time." Michael took my hand, led me to the bedroom, and sat on the edge of the sagging mattress. The springs let out a world-worn, metallic moan. "Besides, we could use a little alone time." He flashed a crooked smile.

Affection tickled the pit of my throat. A more urgent sensation pulsated quite a bit lower. I leaned in and gave Michael a long, meaningful kiss. I might not be ready to make a baby with Michael—or anyone else for that matter. But that didn't mean we shouldn't practice, practice, practice.

———

A loud crash jolted me upright. "What was that?" I fumbled around in the darkness and flipped on the reading lamp.

Michael covered his eyes with his forearms and groaned. "It's just some thunder, Kate. Turn off the light and go back to sleep."

Fat chance of that.

My heart hammered in my chest, beating an out-of-synch rhythm with the rain pelting the roof. I glanced at my watch. Three-fifteen. It could be a very long night. Thunderstorms didn't often declare war on the Pacific Northwest, but when they invaded, they made a statement. A flash of light whitened the room, followed by more deep, rolling thunder.

Michael sat up next to me. "Where's Bella?"

I found her in the bathroom, hiding behind the commode. Saying Bella didn't like loud noises would have been the world's biggest understatement. She had cowered behind my bed every night for a week after the Fourth of July, even on the maximum dose of Xanax. Next year I planned to double the prescription and take it myself. At least then one of us would get some sleep.

With Bella's vet 120 miles away in Seattle, neither of us would find chemical relief tonight. Bella panted and shivered and whined and cowered. Drool dripped from her jaw. Her glassy eyes opened wide, displaying the whites around her irises.

"Come here, girl," I said, murmuring softly. "It's OK."

Bella slinked uncertainly toward me, head hung low. I lightly grabbed the loose skin between her shoulder blades and guided her back to the bedroom. "Come and sleep on the bed with Michael and—"

A jarring bang shook the room, obliterating the rest of my sentence. Bella flew to the bed, but rather than jump on top of it as I had suggested, she tried to squeeze her hundred-pound body into the two-inch space underneath it. Failing at that, she scrambled around the room, looking for any space that might provide shelter: Michael's suitcase, the closet, even under the dresser.

I tried to restrain her, but she struggled against my grasp. I leaned down and whispered into her trembling ears. "Bella, relax. It's just a thunderstorm."

Bella responded by coldcocking me. She bashed her skull into my jaw. My teeth cracked together. My head flew back. Pain jolted my brain like a cattle prod, transforming worry into misplaced anger.

"Knock it off!" I bellowed. I grabbed the scruff on either side of her neck, placed my face an inch from her nose, and glared directly into her eyes. In a voice normally used by sleep-starved mothers of tantruming toddlers, I yelled at my poor, panicked dog. "Calm down. *Now!*"

Bella reacted the way any intelligent being would in her circumstances: trapped in a strange house, surrounded by monsters, and held down by a madwoman. She lashed out like a mental patient resisting a straightjacket. She squirmed, she bucked, she roared, she clawed. I rode Bella like a bucking bronco. Or she rode me. It was difficult to keep track of who was on top in the midst of the chaos.

"Michael, help me! I've never seen her like this."

Michael stood next to the bed, looking helpless. "I guess you were right. We should have brought her crate."

For a moment, time stood still. My mouth gaped open. My head pounded, about to explode. *Of course* I was right. Ever since her prior owner's death, Bella's crate was the only place she always felt safe. But in what universe was it useful to tell me that *now*?

I should have taken some deep breaths. I should have counted to ten. I wasn't even mad at Michael; I was *furious* with myself. Bella was my dog—my responsibility. I knew the abuse she had suffered. I knew she still panicked when stressed. I knew she needed—and deserved—special care. Leaving the crate behind may have been Michael's idea, but I was the idiot who went along with it.

Adrenaline-laced panic overpowered me. Thoughtless words spewed from my mouth like spit from a cobra. "If she gets hurt, it's your fault."

Michael flinched, as if slapped.

Thunder roared through the room again.

Bella wiggled free from my grasp and bolted for the bed. She clawed at the space behind it and ripped her nails against the metal frame. I imagined blood pouring from her soon-to-be-dislocated toes.

Michael finally took action. He grabbed the bottom of the frame and yanked it away from the wall, leaving behind four long, jagged scratches on the hardwood floor. Bella scrambled behind the bed and buried herself—nose to shoulders—underneath the frame. The rest of her body remained crammed into the two-foot space Michael had created behind the mattress.

Bella stopped whining. Her breathing slowed. Her muscles relaxed. The energy surrounding her softened. Lightning still lit up the sky, but in Bella's mind, her world was safe. I wasn't sure burying her head like an ostrich was the most effective survival strategy, but for now, it would do.

My own energy eased as well. I crawled back into bed, rested my head in the crook of my elbow, and stared at Michael's rigid back.

"I'm sorry for yelling at you, sweetie. I didn't mean it; I was just scared. Bella and I are lucky to have you."

Michael didn't answer, but he didn't ignore me, either. He rolled on his back and nuzzled my neck. Hours ticked by. I stared at the ceiling, listening to Bella's soft breathing, Michael's not-so-soft snoring, and the deluge of rain still bombarding the roof. At least a century passed before I fell back to sleep.

THREE

I AWOKE THE NEXT morning to silence. No rain on the rooftop, no purr-like puppy breathing, no soft boyfriend snores. I glanced at the clock. Seven o'clock. The perfect time to snuggle against Michael's warm, rippled chest. I rolled over and reached out my arms, planning to cuddle up to my favorite six-foot-tall bed warmer.

My hands connected with nothing.

No one occupied the space beside me. No one longed for my loving embrace. No one even gave me the cold shoulder in retribution for my prior night's temper tantrum. All that lay beside me were cold, empty bed sheets.

No problem, a fur-covered she-dog would do quite nicely. "Bella, up," I said, patting the bed. No response. I sat up and scanned the room, but found no snoozing shepherds. I peeked in the two-foot-wide storm shelter Michael had created behind the bed. No creatures there either, unless you counted the dust bunnies. Apparently, I slumbered alone.

Bella's single, sharp bark sounded from the kitchen, followed by Michael's voice, goading her on. "That's right, Bella girl. Go wake up Kate."

At seven in the morning? On vacation? I groaned and covered my head with the pillow, determined to ignore them both until a more civilized hour. Like noon.

Three sharp barks later, Michael changed tactics. The bittersweet smell of caramel-laced caffeine wafted into the room. Nice try. It would take more than designer coffee to get me out of this bed.

Like carbohydrates.

The oven door squeaked open. Sugar, cinnamon, and vanilla beckoned me like a siren.

A few frustrated barks, I could ignore. Coffee, I could drink any day of the week. But cinnamon rolls? My mind and my body declared war, fighting for dominance. My mind craved deep, dreamless sleep; my stomach, gooey cinnamon pastry.

My stomach won.

I slipped on a pair of sweatpants and staggered out of the bedroom. Before I could adequately stuff my belly with coffee and pastries, I needed to make a pit stop. I veered to the left and trudged, zombie-like, into the bathroom. I didn't bother to open my puffy eyes; I already knew the room's layout from the prior night's explorations. Instead, I staggered to the far corner, stifled a yawn with my fist, and lowered my bottom into a perfect Half Squat—right before I fell into the toilet.

That was one way to wake up. Muttering words never used in yoga class, I slammed down the open toilet seat, grabbed a towel off the towel rack, and wiped the morning dew off my backside, grateful that Michael at least had the decency to flush. One thing was certain: my eyes were wide open now.

Michael and I had spent multiple sleepovers together, but always at my house, since his apartment didn't allow dogs. Looking around the disaster that used to be the bathroom, I realized that I hadn't fully grasped the dearth of his housekeeping skills.

Red, white, and green gore oozed from an open toothpaste tube and semi-permanently adhered itself to the sink. My small, well-organized makeup bag competed for space with a medley of male personal hygiene products ranging from shaving cream to the world's most disgusting flattened toothbrush to a deodorant labeled "Just for Men."

The rest of the room fared no better. A pair of wrinkled underwear lay bunched in one corner; a wilted black sock occupied another. Juniper-scented soap melted down the edge of the bathtub, oozing an Irish Spring slug trail that led to a bottle of antidandruff shampoo. The pièce de résistance was a tube of medicated cream designed to cure a multitude of fungal infections, up to and including jock itch. *Gross!*

I swallowed back my disgust and joined Hurricane Michael in the kitchen. He grinned at me from the table. "Hey there, sleepy head! It's about time you got up. Miss Bella and I have been waiting for you since five. I knew putting those cinnamon rolls in the oven would do the trick."

I stifled an impolite reply and poured some delicious, caramel-smelling brew into a chipped "I Love Tofu" coffee mug. Two swigs later, I took a huge bite of buttery, hot cinnamon pastry, trying not to imagine globs of cellulite swelling my thighs. Vacation food didn't have calories, right?

Michael sorted through several flyers he'd retrieved from our welcome packet. "What's on today's agenda? We should try to fit in as much as possible before you start teaching tomorrow." He pointed to a map. "How about hiking the trail around Mountain Lake?"

He ruffled Bella's ears. "What do you think, Bella girl? Are you up for a seven-mile loop?"

Bella responded with an enthusiastic bark.

I gaped at them both. "Seven miles? I'd have to ride Bella out. I thought we could hang out here at the center and relax." I punctuated my point by leaning back in one chair and putting my feet up on another.

Michael pursed his lips in a lopsided grin. "Fine. No hike then. We can start with the hot tubs."

Now he was talking. Hot tubbing was my kind of vacation. Sleep in until noon, hang out in the spa, practice some yoga, maybe get a massage or two...

He handed me a full-color pamphlet filled with warm, inviting pictures. Happy-looking adults relaxed in four hot tubs that had been sunken into an expansive cedar deck. Puget Sound's blue waters sparkled in the background. According to the flyer, the wooden building behind the deck housed bathrooms, showers, a steam room, and sauna. I turned the page over and read the section titled "Spa Rules and Regulations."

"Closed for cleaning from eight to ten each morning." No problem there. We could start at eleven. "No lotions, oils, or cell phones allowed." I could live with that. I'd check the Yoga Chick before we left. She probably wasn't waterproof, anyway. "No glass containers or alcoholic beverages allowed." Bummer. But who drank before noon, anyway? "Patrons must sit on a towel at all times."

Huh?

The final line leaped off the page, searing my eyes. "Parents take note: All of our spa facilities are clothing optional." I shuddered from the roots of my hair follicles to the tips of my toenails.

"Michael, these are *naked* hot tubs!" I dropped the offending pamphlet, as if it had scalded my fingertips. "I can't hang out in some *naked* hot tub, especially not with future yoga students." I pointed down at my legs, which appeared to have tripled in size. "Believe me, no one wants to see these thighs naked."

"Don't be silly, Kate," Michael chided. "I love your chunky thighs."

Was that supposed to be a compliment?

"Besides," he continued. "It's not a *naked* hot tub. It's *clothing optional*. Wear your swimming suit."

I rolled my eyes. "Great. Then I'll be the only puritanical prude covered up in a towel, while everyone else gets their jollies by letting it all hang out." I shuddered. "Nope. No way. I'll only be naked with total strangers."

Michael snorted so hard that coffee came out of his nose.

I swatted him on the rear with a towel. "Knock it off. You know what I mean. Now stop mocking me and clean up the dishes. I'll get Bella's food started, and we can take her for a walk while it incubates."

Michael stopped arguing, picked up the plates, and haphazardly stacked them next to the sink. I grabbed the first of my thirty dog food containers and began the chemical experiment that was Bella's food preparation. I opened the eco-friendly, compostible vessel and confirmed that the mountain of powdered medicines I'd added at home was still on top. Then I poured the contents into a large mixing bowl and vigorously stirred, envisioning each separate molecule of kibble being coated with powder.

Next up was adding the water. I carefully measured twelve ounces from the tap and tested it with my finger. Satisfied that the temperature was appropriately warm—not hot—I poured the water onto the powdered food and stirred exactly one hundred times, until the disgusting-looking concoction was the consistency of overcooked oatmeal. I stepped back, assessed my artistic creation, and frowned. Something was off. I stirred some more, then frowned again. "This doesn't feel right. Maybe I should do it over."

Michael—who had finished piling the dishes next to the sink five minutes before—drummed his fingers on the counter impatiently. "Kate, come off it. How hard can it be? I'm beginning to think Rene is right. I know you love Bella. I love her, too. But seriously? You're becoming dog food obsessed."

Six months ago, I'd have thought I was crazy, too. Only the owner of a dog with EPI could understand my anal-retentive dog feeding ritual. Rene even teased that—in addition to my fear of beards—I was developing a brand new Kate-specific neurosis: orthorexia nervosa by proxy. Sufferers of orthorexia nervosa obsessed about the purity and quality of the food they ingested. In my case, I obsessed about Bella's: the ingredients and quality of her kibble, the exact amount she ate daily, and the rigid specificity with which it must be prepared. The only thing I monitored more closely than Bella's input was her output. But I tried not to think about that so close to mealtime.

Neurotic or not, my ritual had proven effective. Six months of obsessive-compulsive food preparation after she entered my life, Bella was only three pounds shy of her goal weight.

Michael pulled on his boots and clipped Bella's leash to her harness. "Kate, we're waiting…"

I tipped Bella's food bowl to check the mixture's consistency. It seemed runnier than normal. "I don't know, Michael. Something's not right. I should make it over, just in case." I pulled container number two off of the countertop, prepared to start over.

Michael snatched it from my hands. "Come on, Kate. Making dog food isn't rocket science, and I should know. I sell it for a living. Let's go!"

I looked skeptically at the goop incubating inside Bella's bowl. Maybe the water was different on Orcas…

Bella let out a series of three sharp barks.

"Are you coming or not?" Michael opened the door and Bella bounded through it. The screen door slammed behind them, leaving me in the cabin, alone.

Michael was probably right. Being neurotic was bad enough; there was no need to act certifiable. I grabbed the Yoga Chick off the counter, checked quickly for messages, then tossed her into my jacket pocket and jogged out the door.

"Hey you guys, wait for me!"

When I caught up with them, I grabbed Bella's leash in one hand and held Michael's fingers in the other. The three of us crunched along the center's network of interconnecting trails as we explored our new territory in the daylight. Bella weaved happily back and forth at the end of her leash, sniffing for hidden treasures, while I took deep breaths of pine-scented air, which was still redolent with ozone from the prior night's storm. Golden oak leaves waved from the branches above and peppered the permanent carpet of pine needles covering the ground.

Last night the grounds seemed desolate; this morning, they bustled. Fellow vacationers sipped mugs of coffee and smiled friendly hellos. Maintenance staff scurried by on electric golf carts. Gardeners harvested, fertilized, and planted cover crops in a huge, fenced-in garden. A sign at the gate read, "Welcome to the Garden of Eden. Visitors are welcome, but please keep pets outside." I smiled at the word play. Eden was the name of Elysian Springs' organic vegan restaurant. The garden must supply at least some of the restaurant's produce.

We wandered along the fence past beds of dark green kale, deep purple cabbage, and beige, peanut-shaped butternut squash. A few feet from the end of the garden, we discovered the free range enclosures of several of the center's happy-looking animal residents. A dozen clucking hens seemed to smile as they pecked at the earth around their whitewashed henhouse. Next door, several ducks splashed happily in a bright blue wading pool, near a pair of fluffy white rabbits who sunned themselves in the corner of a huge fenced-in hutch. We even found a half-dozen floppy-eared goats eating their way through a wall of blackberry bushes in an otherwise vacant field.

We hiked on the center's property for over forty-five minutes, discovering quaint wooden cabins, hidden camp sites, even an old, rusted-out boat that had been abandoned on one of the property's two private beaches. At the end of the beach, we turned left and continued walking—uphill now—away from the water. The trail ended at the edge of a cliff and a campsite labeled "Suicide Bluff." Obviously someone's idea of a joke. A squirrel chirped angrily from above, as if warning us away from his favorite hiding place.

I stood near the bluff's jagged rock outcroppings, entranced by the view. Greenish-blue water extended for miles and birthed powerful waves that crashed over fifty feet below. The smooth, crescendoing sound was both calming and awe-inspiring at the same time. I moved closer to the edge, as if hypnotized.

"Kate, what are you doing? Get away from there." Michael pointed to a sign several feet behind me.

"Danger. Cliffs are unstable. Walking prohibited less than three feet from edge."

As if on cue, a rock broke free and clattered over the edge. I took several large steps back. "Suicide Bluff" suddenly felt more like a warning than a quip. The steep, dark cliffs dared me to come closer. Goaded me. Urged me to jump. An inexplicable chill frosted the back of my neck. I couldn't explain it, but the cliffs felt malevolent—evil somehow. Like they hungered for human sacrifice.

I looped Bella's leash handle around my wrist and pulled her in closer. Gorgeous view or not, I wouldn't come back here again. I didn't trust this place.

"Michael, let's go."

The wary look on his face mirrored my own. He laced his fingers through mine and we hurried away, back toward our cozy little cabin, where the three of us would presumably be safe.

FOUR

I WAS WRONG.

Danger didn't hibernate in dark, rocky cliffs; it napped in warm sun puddles. We almost made it back to our cabin. Another minute or two, and Michael, Bella, and I would have been safely ensconced inside our tiny-but-serviceable kitchen, snacking on leftover pastries. The only obstacle remaining was a multi-acre field dotted with newer-looking cabins.

Each freshly stained structure was architecturally different—designed to look unique. A few were tiny studios, barely more than glorified bedrooms; others were multistoried mansions with wraparound decks and private hot tubs. Some towered over the landscape, offering unobstructed Puget Sound views; others hid, peeking from underneath old-growth Douglas fir trees.

I meandered through the supposedly diverse development with a vague sense of unease—like an unsuspecting stranger visiting a Stepford Wives' neighborhood. In spite of their superficial differences, each building's energy felt exactly the same—and not quite genuine. Each cabin had been sided with uniformly stained cedar shingles and accented with container gardens of dark green flax grass and burnt-orange pansies. Each entry was shielded from mud tracks by recycled rubber mats in a variety of bright, primary colors. The entire area exuded a creepy, not-quite-real energy, feigning diversity while demanding conformity.

No doubt about it, these supposedly upscale cabins paled in comparison with the dingy-but-cute place I now thought of as my own.

Except one.

I stopped and stared at the huge building in front of me—a two-story structure over three times the size of my Ballard home. "Michael, look at that place. Can you imagine the view? It looks right out over the ocean. Bella could lounge on the deck and—"

I stopped midsentence.

This was no good. No good at all.

Bandit, the terrier we'd encountered at the beach near the ferry terminal, napped in a warm patch of sun near the edge of the deck, wearing no oppressive collar to impinge upon his comfort. He opened one sleepy, pirate-patched eye, looked at Bella, and launched.

He dove off the deck, yapping at full volume, and flew down the stairs. His paws hit the grass, and he sprinted across the field toward Bella. His tongue lolled; his ears pressed flat against his head; a huge doggie grin spread across his face.

I hesitated before pulling out the vial of Spot Stop. Michael loved animals as much as I did, so when he assured me that the citronella spray was humane, but effective, I believed him. Still, that didn't mean I wanted to use it. Using force against an animal—

even relatively benign force—was clearly against yoga's principle of nonviolence. I firmly believed in ahimsa. I tried to live by it. But if by using force I could prevent harm? Well, I might have to make an exception.

I moved the spray's nozzle off safety.

"Call your dog!" I yelled across the empty field. I was in luck, or at least I thought so. Somebody heard me. The cabin's door opened and disgorged Bandit's red-fingernailed owner. She stood on the deck, watching, as her dog barreled toward us.

Bandit didn't stop when he reached us. He didn't even slow down. He just kept running. He zoomed around Bella, Michael, and me in ever-decreasing circles, orbiting Bella like a low-flying raptor circling its prey. Only faster. And more determined. And juiced up on cocaine.

Bella didn't move a muscle. She didn't even twitch. She crouched forward, ears pricked at high alert, as if waiting for the right moment to strike.

I prayed to God, the universe, or whoever else was listening. *Please don't let today be the day.*

Bella was famous for her ferocious-looking outbursts, but she'd never actually laid a tooth on another creature—at least not yet. I had a horrible feeling that Bandit might be the first. I envisioned ripping fangs, high-pitched yelps, and spatters of bright red blood in the terrier's future.

I didn't consider what Patanjali—the author of *The Yoga Sutras*—might have done in my situation. I'm sure he would have reacted with much greater aplomb. But in my defense, I was trying to prevent bloodshed.

I looked up at Bandit's still-glaring, still-motionless owner and screamed, "Call your goddamned dog!"

"Oh, for God's sake," she yelled back. "He only wants to play. Ignore him and he'll go away." I watched, horrified, as she stomped back into the cabin and slammed the door behind her.

I was completely out of Bandit-control options. "I'm going to have to spray him!"

"Do it, already!" Michael yelled.

I pointed the nozzle at the circling terrier, silently begged for forgiveness, and pressed down on the plunger, expecting to douse the unsuspecting canine in a fire hose of pressurized chemicals.

A low-pressure squirt of lemon-scented water drizzled out of the opening. Bandit yapped excitedly, entranced by this new game. He alternated between leaping over the ineffectual stream and dodging out of its reach. After less than a minute, the drizzle stopped. The canister was empty. Bandit stopped running and glared at me, clearly disappointed that I'd broken his new water toy.

That was the opportunity Bella had been waiting for. She lunged after Bandit, teeth thrashing and voice roaring. I managed to hang on to her leash—barely—but she pulled me to the ground. Michael tried to prevent doggie homicide by becoming a human shield. He threw his body toward the spinning fur ball but missed and fell face-first into the muck. Bandit alternated between nipping at Bella's toes and vaulting over Michael's prostrate, red-faced, and loudly swearing form.

The cabin's door opened again, and a tall man wearing beige khakis and a blue polo shirt rushed outside. "Bandit, come," he yelled. "I have a cookie!"

The c-word stopped Bandit in his tracks. He peeled off and ran back to the stranger. My new hero clipped a collar on the little beast and tied him to the porch.

Meanwhile, back on the battlefield, Michael, Bella, and I started to shake off our recent trauma. I slowly sat up and tried to catch my breath. Bella whined at the end of her leash, as if mourning the loss of her fur-covered breakfast. Michael rolled from his belly to his back, groaning. Brown muddy guck was smeared from his boots to his eyebrows. He lay on the ground, glowered, and grunted, like a foul-tempered hog wallowing in an unacceptable trough. I tried, unsuccessfully, not to giggle.

"What's so damned funny?" he snapped.

I was saved by the bell—or at least by the ring tone. Bart Simpson's annoying, nasal voice interrupted:

"My best friend's calling me. My friend loves me. You don't got a friend like this."

"What the hell?"

"Ignore it, Michael. It's Rene. She'll leave a message."

"Seriously, Kate? Bart Simpson?"

I shrugged. "Wasn't my idea. Rene programmed my ringtones, and I can't figure out how to change them. She picked this Bart Simpson one for her number. She thinks it's funny."

If he didn't like Bart, he'd *abhor* the "I'm too sexy" ringtone she'd chosen for him. I turned off the phone in case she'd added any other surprises that Michael might not appreciate.

Michael tried to stand up, but his feet slipped in the wet grass and he fell on his rear, right back into the mud. He covered his face with his hands. "Can this trip get any worse?"

I bit my lower lip to keep from answering. Now probably wasn't the best time to point out that the muck on his thighs looked suspiciously like deer dung.

The stranger-hero emerged from his cabin and rushed toward us, carrying two large bath towels. He handed one to each of us, apologizing profusely. "I'm so sorry about that. Bandit's my wife's dog, and she hasn't trained the little monster." His ears turned red. "I'm sure he doesn't mean any harm, but he's definitely a handful."

This must be Bruce, the spouse the Beach Witch had mentioned on the phone last night. If so, they epitomized the phrase "odd couple." He looked at least fifty; she at most thirty. He wore round wire-framed glasses and a poorly done comb-over that didn't quite cover his prominent bald spot. She wore diamond earrings, expensive leather jackets, and waaaay too much makeup. I couldn't help but feel bad for him. Granted, I didn't know him yet, but Bruce seemed like a nice guy, and from what I'd heard last night, I suspected his wife was cheating on him.

I took the proffered towel, stood, and wiped the mud stains off my knees. Michael looked down at his pants, lifted his hand to his nose, and softly swore. The stranger took a tentative step toward us and cleared his throat.

"Let's start over. I'm Bruce. I don't blame you two for being upset about what happened." Michael and I both remained silent. He shifted uncomfortably and continued. "I'm sorry about my wife. She's just so ..." His words trailed off.

Awful. I silently replied. But I didn't say that. Instead, I smiled at him and said, "It's OK. We're Kate and Michael. I pointed toward the hundred pound welcome-dog whining beside me. "And this is Bella. Bella, say hello."

As taught, Bella walked up to Bruce, sat down, and offered him her paw.

"Well aren't you a sweet thing?" He shook Bella's paw and ruffled her ears.

Bruce looked up again. "Are you two here for Emmy and Josh's wedding?"

"No," I replied, then corrected myself. "Well, actually yes, sort of. I'm teaching yoga here this week."

His face broke into a huge grin. "Oh! You're *that* Kate! Emmy told me about you. So nice to meet you, Kate." He pumped my hand vigorously. "I've never done yoga, but I might have to give it a try this week. Emmy's so excited to have a yoga teacher on site. She's hoping you'll teach a private class for the wedding guests from New York."

"I'd be happy to."

"Emmy will be so pleased. She claims that yoga will help us get over our jet lag, but honestly, I think she's looking for ways we can all be in the same room without fighting." He winked. "You know how family can be."

Indeed I did. Dad and I used to fight like cats. I missed those fights still, even almost three years after his death.

My chest felt undeniably heavy, but I kept my voice light. "Tell Emmy I'll drop by the office later so we can set something up."

"Great. You'll love her. She takes after her mother."

Oh, God, no.

I cringed before I could stop myself.

Bruce's eyes twinkled. "That would be Helen, my *ex*-wife. The woman you saw a few minutes ago was my current wife, Monica."

Michael's frown clearly telegraphed his thoughts. *Nice one, Kate.*

I changed the subject. "Hey, can you do me a favor? As you probably noticed, Bella's not great with other dogs. Would you please keep Bandit on a leash?"

Bruce shifted uncomfortably. "I would, but it's not up to me. Like I said, Bandit's my wife's dog. Emmy and I told her about the leash rules already, but she's not exactly a rule follower. Monica's more of a free spirit." Bruce glanced over his shoulder toward the cabin. "I'll try talking to her again." He shook his head slowly. "But if I were you, I'd keep my eyes open, just in case."

———

Michael and I trudged back to the cabin, both exhausted. While Michael showered off the deer dung and Bella snarfed down her breakfast, I listened to the Yoga Chick's voice mail. I expected at least one long-winded message from Rene, but the only message was from the studio. Mandy must have called after I turned off the phone. She didn't sound happy.

"Um, Kate, there was an incident this morning. One of the kids in the Mom and Tot class pulled the fire alarm. I called 911 to tell them it was a false alarm, but we still had to evacuate the building. The firemen just let us back inside."

A second person mumbled in the background. Mandy's voice faded. "Thanks for coming. Sorry for all of the excitement."

She spoke into the handset again. "I gave the students free passes, but you should let Alicia know what happened. The people who live in the apartments upstairs were pretty upset."

I sighed and hung up. I knew exactly which little towheaded tot had pulled that lever—it was the third time this month. And for the third time this month, I cursed Strong and Supple, Serenity

47

Yoga's main competitor, for banning the demon-child and his sweet-and-always-apologetic mother from their classes. No matter how many times I considered it, I didn't have the heart to do the same. Maybe I could anonymously send her a gift certificate to the Pilates studio down the street...

The alarm had already been sounded, so to speak. I'd deal with the fallout later. In the meantime, I tried calling Rene, but the call went directly to voicemail. Now I was worried. Forgoing the opportunity to leave a smart aleck message on my machine was odd enough for Rene; turning off her phone was practically unheard of.

Michael emerged from the bathroom wearing a towel and a smile. Water dripped from his curly, damp hair and ran in enticing rivulets down his chest. He looked at me meaningfully. "I'm still all wound up from that stupid dog incident." He wiggled his eyebrows. "What do you think? Should we burn off some stress?"

In a rare moment of symbiosis, I understood and agreed completely. I laid down my phone, handed Michael our one remaining dry towel, and strode purposefully to the bedroom—to grab my yoga mat.

Michael pulled on some sweats and headed off for a long soak in the clothing-optional hot tubs. I rolled out my mat and began a completely dressed yoga practice.

I sat on the floor, closed my eyes, and deepened my breath. Tension and irritation melted away with each exhale. My jaw unclenched; my fingers relaxed; my shoulders dropped down from my ears.

Several minutes later, I started moving. The injuries to my shoulder—sustained while struggling with my friend's murderer six months before—had finally healed, so I indulged in a strong flow practice designed to burn off excess adrenaline.

I began with several Sun Salutations. The first repetition felt jagged and stiff, but by the third, my breath sounded smooth, regular, stable, and strong. My muscles burned in the most delicious of ways as I moved from Downward Dog, to Plank, to the core-strengthening Chaturanga.

On to some Half Squats to let my thighs join the party. Sweat formed along the back of my neck and dripped down my sides. My quadriceps, hips, hamstrings—even my glutes—quivered in delight-filled torture.

I opened my shoulders in Bridge Pose and turned my body upside down with a short stay in Shoulder Stand. A few counterposes later, I finished with a breath practice designed to balance energy. I lengthened my inhale and exhale for several breaths, then broke each into halves, pausing for several seconds in the middle. This official name for this practice was Krama Pranayama, but I called it Lithium Breathing. Like the medicine for bipolar disorder, Lithium Breathing helped balance my energy, whether it was agitated or depressed.

The practice was exactly what I needed to calm my nervous system. The glass of merlot I drank afterwards didn't hurt, either. I didn't normally drink before lunch, but given the morning's events, I figured a little liquid tranquilization wasn't uncalled for. Besides, everyone knew grape juice was brimming with antioxidants; mine was simply the fermented variety.

By the time I finished sipping the last velvety, plum-scented dregs from my glass, my energy was completely sattvic: relaxed and alert.

When Michael returned to the cabin, he found me curled up on the sofa bed, pen and clipboard in hand, deep into planning the next day's classes. He sported a huge smile. His whole body seemed relaxed; his face flushed and vital.

My energy went from tranquil to hyperaroused in three seconds flat. Michael looked good. Really good. Was his change in demeanor due to the hot tub's rejuvenating bubbles or to the nubile, naked young bodies he'd shared it with? Jealousy prickled the back of my neck.

I jumped up and chattered, trying to act nonchalant. "I'm glad you're back. We should probably get going." I looked at my watch. "It's almost one, and we have dinner reservations at six." I picked up my purse, still babbling. "Let's go to Eastsound, eat some lunch, and buy Bella a crate. If we hurry, we can check out one of those hiking trails you keep talking about."

Michael wasn't fooled. He eased in close and ran his fingertips down my arm. "Hiking's overrated." He nuzzled the back of my neck. "We have plenty of time to get Bella that crate. I had a different activity in mind..."

I could take a hint.

I grabbed Michael's arm and led him toward the bedroom. He leaned in to give me a long, slow kiss and—

Bella erupted.

She leaped from her comfy sun puddle and charged the door. She jumped, scratched, foamed, barked, and growled. Axe-wielding psychopaths had better take note: guard dog Bella was on the job.

Michael pulled back and groaned. Somehow I didn't think the sound was from pleasure.

I shrugged. "Someone's at the door."

"You think?"

Michael waited at the door while I dragged the clawing, frothing monster-beast away and locked her in the bathroom.

A voice yelled over the clamor.

"Open up in there! Police!"

FIVE

MICHAEL FLUNG OPEN THE door. "What are you two doing here?" Granted, I couldn't see his face, but his tone didn't exactly sound welcoming.

Rene didn't seem to notice. "Hey there, gorgeous. Good to see you, too!" She gave Michael a quick peck on the cheek and pressed through the doorway wearing a wide, sparkling grin. Sam staggered behind her, loaded down with enough bags for a month long vacation—for a family of twelve.

Rene tossed her purse on the table. "The chick at the office told us where to find you. I tried calling from the ferry, but you didn't answer, so I decided to surprise you." She opened her arms wide. "Surprise!"

I stared at her, speechless, still recovering from a severe case of about-to-coitus interruptus.

Rene took a step back, crossed her arms, and cocked her head to the side. "You two don't look happy to see me."

"We're not. We were just about to—"

I silenced Michael with a well-placed poke to the ribs. "Of course we're glad you're here. Your timing is perfect. We were just about to go get lunch in Eastsound." Michael didn't correct me. "But I'm surprised. I thought you were sick."

Rene looked down at the floor and chewed on her lower lip. "Oh well…you know…I'm feeling much better now. And Sam's on a break between software projects, so we decided to come after all."

She flashed a plastic smile, begging me to drop the subject. I would normally have forced her to cough up the truth, but this time I hesitated. Rene was hiding something. Any gullible, Santa Claus-loving five-year-old would have seen that. But if the hurt look on Sam's face was any indication, she was hiding it from him, too.

And it couldn't be good.

The woman standing before me was not my best friend. My best friend had a never-ending supply of energy and super-defined muscles—the kind typically seen in rock music videos. Most days, if I hadn't loved her so much, I would have been forced to hate her.

Today I couldn't even drum up a spark of envy. Rene's typically flawless, alabaster skin was a sickly shade of greenish-yellow. Purple crescents underscored the pink, puffy skin underneath her eyes. Her normally confident posture was slumped, tired looking. Even her body looked—dare I say it? Soft.

I wrapped my arm around her shoulder, gave her a hug, and whispered. "Are you OK?"

She whispered back. "Shhh. I'll talk to you when we're alone."

"You two can catch up later," Sam grumped from behind us. "Where should I put these bags? My arms are about to fall off."

"Sorry, Sam." I gestured to the living room. "Put them in there."

Sam dropped Rene's bags on the floor with a disgusted whumpf while Michael released Bella from her temporary prison. Bella gleefully skidded across the floor and greeted Rene with her unique I-love-you happy dance of whines, wiggles, play bows, and kisses.

Sam knelt down, held out his hand, and cooed, "Hey Bella baby. How are you?" Bella looked his direction, flattened her ears, sneezed once, and slinked to the opposite side of the room.

"Bella, say hello," Michael commanded.

Bella refused. She planted all four feet firmly on the hardwood floor and glared, sending Sam an obvious message. *Don't let the door hit you on your way out.*

"I don't get it," Sam said, sounding wounded. "I love animals. I love Bella, for that matter. Why doesn't she like me?"

"I'm sorry, Sam. I think it's your mustache. She's still funny about facial hair."

Sam's mustache was the only reasonable explanation why Bella hadn't taken to him. She certainly couldn't mind the rest of his looks. With straight blond hair, surfer-boy blue eyes, and an avid biker's lean body, Sam was the six-foot-tall Ken to Rene's brunette-haired Barbie.

Bella couldn't fault his personality, either. Somehow Sam had managed not to inherit the pretty boy jerk gene. He was sweet, kind, and—most importantly—he adored Rene to a fault. Add Sam's brilliantly successful software company to all of that personal yumminess and he was—as Rene told anyone who'd listen—the perfect husband.

The disgusting, fuzzy, caterpillar-like growth marring his upper lip was his only glaring flaw. Someday I'd sneak up behind him and shave it off—if I could ever manage to get close enough to touch it without getting sick to my stomach.

Rene waved her hand dismissively. "Ignore her, Sam, and consider yourself lucky. At least Bella doesn't bark at you." She flopped on the sofa bed. A Pigpen-like cloud of dirt, dog dander, and dust mites swirled around her. She sneezed uncontrollably into her hand and looked around the room. "This place is *tiny*. Where's Sam's and my bedroom?"

"You're sitting on it," Michael replied.

Rene's eyes widened. "You have *got* to be kidding me." She sneezed again. "This will never do." She stood up and brushed the newly acquired layer of dander and dog fur off of her pants. "Tell you what, let's go have lunch. Sam and I drove past a Chinese place in Eastsound that looked pretty good. A slice of chocolate truffle pie from the pie shop around the corner doesn't sound half bad, either.

"When we get back, we'll stop at the office and see about getting Sam and me our own place." She scratched Bella's ears. "Maybe Sam will even splurge for a larger cabin for all five of us."

———

The rest of the day went by in a heartbeat. We started at the Chinese restaurant. Michael, Sam, and I stuffed ourselves full of stir fry, while Rene made small piles of fried rice and pushed them around on her plate. After that, we spent the afternoon wandering around Eastsound. Sam and Michael weren't exactly enthusiastic about our choice of girlie activities, but Rene and I enjoyed browsing through the town's many quaint stores.

My budget allowed primarily for window shopping, so Rene spent enough money for us both. She wasn't in the mood to try on clothes—a first for her—but she indulged in a multitude of books, trinkets, and designer chocolates. She even managed to nibble on that coveted slice of pie.

I tried to make good on my promise to buy Bella a new crate, but the local pet boutique didn't carry any large enough for my horse-sized German shepherd. Bella would have to make do with the space Michael had created behind the bed.

Now, five minutes before our six o'clock dinner reservation, we all meandered along the path to Eden, the center's on-site restaurant. Well, three of us meandered. Rene stomped. She pouted and griped and whined and lamented, acting like a starving three-year-old who'd been denied a pink frosted sugar cookie.

"Sold out? How can the entire property be sold out?"

"It isn't, Rene," I replied for the thousandth time. "Sam said there were plenty of campsites available." I nudged her ribs with my elbow. "You might have even been able to score a yurt!"

She grumbled an unrepeatable reply and accelerated. I hurried to keep pace beside her. "I told you, this week is special. It's the grand opening of the new construction, and the site managers are getting married. I'm sure they have a ton of out-of-town guests." I shrugged. "You'll have to live with the sofa bed."

Rene pouted her way up the staircase. "Did you see the dust that came out of that couch? I've already taken a double dose of Benadryl, and my eyes are still swollen like grapefruits!

"Rene, honey," Sam said from behind, "you look gorgeous, like always."

He lied.

Rene looked awful. Even worse than she had earlier. A volcano-sized pimple had erupted on her normally flawless chin. Her watery eyes were laced with a web-like network of red lines. Her face was swollen and blotchy. If I hadn't been with her for the past four hours, I'd have sworn that she'd spent the day crying.

Rene's eyes pleaded with me to agree. "Kate, do I really look OK?"

I paused, searching for something—anything—truthful to say that wouldn't hurt my friend's feelings. I considered fibbing, but lying would go against satya—yoga's principle of truthfulness. Besides in this case, it would be useless. Rene could read me like a country fair psychic. What could I say that would be honest, but kind? Somehow I didn't think assuring her that she looked ten years younger with acne would make her feel better.

A bouncing fur ball solved my dilemma. Bandit jumped up and down at the top of the stairs, barking at full volume. He was restrained, for a change, by a rhinestone-studded leash.

"Well, aren't you a cutie pie?" Rene leaned down to pet him.

I snatched her hand away. "Don't encourage him." I whispered in her ear so Michael wouldn't hear me. "The Beach Witch is here."

"Beach Witch?" Rene asked.

I filled her in on the story as we entered the buzzing restaurant.

An amazing mixture of scents floated into my nostrils and made my mouth water. Spicy arugula, garlic, tomatoes, and a smell that—if I weren't in a vegan restaurant—I would have sworn was melting cheese. Photographs of freshly harvested produce and rescued farm animals decorated the walls, creating a collage of bright red tomatoes, dark purple grapes, deep green chard, and black-spotted piglets. The goats I'd seen mowing the upper pasture adorned the spot above our table. A gray-bearded, hugely smiling man knelt among them, hugging a goat under each arm. The sign attached to the photo read, "Nubian goats provided by Dale's Goat Rescue."

The hostess filled our water glasses and handed us each a one-page paper menu labeled in bold black letters: "Welcome to Eden. Gourmet dining that respects the value of all life." Below the title, several paragraphs described the restaurant's philosophy.

Eden only served food that was one hundred percent vegan (no eggs, dairy, or animal products of any kind), organic, and freshly prepared. Breads and pastries were baked on site daily. Many of the fruits and vegetables served were grown in the center's garden and harvested mere minutes before preparation. The rest were delivered fresh each morning by local farmers.

My stomach rumbled as I imagined the possibilities. Eating out as a vegetarian could sometimes be limiting, even with Seattle's large vegetarian population. Most restaurants had at least one or two meatless dishes to choose from. But a pure vegan menu from which I could order anything I wanted? That was something special. I flipped the page over, wondering how I'd choose between all of the delicious-sounding options.

There weren't any. Options, that is. Eden offered the ultimate in freshness, not variety. All meals were *prixe fixe*—French for lots and lots of expensive food. Each course was created based on the ingredients available that day. Tonight's dinner: Penne Arrabiatta with fresh vegan Romano. I laid down my menu with a satisfied smile. I could live with that.

While Michael, Sam, and Rene finished perusing their menus, I glanced around the room. The limited menu certainly didn't seem to be hurting Eden's business. The space was completely packed with satisfied-looking diners. Not a single table was available.

My eyes stopped at the windows, captivated by the train wreck in front of me. OK, so it wasn't a train wreck, at least at least not by the usual standards, but it was close enough. The entire ocean view window was monopolized by a long table with at least twenty diners. Most wore semiformal outfits and tense expressions, as if it took one hundred percent of their willpower to keep from strangling the person seated next to them. I could practically feel the waves of animosity flow between them.

They had to be the guests of the wedding party.

I came from a very small family. It had been Dad and me—with an occasional visit from Aunt Rita—for as long as I could remember. Still, I learned early on that weddings and funerals brought out the worst in people. In both instances, strangers who'd just as soon stay that way struggled to make small talk on one side of the room, while mortal enemies (aka family members) were forced to pretend that they liked—or at least didn't hate—each other on the other. Add alcohol to the mix and, well, who needed cable?

Psychiatrists didn't need to visit mental hospitals and maximum security penitentiaries to discover the origins of deviant behavior. The perfect Petri dish of dysfunctional human beings incubated in forced family gatherings. As a general rule, I tried to avoid them.

But that didn't stop me from watching someone else's show.

I ignored the conversation at my own table and took inventory of the players before me, trying to decipher who was who.

Bruce and the Beach Witch were obvious. Bruce sipped from a water glass and picked at his salad. He'd ditched this morning's khakis for a dark blue suit, though his poorly done comb-over remained intact. His wife, Monica, wore a bright red cocktail dress cut to show off her ample cleavage and more makeup than the rest of the women at the table combined. A black fur stole nestled comfortably around her shoulders. What kind of self-obsessed narcissist wore fox to a vegan restaurant?

Everyone but Bruce—who raised his water glass—clinked their champagne glasses together. The young couple being toasted at the center of the table had to be the bride and groom, Emmy and Josh. Emmy—a twenty-something pixie with short, dark hair—blushed and cuddled up close to a dark-haired, pony-tailed man that had to be Josh. Emmy's face confirmed my family-gathering-as-torture-session hypothesis. Her posture was tight, almost rigid. Worry lines creased her brow. Her thin, tension-filled lips didn't quite form a smile, in spite of the occasion and its free-flowing libations.

Unlike his fiancé, Josh seemed completely at ease. He slouched comfortably with his arm resting lightly across the back of Emmy's chair. His face was handsome in a scruffy, hippy sort of way—except for the dark smattering of man fur covering his jaw and upper lip. I suspected his new-looking suit had been purchased specifically for the evening's event. He seemed like the type who would be much more comfortable in torn jeans and Birkenstocks.

The woman on Emmy's right looked remarkably like Emmy, if you added thirty years and about the same number of pounds. She wore dark-framed glasses and matching shoulder-length hair that was liberally streaked with gray. She must be Emmy's mother, Helen. Her age, figure, and conservative dark blue dress provided a stark contrast to Bruce's new marital choice.

Helen exchanged a few words with Bruce between deep gulps of champagne, but she pointedly angled her body away from Monica. She drummed the fingers of one hand nervously on the table top and worried her thumbnail with the index finger of the other. Her foot tapped against the floor in a staccato rhythm. I couldn't decide who seemed more tense—the bride or her mother.

Only one other person held my attention. The fiftyish woman sat next to Helen and wore a black pantsuit that matched her short black hair. At first I thought she and Helen might be sisters, but they seemed closer than that—more intimate. She touched Helen's shoulder and whispered into her ear, apparently comforting her. The connection between these two women seemed deeper than blood. They had to be friends.

The rest of the group seated at the table ranged in age from mid-teens to mid-seventies. I recognized some as fellow resort guests. Others were, I suspected, locals. The locals slouched comfortably in loose-fitting clothing. The New Yorkers wore rigid postures and facial expressions that seemed almost as tight as their well-tailored formal wear.

I entertained myself by mentally sorting them into categories: Orcas Islander yes, Orcas Islander no. Orcas Islander yes...

Michael interrupted my pseudo-scientific study of human nature.

"Kate? Care to join the conversation at *this* table?"

I felt my face redden. "Oh, sorry."

"I asked if you'd like to get a bottle of wine." Michael said.

I tried to be a good girlfriend and pay attention, at least long enough to answer Michael's question, but Monica's voice boomed across the restaurant, drawing my attention back to her table like a magnet.

"I'm telling you, Emilee. That was no squirrel outside my cabin, it was a rat!" She gestured toward the kitchen and spoke even louder. "I'll bet this place is *crawling* with the scaly-tailed vermin. We'll be lucky to get out of here without catching the plague."

The room hushed. Emmy cringed and looked down at her wine glass. Josh sat up straighter, but said nothing.

Bruce put his hand on his wife's forearm. "Please, Monica, keep your voice down. I'm sure it was a field mouse."

"Field mouse, my ass. That thing was bigger than Bandit. Probably even has rabies."

Emmy gripped the table so hard her knuckles turned white. Her upper lip trembled.

Michael tapped his finger on my shoulder. "Earth to Kate—are you with us?"

I waved him away. "Shh, I'm eavesdropping!"

Emmy's mother leaned across the table until her face was less than six inches from Monica's. Her lips pulled back in an angry sneer. "I swear to God if you don't—"

The waitress picked that moment to deliver our salads. "Which one of you ordered the dressing on the side?"

"That would be her," Michael said. "The rude one."

I gave the waitress a distracted smile. "It's mine, thanks."

I tried to keep spying on the other table's conversation in between sweet, crunchy bites of baby greens, roasted pumpkin seeds, and dried cranberries, but it was useless. The clamor had died down, and I couldn't make out their words. I turned my attention back to my own meal.

Rene played with her salad, barely touching it.

"Do you want my dressing?" I asked her.

She pushed the plate aside. "No thanks, I'm not in the mood for salad."

I assumed she was saving room for double dessert.

"Let's order some bubbly," Michael said.

"None for me, thanks," Rene replied.

Sam's expression was worried. "Still not feeling good, honey?"

Rene smiled at him wanly. "I'm OK. It kind of comes and goes."

The waitress set a basket of freshly baked bread and roasted elephant garlic on the table. I pulled back the cloth cover, releasing the pungent aroma of warm, spreadable deliciousness.

Rene's face turned pasty gray—the color of contaminated putty. "The garlic smell in this place is pretty overwhelming."

Now I was concerned. The world according to Rene had four major food groups: chocolate, sugar, caffeine, and pasta. Garlic was practically her middle name. Skipping salad to save room for dessert? That was classic Rene. Not savoring the smell of elephant garlic? She must be dying.

I laid the still-steaming slice of bread on my plate. "Are you sure you're OK?"

Rene never answered, or if she did, none of us noticed. We were too distracted by the commotion that erupted across the room.

"You have got to be kidding me!" Monica shoved her chair away from the table and slammed a fork onto her plate. The sharp whack of metal on china shattered the room's formerly jovial atmosphere. "There's no meat in this pasta!" She glared at Emmy, eyes narrow with accusation. "How could you be so inconsiderate? You know I get sick if I don't eat enough protein. I might even pass out!"

Tears streamed down Emmy's face. "It's a vegan restaurant, Monica," she cried. "They never serve meat. I didn't target you deliberately."

Helen jumped up and reached across the table. She grabbed Monica's shoulders and shook her forward and back, like a frustrated parent trying to shake sense into an out-of-control teen. "Monica, this outburst will stop. *Immediately*. You have already hurt this family enough."

Monica's eyes grew wide. She took a step back.

Helen released her grasp, but the unflinching glare she leveled at Monica seemed even more aggressive than her prior assault. When she spoke, she spit out each word, accenting every syllable. "Now sit down. Shut up. And eat your dinner."

The entire restaurant stared in shocked silence. Emmy sobbed into her napkin. Bruce looked down at the table, face so red it was purple. The two dueling women postured defiantly, each daring the other to flinch.

The wall clock ticked on, counting the seconds for at least a century. Monica finally caved. She threw her napkin on the table and wrapped her fur stole tightly around her shoulders. "Enough of this nonsense. Bruce, we're leaving."

Josh slowly stood and patted his bride-to-be's hand, before soothing Monica with an easy smile. "Now, Monica, no need for all that." He turned and addressed the crowd, palms forward in supplication. "Hey there now, folks. It's all good. Go back to your dinners." He nodded to the hostess. "Give everyone a glass of champagne on Emmy and me."

A grateful-looking waitress popped dark green bottles of bubbly and poured everyone extra-full glasses. The crowd resumed their hushed conversations. I pretended to eat my salad, but I surreptitiously watched Josh.

He turned to Emmy, who was still crying. "No worries, Em." He squeezed Helen's forearm and motioned for Monica to sit. "Mellow out, ladies. I'll go get the chef." The two seething women tentatively sat down. Josh ambled to the kitchen and called out, "Kyle, can I talk to you?"

A scowling man emerged from the kitchen. He held a paring knife in one hand and a dish towel in the other.

"I'm busy back here. What's up?"

This pale, lanky man must be the chef Josh had mentioned, though he certainly didn't look the part. With his tie-dyed apron, blond dreadlocks, and oversized striped rasta hat, he looked more like a thirtyish stoner—if said stoner was in a shockingly foul mood.

Josh addressed the Bob Marley dress-alike. "Emmy's stepmom is freaking out over the menu." He scratched the base of his skull. "Would you please talk to her and work it out?"

Josh meandered back the table, easy smile still in place. Kyle marched beside him, looking considerably less amiable.

Monica watched them approach in apparent disbelief. Her lips curled down. Her eyes widened. Her Botox-stiffened brow tried to wrinkle. "You're the chef?" She threw up her hands. "Why am I even surprised?" Evidently both questions were rhetorical, because she didn't wait for a reply.

"This dinner is ridiculous. There's no main course here—just some low-budget appetizers. Bring me meat: lobster or filet mignon will do. I'm not picky."

Kyle wrinkled his lips in disgust. "This is a vegan restaurant, ma'am. We do not serve flesh." He crossed his arms. "Even if I wanted to serve you a carcass—which I don't—I couldn't. I don't store dead animals in my kitchen."

Monica sighed. "Then I guess I'll have to make do. Butcher one of the rabbits in the pen out back. At least then the meat will be fresh."

"Absolutely not!" Emmy cried. "Bugsy and Mr. Hoppins are pets!"

"You don't expect me to eat one of those filthy chickens, do you?"

Kyle stepped his feet wide. "Let me make this abundantly clear. I will not cook flesh. Animals are sentient beings. Not snacks."

I understood Kyle's dilemma. Doggie vegetarianism wasn't an option with Bella's digestive condition, and I cringed all the way to my tofu-eating toenails every time I fed her meat, no matter how humane the source. But a grudging part of me understood Monica's point, too. Food choices were deeply personal, rooted in health, ethics, and spiritual belief systems. Who were Kyle and I to judge hers?

Still, I had a hard time believing she couldn't survive one meatless meal.

Bruce tried to propose a compromise. "How about an omelet, then? You must have eggs, from the chickens."

Emmy replied. "Sorry, Dad. We don't keep the eggs. We feed them back to the hens. It replenishes their depleted calcium supplies."

Even *I* thought that was a little weird.

Monica stood and hooked her purse over her shoulder. "I can't possibly eat here."

"Monica, please." Emmy closed her eyes and took several deep breaths. When she opened them again, her face had a determined look. "Wait a second before you leave. I have an idea."

She walked Kyle a few steps from the table, but still close enough for me to overhear. "I bought some salmon to serve Monica at the family dinner tomorrow. Would you please cook it for her?"

Kyle shook his head adamantly. "Absolutely not. We had an agreement. Cooking an animal goes against everything I believe in. When I agreed to take over the restaurant here, you promised—"

"Please, Kyle?" Emmy begged, crossing her wrists over her heart. "Please? Just this one time. I can't take the fighting anymore. Monica gets worse and worse every day. I swear she's so ..."

Awful, I silently filled in.

Emmy begged for several more minutes. Kyle didn't look happy at the end of their conversation, but he acquiesced. Thirty minutes later, a waitress served Monica a large chunk of salmon with sautéed wild mushrooms on the side. I took my first bite of Penne Arrabiata. Tangy, warm tomatoes burst against my tongue, complemented by fresh roasted garlic and liberal red chilies. The perfect combination of sweet, spicy, and salty. Monica didn't know what she was missing.

Conflict resolved, we all focused on devouring our food. All except Rene, that is. She picked at her pasta, moving it around with her fork and creating Lego-like structures on her plate. Like a chameleon, her skin had changed color again, this time to match the white of our tablecloth. She set down her fork and pushed away from the table. "I'll be back in a second."

I stood up, too. "I'll come with you."

"It's OK." She smiled feebly. "But don't you *dare* touch my dessert."

I didn't notice how much time passed after Rene left our table. I was too busy sipping champagne and gorging myself on peppery carbohydrates. I was vaguely aware of a conversation between the hostess, Emmy, and Bruce, after which all three of them left the room. But to be honest, their activities no longer drew my attention.

The pasta was that good.

Michael, Sam, and I were fighting over the last fragrant clove of elephant garlic when the hostess approached our table. "I'm sorry to interrupt, but the other woman in your party collapsed. We've taken her to the office."

Sam leaped up from the table, fresh-baked bread and spreadable garlic completely forgotten. Michael and I ran close on his heels. We found Rene in the center's main office, seated strategically close to an empty wastebasket. Bruce held Rene's forearm, pressed his fingers against her wrist, and looked at his watch. Emmy hovered beside them, looking concerned.

Sam rushed up to Rene and knelt down beside her. "Honey, what's going on? The hostess said you collapsed!"

"I'm fine, Sam, really. I didn't collapse. I threw up in the bathroom, and when I stood up, I got a little dizzy, that's all. Honestly, I don't know what all the fuss is about. It's just this stupid stomach bug."

She sagged back in her chair. "I haven't eaten since that pie after lunch. I probably have low blood sugar." She swallowed hard. "But the thought of eating..." She shuddered. "Please, everyone. Let's call it a night. I'd like to go back to the cabin and lie down."

"In a minute," Emmy replied. "Let Dad take a look at you first."

Rene made eye contact with me, pointed at Sam under the table, then gestured with her eyes to the door.

Message received.

"Come on guys," I said. "Let's wait outside and give them some space." Sam didn't move. "You too, Sam," I added.

He placed his hand protectively on Rene's back. "I'm not going anywhere."

Rene sat up straighter and smiled at him encouragingly. "Please Sam, I'm feeling a little claustrophobic. Give me a few minutes." She gently nudged him toward the door. "I'm OK. I promise."

Sam followed us out to the hallway, but he remained huddled near the closed door, looking significantly less than happy. I filled the silence with louder-than-normal conversation, hoping to prevent him from eavesdropping.

"You must be Emmy. I'm Kate." I reached out my hand.

Emmy took it. "I'm sorry we had to meet this way."

"Me too," I replied. "I meant to stop by the office earlier today, but I got sidetracked."

Michael, Emmy, and I continued exchanging meaningless pleasantries while Sam paced back and forth, checking and rechecking his watch.

Finally, I asked her, "Your father's a doctor?"

"Yes, a pediatrician. I'm not sure he can help your friend, but he can at least tell us if we need to get her to a hospital."

At the mention of the word "hospital," Sam stopped pacing. He looked at the door knob, ready to pounce.

I needed to distract him, and quick, so I said the first inane thing that popped into my head.

"Hey Sam, I think there's a party later on tonight. Want to go?"

I was pretty sure the obscenity Sam grunted meant no, but at least he stepped away from the door.

Emmy leaned against the wall and groaned. "Oh lord, the open house. I forgot all about the open house." She rubbed her eyes. "Seems like this god-awful night will never end. I've been looking forward to this weekend for months. Now I just wish it was over." She sighed and stared pensively at the restaurant. "Maybe Monica will be satisfied now that she got her way. Maybe she'll give us some peace ..." Her voice trailed off.

She raised her hand as if about to say something important, then let it drop to her side. "Ah, what the hell." She smiled at me.

"We can always get drunk. At least there'll be no shortage of liquor. Dad's making his famous Manhattans."

My stomach clenched. We? Did she say *we*?

I'd obviously made a critical error. I should have distracted Sam by suggesting a different activity. Something less odious than spending more time in the same room as Monica—like tap dancing nude on top of the Space Needle.

"You *are* coming, aren't you? If your friend's feeling better, that is."

I didn't answer.

Emmy's voice grew more insistent. "I know you're probably tired, but I do hope you'll come, at least for a little while. I'd like to introduce you around and drum up some interest for your classes."

I suspected that what Emmy really wanted was a five-foot-three-inch human shield. I didn't blame her, but she'd have to look elsewhere. Nothing short of a volcanic eruption would force me out of my cabin tonight—not to hang out with her dysfunctional family.

I gave her an insincere smile. "We'll give it a try."

The office door opened. Rene limped into the hallway, followed by Bruce.

"What do you think, Dad? Should we call a doctor?" Emmy asked.

"She'll be OK." Bruce turned to Rene. "But remember, if that vomiting continues, let me know. We don't want you to get dehydrated." He handed her a piece of paper. "Here's my cell number. Call any time. If I don't answer, Emmy will know where to find me."

"Thanks," Rene said. She put the paper in her purse and looked at Sam. "I'd like to head back to the cabin."

"We'll all go," Michael replied. "It's time to call it a night."

SIX

Mount Saint Rene erupted two hours later. Multiple times. In multiple rooms. By the third, Michael and I were more than happy to honor Rene's request to give her some space and go to Emmy's event at the Retreat House. I couldn't decide who looked worse as we walked out the door: Rene, who was about to throw up again, or Sam, who was obviously frustrated and heartbroken.

He stomped behind us, erratically bouncing the beam of his flashlight along the path. "I can't believe she kicked us out!"

I gave him what I hoped was a supportive look and tried to soothe him with platitudes. "Well, Rene *is* sick, and misery doesn't always love company. You can't blame her for wanting to throw up in private."

"Give it a rest, Kate," he snapped. "That's not it, and you know it."

I froze, both surprised and insulted. I might let *Rene* get away with that tone. But *Sam*?

Michael cringed and moved several feet away, wisely giving us some space. I glared at Sam across the darkness. "I don't know anything. What are you talking about?"

He shined the light in my face and peered intently, as if searching for answers in the minutia of my expression. After a moment, he lowered his arm.

"You really don't know, do you?" His voice caught. "It must be even worse than I thought."

"Sam," I said softly. "What's going on with you two?"

"I wish I knew. Rene's been acting weird for almost a week now. I've asked her what's wrong at least a dozen times, but she keeps insisting it's nothing—that I'm imagining things." He barely lifted his feet as he shuffled along the dark path. "At first I thought she had the flu. But you know Rene, nothing keeps her down longer than a day or two. She's barely eaten for an entire week. Rene *never* stops eating."

He had a point, but he hadn't told me anything that I didn't already know. I kept listening.

"And she's been acting all furtive."

"How so?"

"Little things, but they add up. Not answering the phone when I call, closing her laptop when I enter the room ... Even worse, she goes to bed early every night. We haven't had sex in five days!"

That got my attention.

A few days of celibacy might not be unusual for most couples, but for Rene and Sam, five days had to be a record.

"I know Rene. She's definitely sick, but that's not the only thing wrong with her. She's hiding something from me, and it's tearing her up inside."

"What on earth would she be hiding?"

Sam stopped walking and silently stared at his shoes. When he looked up, his face was stricken. "I think she's having an affair."

Those were fighting words.

The hair on the back of my arms stood up. In fact, my entire body prickled, as if supercharged with static electricity. Rene had been my best friend for as long as I could remember. She was many things: flirtatious, sarcastic, an inveterate practical joker. Rene could be pushy, nosy—downright intrusive at times. Frankly, she was often annoying as hell. But above all else, Rene was loyal. Sam, of all people, should know that.

"Don't be an idiot, Sam," I snapped. "Rene would never cheat on you. She would never cheat on anybody. And if you haven't figured that out after three years of marriage, then maybe you don't deserve her."

I expected him to snap back. I had, after all, just called him an idiot. But he didn't. In fact, he didn't say anything for several long seconds. When he finally spoke, his voice sounded defeated.

"You're right." He paused, closed his eyes, and took a deep breath. "Of course you're right. But, something's going on with her, Kate. Something bad. And she won't talk to me about it. Believe me, I've asked."

I angled my face away from his mustache, bit back the subtle wave of nausea, and gave him a hug. "I'm sorry, Sam. I wish there was something I could do."

He pulled back. "Actually, there is."

I didn't like the sound of that.

"Rene shares everything with you. You could talk to her and—"

I held up my palms. "Stop right there, mister. I'd do anything to help Rene. You know that. But I will *always* take her side. Even if she *did* tell me what was bothering her, I wouldn't blab it to you. You two need to work out your own relationship issues."

"I know that, Kate, but will you at least talk to her?"

Sam wheedled and cajoled and begged and pleaded all the way to the Retreat House. By the time we reached the door, I had reluctantly agreed to talk to Rene. Honestly, I'd planned to wrangle the truth out of her, anyway. Admitting that fact to Sam was a small price to pay to give him some peace.

Emmy answered the door looking significantly more relaxed than she had earlier. An ever-so-slight slur underscored her bright vocal tone. The sweet smell of vermouth drifted on her breath. I had a feeling that she'd indulged in more than one of her father's famous Manhattans.

"I'm so glad you guys made it!" She stumbled slightly as she opened the door wider. "Let me introduce you to everyone."

We followed her around the gorgeous space, which was packed wall-to-wall with people sipping wine, soda, and a variety of forty-proof beverages.

"The Retreat House is Elysian Spring's showcase," Emmy enthused. "Isn't it beautiful?"

Indeed it was. Floor-to-ceiling windows overlooked the ocean and provided light for a flourishing indoor naturescape of philodendrons, golden pothos, and schefflera trees. The bamboo flooring gleamed with the telltale shine of recent installation and contrasted gorgeously with a large area rug woven in bright reds, blues, beiges, and greens. The carpet's pattern contained colorful stick figures meant to be dogs, horses, or goats, I wasn't sure which.

Emmy noticed my gaze. "That's a Gabbeh."

"A Gabbeh?"

"A style of carpet that was imported from Iran before the trade embargo. That particular rug was created by female weavers in the Zagros Mountains."

"It's beautiful."

"Thanks." She frowned. "Kyle hates it."

"The chef? Why would he care?"

She shrugged. "It's made of wool. If Kyle had his way, the entire resort would be vegan. To me, it's important that our facilities are fair trade, eco-sensitive, and upscale. I get his point about the wool, but I love the idea of supporting Iranian women, and no animals were harmed."

"Well, the whole house is magnificent, Emmy."

"I think so, too. Our older cabins still need work, but we'll get there. The new construction is meant to show investors what we're capable of doing. Tonight's our first event, and so far, it's going wonderfully."

She continued talking about the house with obvious pride. "The Retreat House has a large living space that can host family reunions and small corporate events. It even has a commercial grade kitchen."

"It looks huge."

"It is. Almost three thousand square feet. It can sleep up to sixteen. We're only using two of the bedrooms this week, though. I decided to let Mom and Aunt Toni have the whole house, as long as they were willing to host a few gatherings. Mom needs all the personal space she can get with Monica here." Emmy grinned. "I may snag a third bedroom the night before the wedding, though. Josh needs to miss me a little before the honeymoon."

She pointed toward a table overflowing with breads, fruits, spreads, and desserts. "Help yourself if you're hungry. Mom put out enough food to feed an army."

I patted my stomach. "Thanks, but no. I'm stuffed. Dinner was amazing."

"Well, you at least have to try one of Dad's Manhattans. He stopped drinking years ago, but he bartended his way through college, and his Manhattans are out of this world. He's making them in the kitchen now, if you're interested."

"You don't have to ask me twice," Michael replied.

"Get me one, too," I yelled to his retreating, well-muscled behind.

While Sam and Michael went off in search of libations, Emmy introduced me to the guests. Many looked familiar. Several had been at the restaurant, and a few were staff members I'd seen zipping around on golf carts. Kyle even made an appearance, minus his apron but still sporting that crazy Bob Marley hat.

We eventually made our way to the two women I had assumed were Emmy's mother and her friend. "Mom, this is Kate. She's the yoga teacher I told you about. Kate, this is my Mom, Helen, and my Aunt Toni."

Aunt? So they were related, after all. "Nice to meet you. Are you two sisters?"

Emmy smiled. "No, but they may as well be. Toni and Mom have been friends forever. I practically think of her as my second mother." The two women exchanged a strange look, but Emmy didn't seem to notice. Perhaps it was my imagination.

She turned to her mother. "I'm trying to get Kate to teach a private yoga class for the wedding party, maybe even here at the Retreat House. What do you think?"

Helen opened her mouth to answer but stopped, distracted. The room's energy shifted—from warm and inviting to tense, almost frigid. Helen's shoulders stiffened. Her jaw clenched.

"Mom?"

"I suppose…"

As Helen's voice trailed off, Emmy and I followed her gaze. Straight to the eyes of the Devil herself. Monica completed her grand entrance by removing her fur stole and blithely tossing it over the back of Kyle's chair.

The air suddenly felt thick, unbreatheable. Kyle cringed as if slapped and scrambled away from the dead animal's skin. Monica and Helen made eye contact and froze, not even breathing, poised like she-wolves about to attack. The rest of the room continued making benign conversation, blissfully unaware of the drama unfolding before them.

I told myself that someone needed to diffuse the mounting tension—that the mean-spirited joke I was about to tell was actually a kindness. But truthfully, I wanted to poke fun at Monica. I glanced around to make sure Michael wasn't listening, then I nudged Helen, pointed directly at Monica's cocktail-dressed form, and opened my mouth.

"Now *that's* one rat I'd like to poison."

Two things happened at once: I spoke much louder than I had intended, and the crowd's conversation hushed. My voice rang across the room, clearly audible to everyone within a fifty-foot radius,

Monica and Michael included. Several people broke out in laughter. A few even applauded.

Helen put her arm around my shoulder and gave me a big squeeze. "Ooooh, I *like* this one, Emmy."

Monica was less impressed. She stomped across the room, practically pulsating with anger. Even her diamonds earrings flashed, as if electrified by her fury.

"Laugh all you want," she yelled. "This place is a dive." She pointed at me. "You're one to joke about poison. Your own friend got sick at dinner. That kitchen is probably crawling with rats, roaches, and God knows what else."

The room seemed to explode.

Kyle charged Monica. "Take that back, you bitch! My kitchen's pristine!" He raised his hand, but before he could strike, Josh and another man tackled him from behind and dragged him out of the room by his armpits.

No one restrained Helen. She took five quick steps forward and slapped Monica soundly across the face, leaving four painful-looking red welts across her right cheek. The entire room gaped in shock as a confused-looking Bruce emerged from the kitchen, carefully balancing a tray of martini glasses filled with brownish-pink fluid.

"What in the hell's going on out here?"

"I can't take this anymore!" Emmy wailed. She ran from the room, bumping Bruce in the process. He wavered a moment, tried unsuccessfully to regain his balance, and dropped the tray to the floor in a cacophony of clanging metal, shattering glass, and jarring obscenities. The floor around the tray oozed, as if hemorrhaging a sticky blend of whiskey, sweet vermouth, and maraschino cherries.

"Your filthy tramp is ruining everything!" Helen ran after her daughter, tracking alcohol and crushed crystal behind her.

Monica, for once, didn't say anything. She stared into space and gingerly touched her cheek. Angry tears dripped down her face.

To be honest, I felt like crying myself. This whole catastrophe was my fault. I never should have opened my big mouth.

Bruce left the shattered mess behind, grabbed Monica's arm, and led her out of the room. Most of the rest of the guests, Sam included, surreptitiously gathered their coats and slinked out the front door. Soon, the only people left to clean up the crime scene were Michael, Toni, and me. Toni emerged from the kitchen, carrying several white terry towels. She and I picked up broken glass and mopped up alcohol while Michael watched, wearing a stern expression.

I gave him a tentative smile. He responded by shaking his head in disgust.

I tried to come up with a witty remark or at the very least a lame apology—anything to fill the dead air. But my brain refused to form a single word. Tears threatened my eyes; the sickeningly sweet smell of vermouth burned my sinuses; candied cherries squished under my kneecaps.

Michael finally spoke. "You know, for a yoga teacher you can be a real jerk sometimes."

I cringed inside, but I gave him a tentative smile. "Would you believe I was worse before yoga?" It was true, but perhaps not the smartest comment to make at that moment.

Toni stood up. "I'll give you two a minute."

"Don't bother," Michael replied. "I'm going back to the cabin." The door slammed behind him.

A thousand terry towels and two buckets of soapy water later, I excused myself to go to the bathroom. I stared at my blotchy face in the mirror and tried to gather my thoughts. Michael's not-so-silent reproach was spot on. Frankly, I was embarrassed. Well received or not, well *deserved* or not, my tasteless attempt at humor wasn't at all yogic. Yoga's teachings about communication were clear: Speak less. Speak only the truth. And if the truth will cause harm, say nothing.

Obviously, I should have picked option three.

I owed Monica an apology. I washed my hands, blotted my face, and gathered my courage. One deep breath and I was ready.

I threw open the door, purposefully strode through it—and smashed into Bruce.

"Ouch!" I said, rubbing my nose.

"Oh, sorry." Bruce glanced down the hallway. He looked oddly guilty, given the circumstances. "I didn't see you there." He closed the door to the suite's master bedroom and tucked his hands into his jacket pockets. "Monica wants to leave. I came to get her coat."

"I'm the one who should be sorry," I said. "I acted horribly. I have no idea what got into me. Let me apologize to Monica before you leave."

Bruce's skin paled. "I wouldn't talk to her now. She's not in a good mood." He continued down the hallway, hands empty.

"Bruce?"

He stopped, then turned slowly around. His tone was sharp, as if he were disciplining a disobedient child. "I told you, now is not a good time. When Monica calms down—if she calms down—I'll tell her you're sorry, but for now, you need to leave us alone."

"I will," I assured him. "But I thought you were getting her coat?"

He looked down at his hands. "Damn. I forgot." He turned back to the bedroom.

"It's not in there. She left it on a chair in the living room."

Bruce frowned, turned back around, and continued down the hallway.

I sank to the floor, leaned against the wall, and closed my eyes, trying to shut out this interminable night. A few broken martini glasses were nothing. The cracks in my relationships—both business and personal—might prove much harder to repair.

I huddled on the floor for several minutes. I had no desire to stay at the Retreat House, but it was better than going back to the cabin. As long as I remained here, alone, I wouldn't have to explain myself. I wouldn't have to face Rene's odd evasions, Sam's beseeching eyes, and Michael's recriminations. As long I remained here, alone, the worst thing I had to face was myself.

That was bad enough.

My throat ached with unspoken apologies, but I didn't have enough energy to stand up, much less to make the long, lonely trek back to the cabin. I took some deep breaths and tried to bolster my internal fortitude.

The final impetus to move didn't come from within; it came from the kitchen. Familiar, angry whispers floated down my safe-haven hallway. I told myself not to eavesdrop—that I'd already done enough damage for one night. But curiosity overcame my willpower. I stood up and tiptoed toward the sound.

I flattened my body against the wall and peeked around the industrial grade refrigerator. Monica and Helen were finally having their standoff. Helen held Monica's arm in a death grip, her face tight with anger. "Listen to me, you husband-stealing tramp," she hissed. "If you know what's good for you, you'll mind your own business. If you do anything else to ruin my daughter's wedding, I swear I'll kill you."

Unfortunately for me, Monica and I were the only people who heard her.

SEVEN

The rest of the evening went, not as I'd hoped, but as I should have predicted. Rene and Sam were fast asleep by the time I got home; Michael pretended to be. In spite of my best intentions, I had no opportunity to make apologies, no occasion to unearth hidden secrets. Instead, I spent the seemingly endless night suffering through a haze of late-night dog walks, insomnia, and profound regret.

When I groggily turned off the alarm clock at six the next morning, I resolved to be a better person. As soon as I finished teaching my morning yoga class, I'd take the first step. I'd find the Beach Wi—I mean *Monica*—and apologize for my boorish behavior. I closed my eyes and visualized our encounter.

In my delusional daydream, Monica was also transformed. She was gracious, self-effacing, and charming. We smiled, hugged, and vowed to coexist in harmony. I even imagined a grateful Emmy, who thanked me profusely for helping to reunite her fractured family.

I was kidding myself, of course. But thoughts create reality, right?

I stumbled out of bed and said a quick goodbye to the dog snoozing behind it. Class started at seven, but none of my motley crew would be attending. Michael groaned and rolled over when I tried to wake him; Rene and Sam didn't even do that much.

I tiptoed through the living room and frowned at Rene's sleeping form. *Get ready to fess up, Missy.* Rene may have successfully avoided talking to me last night, but today would be different. Sam was right; something was wrong with her, and I was going to get to the bottom of it.

But not now.

Now I had a yoga class to teach. I slipped the Yoga Chick out of my jacket pocket and placed her on the counter. I doubted anyone would call me this early, but there was no need to risk it. A rude, ringing cell phone would be downright embarrassing in the middle of my own yoga class.

I slipped on my tennis shoes, locked the cabin's door behind me, and hiked through the cool, wet grass to Shanti House, the round wooden yurt I'd noticed the night Michael and I arrived.

I played my flashlight along the trail to the main parking lot, struck again by the architectural diversity of Elysian Springs. To my right stood a micro-neighborhood of slum-like cabins covered by sagging, moss-infested roofs, barely better than the blue tarp campsites parodied in Pacific Northwest bank commercials. The hill to the left featured a gorgeous new development of eco-friendly construction that rivaled the cover of *Traveler* magazine. I couldn't help but smile at the irony. I'd traveled 120 miles to be right back at home.

Elysian Springs, like my own Greenwood neighborhood in Seattle, was seemingly trapped between decay and renewal. The only question remaining was which I'd encounter in my new yoga space: decay or renewal.

I ascended the stairs, turned the key in the door, and flipped on the overhead lights. One word immediately popped into my mind. *Wow.*

Shanti House was clearly one of the center's masterpieces. Huge windows pointed in every direction and provided a 360-degree view of the property's sparkling blue beaches, deep green forests, and expansive recreation areas. Sun poured through the east-facing windows and reflected off the obviously new bamboo floor. The single-room structure was completely unfurnished, except for a small altar and several shelves containing yoga mats, blocks, bolsters, and blankets. Strategically placed candles and a noisier-than-I-would-have-liked space heater added to the warmth and ambiance.

Between the early hour and my prior evening's outburst, I wasn't sure if my class would get any takers, but over a dozen students of various ages, sizes, shapes, and physical abilities chose to attend. Some brought their own yoga gear; others borrowed one of the new-smelling sapphire blue mats provided by the center. Some of my new students were Elysian Springs' employees, including the desk clerk and two people I'd seen working in the garden. Others were guests I'd met at the party the night before.

Once everyone got settled, I asked a few questions to assess the group's prior yoga experience. As I expected, the group was diverse, ranging from experienced practitioners to three women who were trying yoga for the first time. Teaching a mixed-level group class is always a challenge. The trick is figuring out how to design a sequence that keeps new students safe without boring those with more experience. Since no one in the room had acute injuries, I decided to make the class simple, but energizing.

I pulled out my Tibetan chimes and rang them three times, as I did at beginning of every practice. Like one of Pavlov's dogs anticipating a cookie, my own body began to relax.

"Close your eyes and start to settle in. Allow your mind to quiet, and feel the sensations of your breath."

The door opened and Toni, Helen's friend, eased through it. She mouthed the word "sorry" and grabbed a mat. I smiled and pointed to an empty space in the front row.

I began with a few simple kneeling poses to gently warm my students' lower backs as they learned how to link movement with breath. The first pose I taught was Chakravakasana, also called Cat Pose.

"Please come to your hand and knees." I coached the beginners to place blankets under their kneecaps. "Inhale and lengthen your spine, from the crown of your head to your tailbone." As expected, each student gently extended her spine. "Exhale and fold back, bringing your hips toward your heels and your forehead toward the floor. This is called Child's Pose." Although I saw various interpretations of my instructions, each student appeared to find the desired low back stretch. More importantly, their movements looked peaceful and coordinated with the breath.

So far so good.

Twenty minutes later, my disparate group of early morning yogis huffed, puffed, yawned, and stretched their way through the first cycle of Sun Salutes. I kept my instructions short, timing them so that each phrase would fit within a single breath.

"Inhale and raise your arms toward the ceiling. As you exhale, bend forward and place your palms on the floor. Inhale and step your right foot back. Exhale and step your left foot back next to it in Downward Dog."

As intended, the group moved in unison, like synchronized dancers flowing with coordinated breath. The experienced students, Toni among them, closed their eyes and flowed with the grace and ease of consistent practice. The beginners moved tentatively, eyes open, glancing left and right for guidance. Everyone seemed to be enjoying their yoga experience.

Everyone, that is, except a frowning woman in the back row. I nicknamed her the Grumpy Yogini. Michael wouldn't have approved of my choice, but the term fit. Yogini meant female yogi, and this female yogi was certainly grumpy. The tiny, scowling woman wore black yoga pants and a blue tank top with the word *shanti*—Sanskrit for peace—printed on the front. I caught her eye and smiled encouragingly. She looked away, lips thinned. In concentration, I hoped.

After three Sun Salutes, I led the class through several balance postures, a few strengthening prone poses, and some gentle seated stretches. We ended with a breath practice designed to build energy, followed by a ten-minute rest in Savasana, yoga's pose of quiet relaxation.

The sea of supine yogis in front of me looked happy, relaxed, and injury free. Except for the Grumpy Yogini, that is. I tried not to take it personally each time the still-frowning, tank-top-clad woman looked pointedly at her watch. After all, my gentle, breath-centered style of yoga wasn't for everyone. She might be used to

Power Yoga, Iyengar, or—I shuddered at the thought—even Hot Yoga.

I didn't get a chance to ask her. She scooted out the door without making eye contact as soon as we finished saying Namaste—the Sanskrit greeting exchanged at the end of each class.

I pushed any lingering feelings of inadequacy deep into my subconscious, said goodbye to the rest of the participants, and invited them to return the following morning. Most students departed quickly after class, heading off to breakfast and the rest of their morning adventures. Toni stayed and straightened the yoga props.

After the final student left, I sheepishly approached her. "How did everything go the rest of last night?"

"Most everyone left before you and I cleaned up the mess. Monica slinked out the door a little after you did." She smiled. "After that, the rest of the night was uneventful."

My face flashed hot. "I'm sorry I caused such a scene."

"Don't be. You only said what everyone else has been thinking." She continued speaking as we slipped on our shoes and walked outside. "But that's not why I waited for you."

I locked the door and steeled myself, afraid of what she might say next. Was Toni some sort of emissary, sent by Emmy to fire me? Maybe she'd come to tell me that Monica had taken out a restraining order. Heck, it might even be good news. Maybe Michael and I had been banned from the wedding.

Toni smiled. "I've practiced yoga for years, but I've never taken a class like this one. The breath work was amazing!"

I had no idea how tense I'd become until I felt my shoulders relax. She wanted to chat about yoga. Yoga was safe territory. Yoga, I could talk about for hours. "Thanks. The style I teach is called Viniyoga. I'm sure you can find it in New York. If you'd like, I can—"

My words were cut off by a high-pitched scream. The scream of a terrified soprano plummeting off the edge of a skyscraper. The scream of a patient undergoing surgery without anesthesia. The scream of unbridled, tortured terror.

Toni and I gave each other one quick look, then tore across the grass toward the bloodcurdling sound. Frantic voices punctuated each shriek.

"Somebody catch him!"

"He's going to kill them!"

I imagined dozens of unspeakable evils as I ran toward the commotion: teenaged psychopaths, gun-wielding terrorists, duct-tape-wrapped suicide bombers, disgruntled yoga students ...

I rounded the corner and discovered—

A fifteen-pound black and white terriorist.

Bandit had discovered his life's purpose.

Rabbit hunting.

He dug, nipped, ripped, and clawed at the rabbit hutch, trying to get to the creatures inside. A small crowd of people struggled, unsuccessfully, to stop him. Each time someone got close, Bandit leaped out of their grasp.

I wanted to throttle the little devil, but I couldn't blame him. He'd been born for this day. Jack Russell terriers were bred to hunt—raccoons, rats, foxes, and yes, even bunnies. All that stood between Bandit and fulfilling his destiny were a half-dozen two-legged buzz killers and some old, rusty chicken wire.

Bugsy and Mister Hoppins didn't appreciate the game. Cornered by a vicious killer with no means of escape, they had only one option: scream like their lives depended on it, which of course, they did. If someone didn't stop Bandit soon, both rabbits might die. Their tiny hearts couldn't take the stress.

"Where's his owner?" someone yelled.

No one answered. Monica either didn't know about the trouble her dog was causing or—more likely—she didn't give a damn.

Bandit hurled his body at the cage. The rabbits screamed.

My head exploded.

Anger spread like a cancer, metastasizing throughout my body. My heart pounded; my muscles cramped; my nerve endings sizzled. Even my skin pulsated with rage. Allowing Bandit to charge after Bella was bad enough; Bella could defend herself. Letting him attack helpless rabbits? Well, that was war. My peacemaking resolutions went exactly where those terrified bunnies wished they could go: right down the rabbit hole.

That's it. I'm going to kill her.

Bandit's success was ultimately his undoing. He grabbed a loose corner of chicken wire and tugged, opening a terrier-sized hole along the edge of the hutch. The action distracted him long enough for his would-be captors to surround him. A male body flew through the air and landed face-first on the ground.

"Got him!" yelled the triumphant-sounding teenager.

The crowd applauded as their brown-haired hero carried his squirming, whining captive away from the rabbit hutch. The bunnies stopped screaming and huddled together, unharmed.

"Does anyone know who he belongs to?" someone asked.

My teeth clenched tightly together; my lips barely moved. "I do. And I swear to God, if that red-clawed witch doesn't start using his leash, I'll strangle her with it!"

The air became pin-drop silent. Six pairs of shocked, silent eyes stared at me. Even the bunnies wrinkled their noses, as if scowling at me in disapproval.

Oh no. Had I really said that?

Blood poured from my head to my stomach. I glanced around for Toni, hoping to beg for forgiveness. The last thing I needed was for Emmy to hear that I'd threatened to kill her stepmother. Again. But Toni was gone.

I faced the gape-mouthed crowd instead. Part of me wanted to apologize for the outburst. Part of me wanted to explain. Part of me wanted to assure the shocked strangers that my mouth and my intentions sometimes didn't match up. That of course, I'd never strangle Monica. I'd never hurt anyone.

But I was too mortified to speak. So I covered up my embarrassment with pretend indignation. I stomped up to the Bandit-carrying teen and reached toward him with vibrating, claw-like hands.

"Give him to me."

I held tight to the squirming dog's collar, marched to Monica's cabin, and pounded my fist on the door.

I stood at the door for several grumbling, impatient, foot-tapping seconds until Bruce finally answered. Loose, puffy skin pillows hung underneath his eyes. When he spoke, his voice was less than friendly. "What are you doing here? I told you, Monica doesn't want to talk to you."

I held the yapping, writhing terrier up to his face. "Well, I want to talk to her. Bandit was terrorizing the rabbits. She needs to keep him on leash."

Bruce sighed and opened the door wider. "That stupid dog again." He took off his glasses and rubbed the bridge of his nose. "Some days I don't know who's more frustrating: Monica, or that god-awful dog. She must have decided to let him run loose again. She promised Emmy that she'd keep him under control, but sometimes she can be..." He shook his head.

Awful.

Bruce took Bandit from my arms. "You'll have to talk to Monica later. She's not here."

"When will she be back?"

He looked at his watch. "Honestly, I'm not sure. She and Bandit left over an hour ago. She said she was going stop at the restaurant and then go for a soak in the hot tubs. I thought she'd be back by now."

That didn't make any sense. "It's not even nine yet. The hot tubs are closed until ten."

"Emmy gave Monica a key to the spa last night and encouraged her to go after hours."

"She wanted Monica to use the spa when it's closed?"

Bruce shrugged. "Emmy made it sound like a peace offering, but I think she's trying to keep Monica away from the other guests." He frowned. "It's probably for the best. Monica is in a *foul* mood. She was up sick most of the night. When she left this morning, she was hell bent on telling off that chef for giving her food poisoning. I tried to talk her out of it, but there was no reasoning with her."

Monica had been sick last night? She seemed fine when I saw her at the Retreat House. I idly wondered if she had somehow caught

Rene's flu. On a different day, I might have asked Bruce more questions, but I had my own agenda. I said a quick goodbye and walked down the stairway.

I should have taken Bruce's advice and gone back to my cabin. I should have let some time pass. Time in which Monica and I could both have cooled down. But I didn't. I was determined to have it out with her, once and for all.

I set off to find her.

Bruce yelled to my retreating behind. "I'm serious. I'd wait awhile before talking to her!"

I headed toward the center's main recreation area, but I kept an eye out for Monica all along the way. I walked down the hill, past the entrance to the trail system. I marched past the animal enclosures and the now-napping bunnies. I glanced in the restaurant and peeked in the library. By the time I reached the spa area, I'd burned off most of my anger and my rational mind had regained control.

It was clearly time for a new approach. I'd already tried yelling at Monica—mocking her, even—with less than optimal results. I suspected reasoning with her wouldn't work, either, but I had to give it a try.

If Monica and I were going to be trapped on the same island for seven more days, we'd have to come up with a compromise. Maybe she'd be more careful once she learned about the trouble Bandit had caused this morning. Even if she refused to keep him leashed, maybe we could work out a schedule—a safe time for Bella to walk outside. No one who owned a dog could be all evil, could they?

I stopped at the entrance. The sign clearly indicated that the spa was still closed. I cupped my hands around my mouth and yelled, "Hello!"

No response.

I pushed on the unlocked gate. It opened with a low, eerie squeak.

I paused, suddenly wary, and not about my upcoming altercation. The back of my neck tingled. Yoga teachers are deeply attuned to subtle energy. We can even be overwhelmed—hijacked, in a way—by energetic shifts. The energy in this place had been corrupted. It felt jarring. Angry. I considered retreating to my cabin, but something propelled me. Something forced me to move forward.

I reassured myself with idle mental chatter. *Come on, Kate. Of course the energy feels off. Think about who's lurking in there.* My mouth went dry. Perhaps the word "lurking" wasn't the best choice.

I called out in what I hoped was a firm and confident voice. "Monica!" No answer. I left the gate open and eased up the stairs, past a three-foot-tall statue of Ganesh, the Hindu elephant god. Ganesh was the remover of obstacles. That had to be a good sign, right?

I continued ascending, step by cautious step. "Monica, are you there?"

I stood at the top of the steps, waiting and listening. The caustic scent of humidified chlorine burned my nostrils. The mechanized bubble of water jets roared in my ears. "Monica?" My voice sounded tentative, even to me.

I turned the corner, walked halfway across the deck, and froze. Monica was, indeed, floating in one of the tubs. Face down. Completely naked, except for the rhinestone-studded dog leash wrapped around her neck.

EIGHT

I scrambled to the edge of the sunken tub. Deep in my core, I knew that it was too late to save Monica, but I had to try. I looked around the deserted area, willing someone—anyone—to magically appear.

"Help! Somebody, help!" I screamed.

I jumped into the hot, gurgling water, turned Monica over, and shook her, trying not to fixate on the gruesome blue color of her lips or the splotches of red dotting her eyes.

"Monica, wake up! You have to wake up!"

No response.

I jumped out of the water, grabbed her arms, and tried to pull her out, but my hands slipped uselessly across her wet skin. Beads of sweat dripped from my hairline and pooled with the frustrated tears pouring down my cheeks. I was immobilized—trapped between irreconcilable options. I couldn't stay here; I'd never save Monica by myself. But I couldn't leave her alone, either.

I reached for my cell phone, but my hands came back empty. Why did I leave it behind? I frantically scanned the area around me, but I found no phone, no intercom, no connection to the outside world. Only Monica's clothing, piled on a nearby bench.

Maybe Monica brought a phone. I pawed through her belongings, dimly aware of her lingering scent: cigarette smoke mixed with musky perfume. My hands found towels, clothes, cigarettes, and keys, but no electronic devices.

"Help me!" I screamed to the void.

My mind finally grasped the obvious. If I wasted any more time, Monica would be dead for sure.

Time to stop yelling and focus on rescue.

If pulling from above didn't work, maybe I could push her out from below. I jumped back into the water, took a deep breath, and dove under the surface. I pushed up on Monica's inert form with all my strength. My nerve endings vibrated, fueled by the adrenaline of a soccer mom trying to lift a Volkswagen off of her toddler.

Monica's body barely moved.

I burst to the surface and gasped for air. I only had one idea left. Swallowing back sour stomach acid, I yanked Monica's hair out of the way and unwound the leash from her neck. I couldn't let myself think about the deep, reddish-purple bruise slashed across her throat, so my denial-driven mind latched on to her earlobes instead. A sparkling diamond earring glinted from one; a dark chasm plunged into the other. Had Monica lost one of her earrings when she got dressed that morning? Or had she felt it rip from her body as she fought for her life? I imagined her terror, her pain. Her awful, interminable, final seconds. The deck shifted underneath me.

Dad's scolding voice rang through my head. *Focus, Kate. You can do this. It might not be too late. You might still be able to save her.*

I took a deep breath, shook off the dizziness that threatened to overwhelm me, and channeled my inner Bella. I pulled the leash across Monica's chest, looped it under her armpits, and wrapped it around my hands. I imagined myself about to tug, not on Monica's body, but on one of Bella's treasured sticks.

I planted my feet, leaned back, and pulled. Rhinestones bit into my palms. My back and my wrists screamed. But I felt movement. It was working! I bellowed out loud, primordial grunts with each fierce tug. Monica's upper body slid over the edge. I paused, still gripping the leash, and tried to catch my breath. One more tug, and I'd free her hips as well.

Here we go. One … two …

A metallic crash startled me and ripped away my attention. I jumped and accidentally loosened my hands. Monica slid back into the water, leash still looped around her torso. Rhinestone flowers twinkled uselessly as the leash sank to the bottom.

"What are you doing?" A tall twenty-something man stood at the top of the stairs. His mouth gaped open. The floor around him was strewn with white plastic bottles and a now-empty metal bucket. An irrational thought raced through my mind. *You can't possibly clean this hot tub now, there's a body in it.*

"Oh my God—you're killing her!"

"I'm not killing her," I cried. "I'm trying to save her. Now *help me!*"

For a brief moment, he hesitated, unsure whether I was an innocent bystander, a Good Samaritan, or a killer. He still looked undecided when he knelt next to me.

"You grab her arms," I said. "I've got her feet." I jumped back into the water. Together, we pulled Monica onto the deck and laid her on her back.

I didn't think; I just acted. I'd faithfully attended first aid training year after year, praying that I'd never have to use it. I covered Monica's blue lips with my own, gave two quick breaths, and looked up. My gape-jawed assistant sat there, motionless. "Go get help," I ordered.

He didn't move.

"Now!" I yelled.

That jarred him into action. He jumped up and disappeared down the stairs.

A century passed while I puffed into Monica's lips and pressed rhythmically on her chest. My arms, my back—inexplicably, even my legs—burned from the effort. I pumped and I prayed and I pleaded for help to arrive. Emmy came first, along with the man I'd sent for help. Josh and Bruce appeared a few minutes later.

Emmy's voice came through a fog, barely penetrating my awareness. "The ambulance is on its way, Dad."

Bruce shoved me roughly aside. "Get away from her."

He pressed his fingers to the side of Monica's neck. Her lips still glowed that horrendous, almost neon shade of blue.

I waited in silence, knowing what Bruce would say next, but hoping—praying—I was wrong. A low gurgle emerged from deep in his throat. He stumbled away from Monica's body and crumpled to the ground, clutching his chest.

"She's dead. Oh my God, Monica's dead."

———

The EMTs arrived within minutes, followed by two deputies from the San Juan County Sheriff's Department. The paramedics stood helplessly off to the side while a balding, gray-haired deputy held vigil over Monica's body. A younger Asian officer took charge of us five witnesses.

He led us past a small, murmuring crowd that had gathered outside the spa's entrance. The ambulance's lights pulsed in a red-and-white rhythm, keeping time with my pounding head. Disembodied voices crackled over the police cars' scanners. My mind reeled, trapped within a recurring nightmare.

Could this really be happening again?

Just six months ago, I found my friend George's body lying in a pool of blood. Just six months ago, I sat inside a police car, assuring two skeptical detectives that I knew nothing about his death. Just six months ago, I collapsed on my bed, certain that I'd never recover from the trauma. That night, just six months ago, still haunted my nightmares.

I should have been immune, or at least numbed, to violence. I'd been raised by a cop, after all. Stupid criminal stories were Dad's version of Grimm's fairy tales. But listening to Dad's tall tales about Seattle's dumbest lawbreakers was nothing compared to witnessing the true aftereffects of violent crime. I didn't much like my new point of view.

The deputy separated the five of us, presumably to keep us from synching our stories. After allowing me to change into some dry clothes, he sequestered me in the center's library and told me that "Sergeant Bill" would take my statement shortly. By "shortly," he must have meant a few days after Hades turned icy. I paced the small room for well over an hour, reliving the morning and thumbing through magazines I didn't have the attention span to read.

I should have practiced pranayama or done a few yoga poses to calm myself, but I couldn't seem to sit down. All I could do was pace like a caged tiger, back and forth, forth and back, thudding my tennis shoes against the wooden floor in a dull, rhythmic cadence. Hopefully being a trapped animal wasn't my metaphorical future.

I froze.

The police couldn't think *I* killed Monica, could they?

I had to admit, from an outsider's perspective, it didn't look good. I didn't like Monica, that was no secret. My fingerprints were all over her belongings, not to mention the murder weapon. I'd even been found yanking on Monica's water-soaked body.

Oh, crap.

Back to pacing. Back and forth, forth and back.

Ninety panicking, fretting, foot-pounding minutes later, the deputy knocked at the door. "Sergeant Bill's ready to talk to you now."

He led me to Emmy's office, which "Sergeant Bill" had commandeered for a makeshift interview room. Sweat covered my palms and dripped down the back of my neck. I felt like a paranoid teen on her way to the principal's office. I hadn't done anything wrong, but I was convinced I'd be sent to detention, nonetheless.

"Have a seat Miss, um…" The man sitting behind Emmy's desk looked down at his notes.

"Davidson. Kate Davidson." I hesitated, much too nervous to sit. "I'd rather stand, thank you."

His eyes met mine. "I said, have a seat, Miss Davidson." It wasn't a request.

I sat.

While the sergeant reviewed his notes, I drummed my fingers on the desktop and took stock of my future inquisitor. He was short, no more than five-foot-six, and his pants were held up by a belt approximately two sizes smaller than his doughy middle. His receding hairline accented a large, creased forehead.

Nervousness made me goofy—like a dental patient who had inhaled too much nitrous oxide. I couldn't suppress a giggle. I was about to be grilled by the sergeant from *Gomer Pyle*.

He laid down his notebook and scowled across the desk. "Something funny I should know about? Personally, I don't think murder's a laughing matter."

I immediately sobered. "No, of course not."

"Glad to hear it." He leaned back and smiled disarmingly. "This should only take a few minutes."

He pretty much stuck with the basics at first. He told me his name: "Sergeant Bill Molloy, but you can call me Sergeant Bill." He asked me where I lived, why I was on the island, what I'd done that morning, and how I'd happened to come across Monica's body. His lilting, almost melodic voice lulled me into a false sense of security.

I conned myself into believing that Sergeant Bill was just a good old boy, looking for the truth. Dad said I should never lie to the cops, so I answered his questions honestly. But I didn't volunteer any information. My recent altercations with Monica had nothing to do with her murder. Why confuse the issue?

Sergeant Bill took copious notes, nodding and smiling encouragingly. After fifteen rambling minutes, I completed my spiel.

"Well," he said, closing his notebook and laying down his pen. "I think we're about done here."

"You mean I can go?" It couldn't possibly be this easy. I never got away with anything.

He shrugged. "I don't see why not."

Relief washed over me like water in a warm shower. For once, luck and the universe were on my side. I stood up, eased to the door, and rested my hand on the doorknob. Only two more steps and I'd be free. My mind chattered, nervously narrating each action in a silent monologue.

OK, Kate, you're almost there. Stay calm and don't blow it. I took a deep breath. *Turn the knob to the right.* The latch clicked and released. *Open the door.* The hinges squeaked open; a cool breeze caressed my cheeks. As I glanced through the doorway, the empty hall beckoned me—coaxed me toward freedom.

Step one foot forward, and—

"You know, there's only one thing I don't get about your story."

The melodic lilt in Sergeant Bill's voice had completely evaporated.

Tension spread from my toes to my scalp. I tried to suppress—or at least camouflage—a mounting sense of panic. I took a deep breath and turned to face him. Sergeant Bill leaned forward, elbows on the desk, fingers laced together. He didn't look at all friendly.

I forced my lips into a smile and tried to look innocent.

"What's that?"

"Why is it that six different witnesses say you threatened to strangle the victim this morning?"

Sergeant Bill wasn't smiling anymore. Then again, neither was I. We stared at each other in silence.

"Why don't you close that door and sit on back down."

NINE

AFTER THAT, HIS QUESTIONS became significantly more pointed. My answers, more tentative. I knew my Tofurky was cooked when he suggested that we continue our conversation at the police station. My body flashed hot, then cold. I squeezed my arms tight to my body and suppressed the urge to bolt.

"Am I under arrest?"

"No. Not yet."

At least that was something.

He narrowed his eyes. "Should you be?"

I consciously relaxed my fists and tried not to blink. "No. Definitely not."

Sergeant Bill's plastic smile didn't reach the wrinkles around his eyes. "Well then, there's no need to make this difficult. All you need to do is come to the station, answer a few more questions, and you'll be on your way."

He couldn't fool me that easily. If nothing else, Dad's stories had taught me that smart criminals never threw away their rights. "I don't have to go with you."

Sergeant Bill shrugged. "That's true. You don't. But unless you have something to hide, there's no reason not to." He leaned back and jiggled the cuffs on his belt. "I'd hate to come back here with an arrest warrant."

On the other hand, *I* wasn't a criminal. And I didn't want to act like one.

I should have refused to go anywhere without a lawyer, but I felt oddly compelled to obey. As if by obeying, I could convince Sergeant Bill that I was a good girl—much too good to commit murder.

"OK. Give me the address and I'll meet you there."

He pushed back his chair and thrust the notebook into his pocket. "We'll drive together."

Instead of one phone call, he allowed me one stop—at the cabin, to tell Michael where I was headed.

Worry lines creased Michael's brow. "Kate, don't say anything. I'll follow behind and meet you at the station."

I'm not sure who I was trying to convince: Michael or myself. "I'll be fine, Michael. The only thing I'm guilty of is trying to save Monica's life." I tried to smile, but my stressed-out lips barely curled upward. "Stay here with Bella. I'll be back as soon as I can."

Michael followed us outside. Sergeant Bill opened the door to the back seat of his car and gestured for me to get in.

"Can't I at least sit in the front?"

"It's against regulations, Ma'am." I didn't argue. Good girls didn't argue.

The door slammed shut.

The space around me felt suddenly smaller—more claustrophobic. I tried to lengthen my breath, but it refused to comply, remaining shallow and high up in my chest. I wasn't under arrest, so why did I feel like a prisoner? I reached over to roll down the window.

I couldn't.

There weren't any window controls, no door handles, either. I couldn't even climb to the front seat, unless I figured out how to wedge my body underneath the car's screened divider.

"It's kind of lonely back here," I quipped. "How about some music?"

Sergeant Bill ignored my request and all subsequent attempts at idle chatter. We drove in silence for forty-five minutes. Forty-five minutes during which my imagination went wild, listing all of the evidence against me. I almost convinced myself I was guilty.

I'd threatened to kill Monica in front of several witnesses. Twice, if you counted the rat poisoning comment. I was all talk, no action, but no one on Orcas knew that.

That gave me motive.

A witness found me bent over the body, holding the murder weapon.

That gave me means.

I was alone with Monica's body for several minutes before anyone found us.

That gave me opportunity.

If I wanted to look innocent, I shouldn't have touched anything. I shouldn't have wasted time looking for cell phones. I should have immediately left the spa and run screaming for help. But what if Monica had still been alive? I couldn't leave her there, floating. Not when there was even a remote possibility that I could save her. So I'd done everything I could think of to help—all while making myself look guilty, at least to Sergeant Bill.

But I knew something Sergeant Bill didn't. I knew I was innocent. I may have had means, motive, and opportunity, but so did the real murderer. I didn't know who that was—yet—but I was damned sure going to figure it out. Washington was a death penalty state. My life might depend on it.

The car turned right and bumped along a long, dusty gravel road that ended at a squat wooden building. The sign out front read "San Juan County Sheriff: Orcas Island Station." Sergeant Bill pulled into one of the four parking spots and turned off the ignition. He released me from my mobile prison cell and uttered the first words he'd said to me since we left Elysian Springs.

"After you."

He nodded at a middle-aged blonde seated at the reception desk and led me to a small, airless room containing a metal table and two chairs. The room's baby-vomit-green walls were completely bare, with nothing, not even the requisite two-way mirror, to make the space feel inviting.

Sergeant Bill slowly lowered the blinds. Each screeching pull on the multistringed cord sucked out more of the room's oxygen. Each disappearing sliver of light siphoned off more of my confidence. My heart hammered. My mouth felt dry. Even my skin itched. I hadn't done anything wrong, so why did I feel such an overwhelming need to confess?

"Can I get you something? Coffee? Water?"

"Coffee would be great. Thanks." The last thing my already hyperaroused system needed was caffeine, but holding the hot mug might soothe me. At the very least, it would give me something to do with my hands.

He left the room and said he'd be back shortly. The door clicked behind him. I turned the knob, just to be sure. Locked.

I had no idea how much time passed as I sat in that small, suffocating room, but it was long enough for my conscience to go crazy.

Maybe I *was* guilty, in a way.

My actions didn't warrant a life sentence, but they were nothing to brag about, either. Yoga's philosophy advocates nonviolence—in actions, words, and thoughts. I didn't lay a hand on Monica, but my words certainly carried a punch. And my thoughts, well they'd been downright malicious. I'd practically *dared* the universe to hurt her.

All of my recent sins haunted me while I waited in that putrid room. The longer I sat there alone, the guiltier I felt, which was probably Sergeant Bill's plan all along.

After at least a decade, Sergeant Bill returned and placed a paper cup of metallic-smelling brown liquid on the table. He skipped the preamble and got right to the punch.

"Look, no one thinks you *planned* to hurt that woman. Everyone I talked to said she was a real bitch. You just got angry—out of control. Maybe even temporarily insane." He sat down and crossed his ankle over his knee. "I want to help you, but I can't. Not unless you allow me to. Make it easy on yourself and confess. I'll do everything I can to help you get a reduced sentence."

The sheer ludicrousness of the situation finally occurred to me. "Yes, I was mad at her—*over a dog*. Why would I kill her over that?

I barely knew her! Besides, like you said, Monica was a real..." I stopped myself. "Not many people liked her."

"Yes, but you were the only person found choking her."

And that's when I panicked. A chemical thunderstorm raged through my system. My adrenal glands opened, flooding my body with adrenalin and cortisol. My heart pounded. My blood sugar plummeted. I felt dizzy, frustrated, and terrified all at the same time.

I pounded my fists on the table and yelled, "I didn't choke her!"

Sergeant Bill uncrossed his ankle and raised his eyebrows. "That's quite a temper you have there, miss. Did you lose control like that this morning? Is that why you strangled that poor woman?"

Two horrifying images flashed through my mind. The first was a thirty-two-year-old, pony-tailed yoga teacher gripping the bars of an eight-foot-square prison cell. The second was the confused face of the unadoptable German shepherd she'd left behind. The fire in my system fizzled, suffocated by heavy, cold dread.

At first I said nothing. I clutched the arms of the chair, stared at the table, and took several lengthened breaths. Then I consciously relaxed my hands. Finally, I stalled for more time by sipping the tepid battery acid inside my coffee cup.

By the time I looked up, I had no energy left for false bravado. "You're right. I have a terrible temper. Always have. I'm not proud of it." Tears blurred my vision. "But I've never been violent, not once. I swear to you, I didn't kill Monica. I tried to save her life."

Sergeant Bill wrinkled his brow, leaned back, and stared at me for at least a century. He gave a single, distinct nod.

"I believe you."

I tried to read his expression, but I couldn't be sure. Did he *really* believe me, or was this another one of his tactics?

He sat forward again and laid his palms on the table. "Talk to me, Miss Davidson. Tell me exactly what happened this morning." He held up a finger. "And this time, don't hold anything back."

Lord only knows what would have happened next. I certainly wasn't about to exercise my right to remain silent. Frankly, I would have done just about anything to leave that oxygen-deprived room. I opened my mouth, about to admit everything—beach walk, death threats, and all.

"I never meant to—"

The door burst open and a tall, bearded man strode purposefully into the room.

"Hello, Bill. You may as well stop right now. My client is done talking."

His client?

If he was a lawyer, I was a supermodel.

The gray-bearded man wore filthy jean overalls hooked over a red flannel shirt. An unpleasant smell emanated from the soles of his work boots. I'd never met this man, but I knew him. His picture had hung above my dinner table at Eden.

What was the goat rescue guy doing here, claiming to be my attorney?

Sergeant Bill looked annoyed. The goat man, amused.

I'm pretty sure I looked like I was about to be sick.

My horrified eyes locked on the stranger's beard. I saw something in it—something different than the usual collection of saliva and food crumbs. Something was lodged in that disorganized tangle of facial hair, right next to his chin. It only moved when he talked, right? Surely it wasn't ... it couldn't be ... *alive*?

I looked to the side and tried not to gag.

"Who are you?" I asked between swallows.

The goat man's reply sounded stern, in spite of his disarming, hillbilly twang. "Miss Davidson, I highly recommend that you shut that pretty little mouth of yours." He turned to my inquisitor. "My client has nothing to say to you, Bill. So unless you plan to arrest her, you'd best be letting her go now."

Sergeant Bill sighed and rubbed the bridge of his nose. "Fine, Dale. You win. But she'd better not leave the island."

Dale, the goat lawyer, gestured toward the door. "Give us a second, honey. Your friends are outside."

Just the invitation I was waiting for. I scurried out of the room and joined Michael, Rene, and Sam in the lobby.

Michael wrapped me in a long, hard hug. "Kate, are you OK?"

"I'm fine. Stressed out, but fine." I pointed to the interview room. "Who's that guy in there claiming to be my lawyer?"

"He's a lawyer?" Michael looked confused.

"He must be John's friend," Rene replied.

I rubbed my temples and groaned. "I thought this day couldn't get any worse. You called John?"

I understood why. John O'Connell had been my father's partner at the Seattle Police Department. Even more importantly, he was my friend. He practically adopted me when Dad died. After twenty-five years on the force, John, more than anyone, would know where to find me a Get Out of Jail Free card.

Still, it was hard to know which would be worse—death by hanging or a life sentence of listening to John's lectures about my newest run-in with the law. I supposed I could always choose lethal injection...

"Don't be mad, Kate," Rene said. "I called him. We didn't know what else to do. John said you needed a lawyer—immediately. He told us to head to the station and wait for a friend of his."

Michael took over telling the story. "We left right away. That farmer guy walked in a couple of minutes after we got here." He shook his head. "I still can't believe he's an attorney."

"Maybe John's developing Alzheimer's," I quipped.

"Funny, Kate." Rene smiled, but her eyes remained sober. She put her hand on my arm. "Hon, you need to take this seriously. You might be in real trouble. Is it true that you threatened to strangle the woman who was killed?" Her face turned green. "Oh no, I think I'm going to be sick."

She covered her mouth and bolted for the bathroom. By the time she reemerged a few minutes later, Dale had ambled into the lobby. His voice was significantly louder than I would have expected, considering he was bound by attorney-client privilege.

"It was just like I thought. Bill doesn't really think you killed anyone, but he had to bring you in to keep up appearances, it being an election year and all." He reached out his hand. "I'm Dale Evans, by the way. I'm your attorney. You must be the infamous Kate." He paused mid-shake, pulled me closer, and peered directly into my eyes. "You *didn't* kill anyone, did you?"

"Of course not. Why would I kill someone over an off-leash dog?"

He smiled and released his grip. "That'd be a new one, grant you that." He flashed a huge smile at the obviously eavesdropping receptionist. "Hey there, Dolores. How're you doing? Beautiful day, isn't it?"

She quickly looked down and resumed typing.

Dale put his arm around my shoulder. "Don't worry, honey. Bill's a little slow on the uptake, but he's good folk. He'll figure out who killed that poor woman. You'll be on your way back to Seattle in no time."

I'm sure he meant to comfort me, but the effect was exactly the opposite. As Dale's arm wrapped around my shoulders, his beard moved dangerously close to my face. That thing—I prayed it was a thing, not a creature—was still lodged between several wiry gray hairs. It moved as he spoke; it jiggled with every syllable.

This would never do.

I raised my hand to brush the tiny object away, but I couldn't make myself touch it. I wiped at my own face instead, hoping Dale would get the hint.

He didn't.

My eyes begged Michael for help, but he just looked at me and shrugged. I felt my lips quiver. My skin started to crawl. I tried to inconspicuously back away, but Dale hugged me in closer, almost touching me with that greasy, gray scraggle of man fur. I gulped and tried not to panic. "Dale, there's um...something, um ...something on your chin."

"Oh is there, now." Dale backed away and brushed at his beard. A piece of brownish-yellow straw fluttered lifelessly to the floor. "Sorry about that. I was cleaning out the goat pens when John called." He looked down at his clothes, as if noticing them for the first time. "I didn't take time to get all gussied up. John said you were smart as a whip, but that you'd be a pain-in-the-ass client. He said you probably wouldn't keep your mouth shut, so I hopped in my truck and headed straight to the station."

116

He chuckled. "Quite the excitement, your little murder is. We don't get a lot of crime around here, 'cept maybe some shoplifting now and again. Heck, most people don't even lock their doors. They get a big, mean-looking dog and call it good. Last major criminal around these parts was the Barefoot Bandit."

He walked to the reception desk and winked at the still-eaves-dropping woman behind it. "Now *that* was some excitement, wasn't it Dolores? That young kid running around stealing air-planes and all." Dale poured a glass of water from a pitcher on the desk and drank it in several thirsty gulps. "Been years since we had a murder on the island." He crumpled the paper cup and tossed it the trash. "This'll be fun."

Michael and I gaped at each other incredulously, for once in complete agreement. I didn't know why John had sent this man to represent me, but I knew I could find someone better. I *had* to find someone better. But first I needed to fire Dale without hurting his feelings.

"You've been great today. I appreciate your help. But the thing is … um … maybe I need a different lawyer. You know … maybe one from Seattle."

"Sorry, hon. You're better off with a local. People 'round here don't take much to strangers."

Obviously, I hadn't made myself clear.

"I'm sorry. I know you're a friend of John's, and I'm sure you're very talented, but I don't think you're the right person to represent me. You said yourself, there hasn't been a murder on Orcas in years. I need someone with more criminal experience."

Dale stopped slouching. His eyes sharpened. The twang in his voice disappeared. He leaned in close and whispered, so as not to be overheard. "Ms. Davidson, I can assure you that I am completely qualified to handle your case. I moved to Orcas six years ago, but before that I spent twenty years as a defense attorney in Seattle. I obtained acquittals for ninety percent of my clients, and unlike you, most of them were guilty. Now be quiet and follow my lead."

Dale slouched again, smiling. Deep wrinkles softened his eyes. His voice boomed throughout the room. "Now how 'bout we go find ourselves a cup of coffee and figure out how to get you out of this mess."

TEN

WHEN WE EMERGED FROM the building and walked out to the parking lot, all four spots had been taken. Sergeant Bill's police car was still parked in the spot nearest the door. Sam's Camaro and Michael's Explorer occupied the two shady spaces in the middle. A broken-down-looking orange Plymouth pickup littered the space on the end. Dale's, I assumed.

Dale gave me directions to his office while Michael let Bella out of the car to take care of her biological duties.

I pointed to Sam's car. "Why didn't you guys all come together in the Explorer?"

Rene smirked at Sam. "Mr. Macho here is afraid to ride in the same car with Bella."

"Do you blame me? That dog hates me!"

Dale followed Sam's gaze to the sniffing explorer-dog and broke out in a huge, hairy grin. "Well hey, there, beautiful. Come on over and say hi!"

Sam grabbed his arm. "Don't get close to that dog. She hates men with facial hair."

Dale looked affronted. He shook off Sam's grasp and walked straight toward Bella. "Don't worry, I'm great with dogs."

I had a terrible feeling those might be Dale's last words.

Bella looked up from her sniffing, spotted Dale, and moaned. She took a tentative step toward him.

Dale crooned in reply. "Oh, sweetie..."

I tried to step between them, but my legs seemed to move in slow motion, and there was no stopping them anyway. Dale and Bella pined for each other like star-crossed lovers kept apart by an evil stepmother. Dale staggered toward Bella; Bella lurched toward Dale. Michael dragged behind her like a not-heavy-enough anchor. They closed the distance separating them in three seconds flat.

I watched, shell-shocked, as the drama unfolded. Dale knelt on the pavement, reached out his arms, and pulled Bella in close. She responded by licking his face and nibbling at his beard.

Sam gaped at them both. "What the hell?"

Bella wiggled, wagged, whined, and drooled all over Dale's chin. Dale raked his fingernails up and down her spine. Neither man nor beast had ever looked happier.

"Told you," Dale said. "I love dogs!"

Sam crossed his arms and glared. "Un-effing-believable."

Bella stopped wiggling and turned toward Sam's voice. She flatted her ears and lifted her upper lip, exposing several sharp white teeth. The expression wasn't at all friendly. I could have sworn that I saw Rene raise her lip too, but I must have imagined it.

"I'm so sorry, Sam," I said. "She never shows her teeth like that. She must sense that you're uncomfortable."

Sam kept his eyes firmly locked on Bella's. "That's the third time she's done that to me today." He shuddered. "I swear that dog's going to kill me in my sleep."

Rene's evil grin brightened her sallow complexion. "Don't be ridiculous, Sam. I sleep right next to you."

"What difference does that make?"

"Bella's much too smart to leave a witness." Rene paused and wiggled her eyebrows for emphasis. "She'll wait until the two of you are alone."

Sam took several steps back.

I gave her a dirty look. "You're not helping."

"Come on, Kate. Someone has to lighten the mood around here."

———

Several minutes of human-canine bonding later, Dale left and told me to meet him at his office. I gave Rene a quick hug, asked her to go back to the center, and promised that Michael and I would return to the cabin in a couple of hours. As Rene sagged into the passenger seat of the Camaro, Sam pulled me aside. Worry lines creased his brow.

"I feel selfish for asking. You've got your own problems right now ..." His voice trailed off.

I squeezed his hands. "Don't worry, Sam. I'll talk to her tomorrow."

"Thanks, Kate."

I tried not to worry as I watched them drive away. Whatever was going on with Rene, it would have to wait until tomorrow. In the meantime, I joined Michael and Bella in the Explorer for the quick drive to Eastsound.

Ten minutes later, Michael pulled up near Dale's address, parked in the shade, and cracked open the windows a couple of inches. The weather was cloudy and cool—perfect for Bella's late-afternoon nap. I gave her a quick scratch behind the ears and re-filled her water bowl. "We'll be back before you know it, sweetie."

We walked a half-block north to the Eastsound Professional Building—a rundown, five-business strip mall that contained the offices of two real estate agents, a tax accountant, a psychic advisor, and "Dale Evans, Goat Rustler and Attorney at Law." Or at least that's what the sign on the door said.

Dale invited us into a paneled room decorated with pictures of goats. Lots and lots of goats. Some posed with human companions. Some wore hats and glasses. One even balanced precariously on the roof of Dale's rattletrap pickup. A photocopy of Dale's law degree was haphazardly taped above a poster advertising The Great Goat Olympics. A dancing goat bobblehead nodded encouragingly from a scarred wooden desktop.

He motioned for us to sit at a folding table and said he'd be back momentarily. When he returned, he carried a pot of freshly brewed coffee, a bowl of spreadable cheese—goat cheese, of course—and a plate piled high with rosemary scones. "We'll talk about your case in a minute. First, we eat. I don't work on an empty stomach." He set the platter of goodies on the table and motioned toward a cabinet near the window. "Grab yourselves a mug."

The cabinet's assortment of coffee mugs continued the goat theme. Dale's choice was a blue ceramic mug with the title "Goat Whisperer." I selected a pink-lettered "Crazy Goat Lady" travel mug and handed "Stubborn Old Goat" to Michael.

"I only have honey for the coffee," Dale said. "Hope that will do."

It would do nicely.

Four o'clock was well past my normal lunchtime, and now that I thought about it, I hadn't eaten breakfast, either. Between finding Monica's body and trying to keep myself out of prison, snacking hadn't been my highest priority. But now that I smelled the pungent aromas of rosemary and chèvre, I realized that I was famished.

I grabbed the largest pastry off the plate and slathered it with cheese, for once not worried about my waistline. I gulped the first one down so fast that the herbaceous, tangy concoction barely touched my tongue. The second one, I savored. Its flakey richness settled in my belly, grounding me.

Michael listened silently while Dale built my trust with dense carbohydrates and light-hearted small talk. He skillfully listened to stories about my life and allowed me to pepper him with personal questions about his own. In spite of his nearly white whiskers and my earlier reservations, I found myself beginning to like and trust this unusual man.

"Why goats?"

"Goats are amazing creatures. Intelligent, social, and ornery as hell." He winked. "Kind of how John described you."

I ignored the editorial comment and stirred another teaspoon of honey into my coffee.

"Besides, goats may be willful as hell, but they never talk back, and they're a heck of a lot smarter than most of my clients."

"Do you do much defense work?" Michael asked.

"Not any more. I stopped being a defense attorney years ago. I'm pretty much a paper-pusher these days. You know, divorces, wills, property disputes, that sort of thing." He hitchhiked his thumb toward me. "I'm only taking this one on as a favor to John."

"How do you and John know each other?" I asked.

"We worked together, or rather, against each other. John and I sat on opposite sides of the courtroom plenty of times when I was a public defender. Your father, too."

That got my attention. John and Dad did their homework. If Dale got acquittals on the cases they worked, he must be good.

I hesitated before asking, but I had to know. "I don't want to offend you, but I have to ask. What's with the country bumpkin routine?"

He chuckled. "I had you going there, didn't I?" He took a long drink of coffee then set the mug on the table. "You ever lived in a small town?"

I shook my head.

"I did. I grew up in one." He resumed his affected hillbilly twang. "Marlington, Kentucky. Population six hunnert and seventy-three." He smiled "Orcas is bigger than Marlington, but the culture's the same. The locals are friendly, but they don't trust strangers. And by 'strangers' I mean anyone who wasn't born on the island. But when I turn on the country charm, people loosen right up."

He crumpled his napkin and tossed it in the trash. "I'm not really fooling anyone, but people find it amusing. It gives them an excuse to cut me some slack. Besides, I spend more of my time on animal rescue than law these days, so my Farmer John act isn't all that untrue."

"How'd you go from Seattle attorney to Eastsound goat rustler?"

Dale's easygoing smile disappeared. "That, my dear, is a long story." He pushed his plate to the side. "Let's just say some creatures are more worth saving than others." He stood up and moved behind the desk. "Lunch break is over. Pull your chairs over here, and let's get to work."

My curiosity was piqued, but I didn't ask any more questions. The wide expanse of desk Dale placed between us sent a clear message: the time for personal chitchat was over.

He pulled out a legal pad and uncapped a pen. "Before we start, John made me promise to tell you something."

Here it came. One of John's infamous lectures.

"He told me about that mess you got into when your friend was killed a few months ago."

Wait for it...

"And he doesn't want you playing amateur detective this time." Dale raised his hands to make air quotes. "I believe John's exact words were, 'Katydid, mind your own business. Stick with your stretching exercises and let the police do the investigating. That's an order.'"

I kept my expression neutral.

"So, Miss Kate. Are you going to obey?"

My body stiffened at Dale's choice of words. "Obey" wasn't part of my lexicon.

Michael reached under the table and squeezed my hand. "John's right, Kate."

Even the bobblehead goat nodded in agreement.

Well, I had news for all of them, billy goat chauvinist included. If being accused of murder wasn't my business, I didn't know what was.

I considered arguing, but what was the point? I hadn't met a man yet—at least not one worth knowing—that didn't want to protect me, especially from myself. I'd never fool Michael, but I might stand a chance with Dale. He didn't know me.

I released Michael's hand, crossed my left fingers under my leg, and made the scout's honor sign with my right. "Don't worry. I learned my lesson last time. Bella and I almost got killed. I'll let the police handle this." Clients lie to their attorneys all the time, right?

Michael looked skeptical.

Dale looked downright disappointed. "Huh. I thought you had more spunk than that."

"But you just told me to stay out of it!" My voice may have sounded a *tiny* bit more petulant than I had intended.

Dale shook his head emphatically. "No, Miss Kate, I did not. You need to listen more carefully. *John* told you to stay out of it. I simply relayed the message. I never said I agreed with him."

He couldn't be serious. "You mean you *want* me to try to solve Monica's murder?"

Dale leaned forward and put his elbows on the table. "Normally, I tell my clients to shut up and lay low. But normally, my clients are guilty. In your case, I think we should try to find out

126

who the real killer is before Bill gets his act together enough to arrest you."

Michael jolted. "Arrest her? You said that sergeant didn't think Kate was guilty."

Dale shrugged. "He doesn't. But he's not positive she's innocent, either. This island survives on tourist income. No one's going to want an unsolved murder—especially one of a tourist—on the books. Bill's going to be under a lot of pressure to arrest someone." He turned toward me. "All of the evidence so far points to you, Miss Davidson."

White flour and goat cheese congealed in my stomach. "I'm in trouble, aren't I?"

Dale set down his pen and looked at me sympathetically. "I'm sorry, Kate, but yes. You're in trouble. So far, the case against you is weak. You don't have a history of violence or a compelling motive. But that doesn't mean you won't get arrested. Even if the case never goes to trial, your life—at least for the next few months—could turn into a living hell. Your reputation may never recover."

I didn't say anything. I was afraid that if I opened my mouth, I might get sick.

"Our best bet is to find Bill a different suspect—the right one this time. I'm not saying you should do anything to put yourself in danger, but you're stuck on Orcas for now, anyway. You may as well stay at Elysian Springs and keep your ears open." He held up his hand. "But let me be clear: I only want you to listen. Do *not* actively investigate. You could destroy your case. If you hear anything interesting, call me. I'll follow up."

Michael didn't agree, but he didn't argue, either.

Dale turned the notebook to a blank page. "Now, tell me exactly what happened this morning."

I related my version of the weekend's events, from beach encounters, to Helen's and my idle threats, to Monica's body floating face-down in the hot tub. Dale listened intently, taking notes. When I finished, he tapped his pen on the notebook.

"Well, that pretty much explains our problem."

"What do you mean?"

"The witness who found you heard screaming, all right, but he thinks it came from the victim. He heard a woman cry for help and rushed to the top of the stairs. When he got there, the screaming had stopped, and you were huddled over the body."

"I was the one who screamed, not Monica."

"I understand that. And the witness doesn't completely disagree. He says he doesn't know what you were doing, at least not for sure. But add what he saw to the half-dozen people who heard you threaten the victim, and it doesn't look good."

Michael started pacing. "I told you, Kate. I told you that temper was going to get you in trouble." His tone may have scolded, but his expression held nothing but concern. "There had to be someone else there, someone who saw, or at least heard, something." He ran his fingers across his scalp. "Think Kate, did you see anyone? A maid? A groundskeeper? A guest maybe?"

I'd been asking myself that same question for hours. "No. No one."

Dale frowned. "Well then, we've got our work cut out for us, haven't we?"

No doubt about it. I needed Dale's help. Help that, in spite of his low-budget office furniture, couldn't possibly come cheap. I was making ends meet—barely—with the studio now. I had no extra income to pay for a lawyer.

"Dale?"

"Yes?"

"I appreciate your help. Really, I do. I trust you. I'd like for you to represent me. But I don't have much money. I don't know how I'll ever pay you."

Dale closed the notebook and laid down his pen. His unflinching look demanded the truth. "Did you kill that woman?"

"No. I didn't. I swear."

"Then don't worry about money. Let's figure out how to get you out of this mess."

ELEVEN

WHEN MICHAEL AND I pulled into the ghost town formerly known as Elysian Springs two hours later, the parking lot was about three-quarters empty. No maids laundered bed sheets; no hikers meandered along trails; no groundskeepers scurried on golf carts. The office, spa, and restaurant all sported closed signs. Where was everyone?

We found Rene and Sam sitting on opposite ends of the sofa bed, avoiding eye contact. According to Rene, the police had finished questioning everyone around six and cleared the spa for reopening—minus the hot tubs, of course. As soon as the detectives left, Emmy and Josh shut down all of the center's nonessential operations for the rest of the night. They promised to reopen in the morning.

None of us had much of an appetite, so we hunkered down in the cabin and tried to avoid each other. We acted like prisoners in solitary confinement, only sharing the same space. Rene flipped through a magazine, uncharacteristically quiet. Sam brooded in a corner. Michael played solitaire, looking withdrawn and cranky; Bella restlessly panted and paced.

I distracted myself by making some phone calls—an act I immediately regretted.

I started by dialing John O'Connell's home number.

"What in the f—were you thinking, Kate?"

I inserted a mental beep at the sound of John saying the f-word. John often lectured, but he rarely chastised. And he never swore, at least not in front of me. In John's eyes I was a thirty-two-year-old schoolgirl in need of protection. He'd never expose me to the evils of profanity. He must be even more worried than I thought.

The sharp cadence of boots pacing on hardwood cracked through the phone line. "Talking to the police without a lawyer? What are you, stupid?"

He was right of course, and I suspected the question was rhetorical. But I'd had a hard day, and I was feeling a little grumpy myself. "I was thinking that I was *innocent*, John."

The sound of John's pacing was replaced by the telltale squeak of denim on leather. I imagined him seated behind his imposing oak desk, glowering at me. "Yeah, well, innocent or not, Dale seems to think you're in trouble."

"Dale talked to you? Hasn't he ever heard of attorney-client privilege?"

"Don't worry, your secrets are safe. Dale refused to give me any details." John grunted, obviously displeased. "But I still got more information out of him than that bumpkin sergeant."

I sat up straight. "What did Sergeant Bill tell you?"

"Nothing. At least nothing useful. And I wouldn't share it with you if he did. You'd just go off on one of your harebrained schemes again."

"John, I—"

He didn't give me a chance to finish. "Don't you worry, Katydid. Don't you worry a bit. I'm not about to let those backcountry hicks railroad you into a murder conviction. I've got some vacation time coming. I'll be there to fix all this tomorrow."

Lord, that was all I needed. John would put me in handcuffs and barricade me in the cabin for sure. I tried to sound reassuring. "There's no need to come up here, John, at least not yet. I haven't been arrested, and Dale has everything under control. Stay in Seattle for now. Save that vacation time, in case I need your help later. I'll make sure Dale keeps you informed." *Of as little as possible.*

John grumbled and griped. He snapped orders and reprimands. He gave ultimatums. But he eventually agreed to stay in Seattle, at least for a day or two.

Next I checked in on Serenity Yoga.

Unlike John, Mandy didn't even bark a hello.

"Kate, I know you're on vacation and all, but you have to return my calls! I've left at least a dozen messages!"

I glanced at the Yoga Chick's message indicator. Six missed calls, all from the studio.

"Sorry Mandy. I left my phone in the cabin and just got home a few minutes ago." I opted not to tell her that I'd spent the day trying to convince a potbellied policeman I wasn't guilty of murder. "What's up?"

"While you were off enjoying your vacation, I was stuck here with a mess, that's what's up. That new Morning Flow Yoga teacher forgot to set her alarm. Her students waited outside in the pouring rain for twenty minutes before they gave up." Mandy's voice grew softer. "Honey, not now. Mommy's on the phone." She came back on the line. "I was supposed to work on the twins' Halloween costumes today, but I had to spend my entire afternoon trying to placate fourteen very annoyed yoga students."

I cringed. "You gave them all free passes, right?"

"Yes, but I doubt some of them will come back. Three have already demanded refunds." She paused. "And you know what's worse?"

No, and I probably didn't want to. "What?"

"The instructor wouldn't even help me contact the students. She said we should all mellow out. That anyone can forget to set an alarm. Unbelievable."

A high pitched wail screeched in the background.

Mandy yelled in reply. "Stop poking your brother this instant!"

"Um, Mandy—"

"Kate, I need to go. But you have to do something about that instructor."

I sighed. "I'll talk to her when I get back."

If I get back.

But that was a possibility I didn't want to think about.

I thanked Mandy for her help, hung up the phone, and collapsed into bed. I tried to soothe myself with my favorite bedtime pranayama practice, Kate's Sleeping Pill, but it had no effect. Even after twenty minutes of deep, segmented breathing, I still couldn't relax enough to close my eyes. Instead, I rolled to my side and stared at the closet, wishing I could magically transport myself somewhere—anywhere—else.

I didn't think it was possible, but sometime, long after midnight, I fell asleep.

————

My alarm went off at six the next morning. I hit the snooze button, closed my eyes, and snuggled back under the covers. My world felt cozy, comfortable, wrapped in a soft cotton blanket. Michael breathed rhythmically beside me. I reached behind the bed and stroked the silky spot behind Bella's ears.

I was … happy.

And then I blinked.

Reality crashed down, destroying my temporary oasis. I remembered it all: Monica's body, my futile efforts to revive her, that suffocating interrogation room. My arms and abdomen ached, sore from yesterday's useless CPR attempt. My shoulders knotted with tension. My eyes burned with exhaustion and held-back tears. How could anyone believe I was capable of murder?

I managed to drag myself out of bed and limp past the mostly empty parking lot to Shanti House. No one had officially fired me yet, so I assumed my morning yoga class was still on.

I unlocked the door to the yurt, turned on the lights, lit the candles, and waited.

And waited.

And waited.

As I looked around the empty room, I only knew one thing for certain: being accused of murder killed your yoga business. On the bright side, if I *did* end up in prison, Death Row Yoga would have a captive audience.

By the time class was scheduled to start, the room held only one brave student: a mid-thirties gentleman who had arrived at the center late the night before. He didn't ask about Monica's murder, and I didn't volunteer. If he didn't realize he shared yurt space with a suspected murderer, who was I to tell him?

I waited until five minutes after the session's posted start time, then rang the Tibetan chimes three times to clear the room's energy and focus my mind. I smiled at my single, intrepid student. "Close your eyes and settle in. Feel your body connect with the earth and—"

The door opened. The Grumpy Yogini entered, still wearing the same frown as the day before. She rolled out her black rubber mat, sat cross-legged on a blanket, and closed her eyes.

At least *someone* was willing to give me a second chance.

I started class with a Sanskrit chant designed to promote healing and peace. I typically avoided teaching chant in group yoga classes. Many American students were uncomfortable with Sanskrit's unusual sounds; others didn't like singing in public. But frankly, that low, soft melody wasn't for my students; I sang it solely for me. My heart needed the peace-inducing vibration of sound.

I described the call-and-response process we'd follow. "I'll chant each phrase two times. The first time, I'll do it alone; the second time, you'll join me." I touched my palms together in front of my chest. "Inhale, and open your arms out to the side." Both students followed my instructions. "Exhale and touch your palms to your heart." I chanted as they moved.

"Anamaya shanti."

As we opened our arms on the next inhale, I recited the chant's English meaning.

"May my body have peace."

We swept our palms back to our hearts and repeated the chant together.

"Anamaya shanti."

We followed the process four more times, inviting peace to body, breath, mind, heart, and spirit.

The movements we practiced next were slow, easeful, and soothing. Instead of walking around to observe my students, I laid out a mat and practiced with them, stopping occasionally to check their form. It wasn't my best teaching effort, but it was better than the alternative. If I stopped moving long enough to think, I'd burst into tears.

We started on hands and knees. "Inhale and lengthen your spine. As you exhale, lower your hips to your heels, your elbows and forehead to the floor. This is called Child's Pose."

Connecting movement and breath forced me to stay in the present moment. A moment without frustration, death, and interminable questions. A moment in which I had everything I needed, right there inside of me.

I barely noticed our transition to standing, but as I led those two brave souls through Uttanasana, Standing Head to Knees Pose, my low back relaxed. As we twisted, my neck, my shoulders, even my belly, released. When the final vertebra cracked into place, I felt like Kate again.

My world was still far from perfect, but somehow I knew I'd survive.

I abandoned my yoga mat and walked among my two students. I coached and corrected their form. I even hazarded a smile when the Grumpy Yogini lifted her hips into Bridge Pose.

The second-to-last pose was a restorative posture called Bound Angle Pose. My two students lay face-up on the floor, bodies draped over emerald green bolsters, arms opened out to the side. Their knees were bent; the soles of their feet touched together. As I watched them relax, I asked them to imagine a warm light entering their hearts.

My own heart opened.

Ostensibly, I was the teacher, not the student, but I was still the one transformed. For the first time in almost twenty-four hours, I could breathe.

My male student looked calm, peaceful, and happy as he walked out of the building. The Grumpy Yogini looked—grumpy. At least this time she didn't check her watch in Savasana. She didn't have to. She rolled up her mat and left shortly before the rest period began.

Time to close up shop and head back to the cabin. I blew out the candles and turned off the space heater. The floor wasn't dirty, but I swept it anyway. The simple act grounded me and demonstrated my respect for the space.

The mop's soft, rhythmic swishes soothed my nervous system. Morning light poured through the east-facing windows and warmed my skin. After the last errant dust bunny had been whisked away, I leaned on the mop handle and stared out at the ocean, lost in my own melancholy thoughts.

"Excuse me, Kate?"

I cringed at the sound of Emmy's voice. *Looks like I'm fired after all.*

Losing a week-long job should have been the least of my worries, given the circumstances, but I was still afraid to face her. What if Emmy thought I killed Monica? What if she hated me?

I slowly turned around, steeling myself for an angry confrontation.

I needn't have worried.

The person standing before me didn't look upset, she looked terminal. Her sunken eyes were underscored by dark shadows. The skin on her face seemed paradoxically puffy and dehydrated at the same time. Her normally pixie-like hair wilted lifelessly from her scalp.

Facing Emmy's anger would have been nothing. Uncontrollable rage might have been an upgrade. Anything would have been better than witnessing her despair.

"Kate, this is a disaster."

"I know. It's terrible." I leaned the dust mop against the window and took a few tentative steps toward her. I wanted to give Emmy a hug, but I wasn't sure how she'd react. She could easily think that I killed Monica. Call me crazy, but I had a feeling she might not be eager to cuddle up with her stepmother's murderer.

I kept an imaginary yoga mat's distance between us. "I'm so sorry about Monica. I can't even fathom how hard this must be. But I swear to you, I didn't—"

Emmy lifted her hands, palms forward. "I know, Kate, I know. You didn't hurt Monica. Why would you? You barely knew her." She paused. "Besides, Monica's death isn't the disaster I'm talking about."

It wasn't? What other disaster was there?

"I mean, sure, it's sad about Monica and all. I feel terrible for Dad." She swallowed. "But it's worse than that. Elysian Springs might have to close."

My expression must have betrayed my thoughts.

"I'm sorry. That sounded cold. But I barely knew Monica, and what I *did* know I didn't like. She destroyed my parents' marriage. The center, though..." Her voice faltered. "Elysian Springs is Josh's and my life."

"I understand that, Emmy. My yoga studio is my life's work, too. But closing the center for a few days, even a week—well, that hardly seems tragic."

She shook her head. "No, you don't get it. I mean close forever. As in go out of business."

Her words startled me. "How can you even think about permanently closing? This is your grand reopening. Alicia told me the center's business is about to skyrocket."

Emmy didn't make eye contact. "The thing is... Alicia... well, she doesn't have all of the information."

I felt myself stiffen. "Exactly what information might Alicia be missing?"

Emmy cringed.

OK, so maybe I sounded a *tiny* bit prickly. But Alicia was my friend, as well as my studio's landlord. She had invested considerable money in this venture, and I had a feeling she might have been duped. I wasn't worried about Alicia's finances; she'd never invest money she couldn't afford to lose. Still, that didn't give anyone—not even a pixie-haired bride-to-be—the right to take advantage of her.

Emmy's words tumbled out faster. "You have to understand, Kate. Alicia invested early—almost eighteen months ago, when Josh and I first took over. We knew the place needed some work, but we had no idea how much. We thought it mainly needed a facelift."

I nodded for her to continue. "We opened with the existing cabins, lined up Alicia and a few other investors, and started rebuilding. I knew money would be tight, but I thought we could limp along until the renovations were finished." She frowned. "Problem is, they may *never* be finished, unless we get more money. Josh and I have spent all of the original investment money. We drained our personal savings. We even sold Kyle the rights to the restaurant. But there's still so much work to do."

She laced her fingers together, as if begging me to understand. "I appreciate your friend's investment, really I do. I promise you, we spent every penny of her money on the renovations. But unless something changes soon, it won't be enough."

I hesitated, torn between sympathy for Emmy and loyalty to Alicia. I, of all people, knew how hard building a business could be. I'd almost gone bankrupt after I opened Serenity Yoga.

Emmy stared out the window toward the Retreat House. "I had an incredible vision for this place. Elysian Springs was going to be the Northwest's premier upscale, eco-friendly retreat center." When she turned back around, she wore a sad smile.

"We were this close." She held her thumb and forefinger an inch apart. "I invited some potential investors to visit the property this weekend, and we completely sold out. But then Monica went and got killed. Half of the guests checked out yesterday. That was bad enough. If her murder goes unsolved, the new investors will bolt." Her whole body seemed to shrink. "We'll never make it."

I didn't know what to say, so I remained silent. Emmy paused for a moment, then straightened her spine. Her shoulder blades drew together; she held my gaze without blinking. "That's where you come in."

Two thoughts raced through my mind. First, if Emmy thought I'd confess to murder to save a glorified hotel, she was crazy.

Second, she wasn't exactly wallowing in grief over Monica's death.

Could Emmy be Monica's murderer?

I took several steps back.

Emmy took the same number of steps forward. "I'm sure I seem callous—inhuman even. But pretending to mourn Monica won't bring her back. I can't do anything to save Monica, but I intend to protect Josh's and my future. To do that, I need your help."

I had no idea what she wanted, but I doubted I'd like it.

"What do you mean?"

"Alicia told me about the murder you solved in Seattle."

I was right. I didn't like it at all.

"That was a mistake, Emmy. I practically got killed. This time, I'm leaving the investigation to the police." I lied, of course. I liked Emmy, but that didn't make her innocent. I wasn't ready to clue her in on my plans.

Emmy frowned. "The police won't move fast enough. Bill's a great guy, but he's no homicide detective. The cops around here spend most of their time breaking up fistfights and pulling deer carcasses to the side of the road."

"What makes you think I'll do any better? People might at least talk to Sergeant Bill. I'm a suspect, remember? No one's going to open up to me."

"That's where you're wrong," Emmy replied. "You're the perfect person to ferret out the truth. You yoga teachers are like hairdressers. People trust you. They tell you their secrets without even realizing it. And I can help. I'm the boss *and* the bride. If I tell people to attend your yoga classes, they won't be able to say no."

I gestured around the empty room. "They certainly said no this morning."

"The whole resort's a dead zone right now. People are skittish, but I can fix that. I'll tell everyone that you're not really a suspect—that Bill questioned you to keep the real murderer off guard." For the first time since entering the yurt, Emmy smiled. "No one will doubt me. I can be *very* persuasive when I need to be."

She was certainly convincing me.

"I'll get you access, you keep me posted on what you learn." She held out her hand. "Deal?"

I hesitated. I was already planning to look into Monica's death, and having an inside contact would certainly make that easier. Besides, Emmy wouldn't ask for my help if she were the killer.

Would she?

I reached out my hand and grasped hers. "Deal. I'll keep you posted." *As long as I don't learn anything that implicates you.*

"Great." Emmy glanced at her watch. "The morning meditation group will need this space soon. Let's go to my office and talk specifics."

TWELVE

As EMMY AND I walked toward the buildings that housed the spa, the main office, and Eden, I quizzed her about her life.

"You're originally from New York, right?"

She nodded.

"How'd you end up on Orcas?"

She smiled. "It's the classic story. Girl meets boy. Girl falls in love, ditches her old life, and travels across the country to be with him."

I smiled. "Tell me more."

She shrugged. "Not much to tell, really. I took it pretty hard when everything went south for my parents two years ago. Monica wasn't that much older than me. The thought of her and my dad..." She shuddered. "I needed to escape all of the drama and I liked doing yoga, so I figured why not meditation? I signed up for a four-teen-day silent retreat here at Elysian Springs."

"I could never do that."

"Turns out, neither could I. I hated it. I spent most of our silent time wandering around the grounds, searching for anyone who was willing to talk to me. Josh was one of the groundskeepers. Let's just say he proved *very* entertaining." She blushed. "It didn't take long for me to figure out that I liked Josh, but what I truly fell in love with was the site.

"At first we both thought our romance was one of those summer vacation flings, but we stayed in touch. When Josh told me that Elysian Springs was about to go out of business, I figured it was Kismet. I had a business degree; he knew the site. We got some investors and started rebuilding."

She came to a stop outside Eden. "And the rest, as they say, is history. Come on up with me. I need to talk to someone."

We walked through the door into the almost-empty restaurant.

Two nights ago, Eden buzzed. This morning, it whispered.

About me.

I didn't see any familiar faces among the smattering of diners, but they definitely knew me. As soon as I entered, conversations hushed. The waitress busied herself, shining and reshining the silverware. Most of the diners stole quick glances my way, then stared down at the table, seemingly fascinated by the dregs of their coffee. One woman nudged the man seated beside her and said in a stage whisper, "I think that's her!"

Emmy pretended not to notice the room's obvious discomfort. She smiled and cheerfully greeted each patron while I huddled close to the wall, whole body flushed in embarrassment. I understood now why Bella took comfort in small, dark spaces. I wanted to crawl under a table myself.

Emmy made her way to the kitchen and leaned inside.

"Kyle, can you talk yet?"

"Give me ten minutes," he replied.

Now I was in cahoots with the chef, too?

Emmy and I moved to her office.

"Why are we talking to Kyle?"

"Hang on. You'll see in a minute."

Kyle eased into Emmy's office ten minutes later, carefully balancing a basket of pumpkin muffins and a tray with three steaming soy lattes. He set a cobalt blue mug in front of each chair and placed the muffins on Emmy's desk. My stomach rumbled.

"Help yourself," he said.

I grabbed one of the warm, amber-colored pastries, broke off a large chunk, and inhaled the spicy scents of cinnamon, ginger, and clove.

Kyle spoke to Emmy, but he gestured toward me. "So, did she agree to help find the killer?"

Emmy smiled. "Yep. Told you I'd convince her."

"You *told* him?" Pieces of partially chewed pumpkin spewed down the front of my shirt. "Emmy, what were you thinking? For all we know, he's the murderer!"

Kyle's jaw dropped open. "Me? You're the one who spent most of yesterday in police custody."

"Knock it off, you two," Emmy chastised. "Accusing each other isn't helpful, or even reasonable. I had more reason to kill Monica than either of you."

She had a point, but it wasn't in her favor.

I grumbled and wiped bits of gooey, masticated pumpkin off of my shirt. "Who else have you told, Emmy? The rest of your family?

Everyone on staff? Maybe we should have Josh announce it over the loudspeaker."

Emmy held up her palms. "Oh no, Kate. Please. We can't tell Josh."

I stopped wiping and gaped at her. "You suspect *Josh*?"

"Of course not. Josh would never hurt anyone. But he'd never understand."

Neither did I, for that matter.

"I love Josh, more than I've loved anyone in my life. But he's so ... *mellow*." Her vocal tone clearly indicated that was a bad thing. "If I told Josh about this, we'd end up fighting again." She frowned. "That is, if you can call me screaming while Josh ignores me fighting."

"You've been arguing?"

Emmy's face flushed. "See, Kate, you *are* good at getting people to blurt out their secrets." She blew the steam off her latte and took a cautious sip.

I waited for her to continue.

"Josh and I have been fighting about Elysian Springs. He needs to wake up and face reality; we're almost out of money."

"If you hadn't wasted so much on the new construction ..."

Emmy slammed her mug on the desk, splashing foamy beige liquid across its surface. "Drop it, Kyle," she snapped. "I already know what you think."

Kyle flinched, but he didn't reply. He stared at her, eyes wide open. Even his dreadlocks seemed to quiver in surprise.

Emmy bit her lower lip and stared silently down at her lap, as if embarrassed by the outburst.

"Emmy?" I asked. "You OK?"

After a moment, she uncurled her fingers from the mug's handle, mopped up the mess with her napkin, and steadied her voice. "Sorry. It's a sore subject." She crumpled up the soiled napkin and laid it down on the table. "Look, I'll admit, I got carried away with the new buildings, but I'm trying to appeal to an upscale clientele. No one knew that the existing structures had so many problems."

"Is that what you and Josh fight about? The money?"

Emmy sighed and shook her head. "I wish. That would be easier. We fight because he doesn't *care* about the money. He lives in a fantasy world. Josh thinks the universe provides, but only if you believe in it. He says I need to *relax and have faith*." She punctuated the last four words with finger quotes. "He wouldn't be mad at me if he knew I was trying to solve Monica's murder; he'd be disappointed. I can't stand the thought of disappointing him."

I looked at Kyle. "What's your stake in all of this?"

"You saw how empty the restaurant was this morning. It should have been packed. Business was so slow that I sent all but one waitress home. I'm barely making it as it is. If the resort goes under, I'll be out of business for sure."

I broke off another chunk of spicy, sweet muffin, slowly chewed, and considered my options. I didn't know Kyle, much less trust him, but Emmy wasn't exactly one of my childhood friends, either. Since the Cat Pose was already out of the bag, so to speak…

"OK. Let's talk." I gave Emmy a stern look. "But don't tell anyone else." I glanced at the desktop. "Can I borrow a pen and paper?"

Emmy handed me a clipboard.

"Let's start with you, Emmy. Tell me what you know so far."

Emmy's version of events started when she learned that Monica had collapsed in the hot tub and ended with a family gathering last night at the Retreat House.

"Everyone pretended to be shocked and upset, but Dad's the only one truly grief-stricken."

"Anyone act unusual?" I asked.

"What's 'usual' about finding out that someone you know has been murdered?"

She had a point.

"But no, I didn't notice anything strange." Emmy stood and wandered pensively around the small office. "Nobody in the family liked Monica, but I can't imagine one of them hurting her. And why would one of the staff members?" She chewed the edge of her thumbnail. "Maybe Mom's right. Maybe it was some drifter."

Kyle interjected. "Or the thief."

"Thief?" I asked.

"A few things have gone missing," Emmy replied. "Some tea, a couple of plants, a few bottles of wine. Someone even took a bag of cleaning supplies."

"You think someone killed Monica over a bottle of window cleaner?"

Emmy sat back down. "The eco-friendly supplies we use are pretty expensive, but you're right, it does seem crazy."

Kyle interrupted. "Don't forget to tell her about the stolen drugs."

That got my attention. "What drugs?"

"I told you, Kyle. Those prescriptions weren't stolen; Mom forgot to pack them." Emmy opened a packet of raw sugar and absently stirred it into her coffee. "My mother's not the most organized person, especially when she's nervous. And she's always nervous when she travels. She inevitably forgets something."

Emmy removed the spoon, tapped it lightly against the edge of her mug, and laid it on the table. "Mom and I went to Europe a few years ago. Mom brought shirts, two cameras, and plenty of underwear, but not a single pair of pants. We spent half the vacation clothes shopping. This time she claims some prescriptions went missing."

"What kind of drugs were they?"

Emmy shrugged. "That's just it. She's not sure. Mom throws the entire medicine cabinet into her suitcase when she travels. She didn't even notice anything was missing at first because she had several days' worth of tranquilizers and heart medication in her carry on. I suspect all of the 'missing' drugs are right where she left them—on her bathroom counter."

"I'm not so sure you should write it off, Emmy," Kyle said. "Lord knows what else has been stolen that we haven't noticed. Someone might even be skimming from the till. You're not exactly security conscious."

"I suppose." Emmy sighed. "We treat the staff here like family. I thought we could trust them."

Drugs and money sounded like good motives to me. I made a note to follow up with Helen about the missing prescriptions. "Kyle, what about you? What did you notice yesterday morning?"

Kyle's day started when he began preparations for the eight o'clock breakfast service and ended when he heard sirens.

"You didn't see Monica?"

"No, why would I?"

"When I spoke to Bruce yesterday morning, he said Monica was planning to talk to you."

"The hostess told me that Monica stopped by the restaurant, but I never saw her. I went to the garden to cool off."

"Cool off?"

Kyle's face turned almost as red as the stripes on his hat. "That daytime hostess has one job. One. Simple. Job. Greet people at the door and make them feel welcome. And she's not even very good at that." He glowered at Emmy. "I never should have let you talk me into hiring her. Would it kill her to smile every now and then?"

"Her name's Jennifer. And she's shy, Kyle. She'll open up eventually."

"So you say." He continued grumbling. "She showed up late yesterday morning, and we were swamped. The waitresses had enough trouble keeping up with their own work. They didn't have time to do hers, too." The small muscles in the corner of his jaw quivered. "I was furious. If I'd stuck around, I'd have yelled at her in front of everyone, so I left my sous chef in charge and went to the garden to harvest some herbs for the lunch service. I was finishing up there when I heard the sirens." He shuddered. "After that, everything turned into a circus."

I watched him intently, trying to read his expression. "Monica never found you after she left the restaurant?"

He paused, but only for a second. His eye contact never wavered. "No. As far as I know, she went right to the spa."

"Well then, Kyle, your hostess may have been the last person to see Monica alive."

THIRTEEN

KYLE, EMMY, AND I spent the next twenty minutes plotting strategy. With over a hundred staff members and guests as potential witnesses, we had to no choice but to prioritize. Ultimately, we each focused on what we knew best. Kyle took the restaurant staff, Emmy the retreat center employees. I chose to connect with the most likely suspects—the wedding guests from New York—via some private yoga classes. It was as good a start as any.

Teaching yoga would give me the perfect opportunity to study Emmy's family. Effective yoga teachers are master observers, trained to watch students for even the subtlest signs of physical or emotional discomfort. In this case, I'd be on the lookout for subconscious signs of guilt, searching for a murderer the way a pathologist scans slides for a cancerous cell.

Besides, Emmy was right. People *did* open up to their yoga teachers, often more than they realized. Contrary to popular belief, yoga isn't about contorting your body into pretzel-like positions. Yoga's ultimate goal is to focus and clarify the mind. An effective yoga class leaves students' bodies strong, yet supple; their energy relaxed, yet alert; their hearts open—yet often vulnerable. The first rule of yoga ethics is to *never* abuse that vulnerability. I could only hope trapping a murderer was somehow an exception.

When the three of us parted company, we agreed to meet again after my class the next morning. Emmy promised to schedule the private session with her family as soon as possible.

In the meantime, I headed back to the cabin.

The aromas of sweet maple syrup and smoky vegan soysage greeted me at the door. Michael poked his head out from the kitchen. "Thank goodness you're finally here! We were about to give up on you."

I walked inside, gave Michael a hug—and almost had heart failure. A tornado had obviously touched down in the kitchen. Globs of pancake batter oozed down the cabinets and congealed on the counter. Grease spots stained the wall. Every plate, cup, pot, and utensil in the cabin—and few more Michael must have stolen from somewhere—was either currently in use or stacked haphazardly next to the sink. Dried batter and cooked-on food coated every dish.

"I made pancakes!"

"I see that."

My stomach still bulged from pumpkin muffins and caffeinated soy milk, but I didn't have the heart to disappoint him. I sat down for my second breakfast of the morning and tried to ignore the disaster in the kitchen.

Rene halfheartedly moved the food around on her plate. "Sorry, Michael. I'm still not feeling well."

"It's not bad for fake meat," Sam volunteered.

Michael poured me more orange juice. "What do you think, Kate?"

"It's quite good," I said. Which it was. "I'm not very hungry, though." Which I wasn't.

"Nonsense." Michael stacked two more pancakes and three more soysages on my plate. "Eat up, you'll need your strength."

"Why's that?"

"House rules. I cooked, so you have to clean up."

Michael smiled sweetly. I suppressed a groan.

At least thirty thousand calories later, Rene and Sam relaxed in the living room. Michael hung out in the kitchen and watched me clean. He wrapped his arms around my waist from behind and nuzzled my neck. "This is so great. I can imagine doing this every morning, can't you?"

It took every fiber of my willpower not to burst into tears.

Like Michael, I had created a mental movie of our future life together—only mine was a horror flick. Globs of dried toothpaste all over the sink, bruises on my nether parts from left-open toilet seats, shriveled up hands, shrunken from overexposure to dish soap. Only three days into our first experience cohabitating, and I was convinced I might lose my mind. How did Rene keep her sanity?

"Uh, Kate ... I think we should talk."

Uh oh.

"I've been meaning to ask you something."

Oh good lord, here it comes.

My throat constricted. My heart pounded. My lungs convulsed, suddenly starved for oxygen. Michael was about to pop the question. The question that permanently cemented or forever tore apart relationships. The question that forced you to choose: move forward, or permanently retreat. I didn't want to retreat. Not at all. I loved Michael more than I knew how to express. But what if I wasn't ready to move forward?

My mind flashed on the story of the farmer who lassoed a deer. His plan was simple. Cage it, fatten it like a Herford calf, then eat grain-fed venison for the rest of the winter.

Bambi had other plans.

The normally quiet, docile creature let out a primal scream and attacked, kicking, trampling, goring, and biting. Anything to get out from under that noose.

Bambi eventually escaped without injury. The farmer barely escaped with his life.

Michael should seriously consider lowering that rope.

I stepped out of his embrace and tugged at my shirt collar. "It's really hot in here, Michael. I think I'll take Bella for a walk," I yelled into the living room. "Rene, get off your butt and grab Bella. We're going for a walk."

Michael looked hurt. "Kate, I was talking to you."

"I know. We'll be back in a few minutes—a half hour at most. I need to get some air."

I backed away from him, panicked. "Rene, let's go!" I slammed the door on his voice and ran toward the trail. A minute or so later, Rene and Bella joined me.

"What was that all about? Michael looks pissed."

"Nothing. Let's walk."

Rene, for one of the few times in her life, indulged me.

For the first treasured minutes, I shook off my panic attack by immersing myself in the dense, tree-lined forest with all of my senses. October's cool sun peeked through the trees and cast rippled gray shadows over an undergrowth of feather-like sword ferns, spotted mushrooms, and yellow-green moss. A musty-smelling mulch of pine needles and fallen aspen leaves scented the air. A soft breeze ruffled my hair. I even imagined that I could taste the prior night's rain on the back of my tongue.

Bella explored the trail ahead—on leash of course—while Rene and I walked quietly together, our silence broken only by the steady crunch, crunch, crunch of our shoes. The stillness felt so restful, so complete, that I almost forgot I was a murder suspect.

Almost.

But I didn't forget my promise to Sam.

I didn't know what to do about my relationship with Michael; I had no idea who murdered Monica; but I was damned sure going to solve the Mystery of the Recalcitrant Rene.

Whatever was going on with her, it certainly wasn't an affair. Rene looked nothing like a woman newly in love. Puffy half-moons underscored her eyes, despite a thick layer of expertly applied makeup. Worry lines creased her forehead. She sagged, almost wilted, under her new Louis Vuitton jacket. Her pink UGG boots moved along the trail in a slow, foot-dragging shuffle.

No doubt about it. My friend needed help.

"Rene, what's going on?"

"Nothing, Kate, I'm fine." Her lips turned up, but the expression looked more like a grimace than a smile. Tiny puddles of liquid pooled above her lower lashes.

Were those tears?

Rene never cried. It simply wasn't part of her emotional vocabulary. She joked, she teased, she made sarcastic remarks. She used any defense mechanism possible to avoid showing weakness. Her constant, inappropriate teasing often drove me insane.

But she never cried.

I grabbed her shoulders and forced her to face me.

"This isn't just the stomach flu, is it."

She didn't answer.

The deepest part of me was terrified to ask the question. The deepest part of me didn't want to know.

"Honey, are you sick?"

She avoided my question by pretending to take it literally. "Obviously. I vomited all through dinner the other night. Remember?"

"Stop messing around. That's not what I meant, and you know it. Now tell me the truth. Are. You. Sick?"

For the few frozen seconds until she replied, I forgot to breathe. Bella sensed my tension and stopped sniffing. The no-longer-restful-but-still-horrifyingly-complete silence pounded my eardrums. Rene was my touchstone, my support system, my tormentor, my friend. She couldn't be sick. Not seriously. She just couldn't.

Rene stared at her feet, completely still, as if harnessing all of her courage to form the words. "I'm not sick, Kate. It's worse than that. The thing is … well …" Her throat convulsed. "I think I might be pregnant."

That was it?

I grabbed her hands. "Rene, honey, that's *good* news!" Granted, I wasn't ready for children of my own, but *I* was still single. The minute Rene said "I do," she started the inevitable cycle: marriage, kids, old age, and death. Rene and Sam had been married for three years. Getting pregnant was the obvious next step.

Rene yanked her hands from my grasp. "God, Kate. How could—" Her voice cracked. "How could you not get it?" Mascara-stained tears dripped down her face.

She was right. I hadn't gotten it. But I did now.

"This *isn't* good news, is it?"

"No, Kate. It's not good news at all."

"I'm listening."

Rene moved next to Bella, knelt down, and slowly rubbed the soft spot behind her ears. The rhythmic motion seemed to give her comfort. "Remember how I said I never wanted kids?"

I nodded my head yes.

"Well, I meant it. I never even liked dolls as a child, other than Barbie, and that was only because she wore cool clothes." Bella sighed and relaxed into Rene's touch. "But Sam wants kids less than any-one I've ever met." She swallowed. "He even planned to have a va-sectomy after we got married, but he never got around to it."

I hated myself, but I had to ask. "Then why didn't you guys use birth control?"

"We did. I'm not *that* stupid. The pill doesn't always work, you know."

She was right. Birth control pills were only ninety-nine percent effective. Leave it to Rene to be part of the one percent.

"Kate, what if Sam wants me to … you know." Her expression was tortured. "Sam will want me to end the pregnancy."

I knelt on the ground next to her. "Forget Sam for a minute. It's your baby. It's your *body*. What do *you* want?" I had no idea what I'd do in Rene's situation, but I knew this much. Whatever she decided, I'd be there, every step of the way. If Sam wasn't man enough to step up, I sure as hell would.

Rene rubbed her eyes, smearing deep black mascara across her cheeks. "I can't believe this, Kate. I thought I'd never, *ever* want a child." She paused. "But I want *this* baby." She said the words again, as if surprised to hear them out loud. "*I want this baby.*"

I smiled and tried to look confident. "Well then, Sam will, too." I hoped I was right.

Rene stood up and brushed off her pants. "I don't think so, Kate. I know Sam loves me. Lord knows, he puts up with enough of my crap. But when we decided to get married, he made one condition clear. No kids. No way. No exceptions." She teared up again. "He might even leave me."

I didn't know what to say, so I stalled with a question.

"What did the doctor say? Does the baby seem healthy so far?"

"I haven't gone to a doctor yet. I made an appointment a few days ago. I even drove to the doctor's office, but I chickened out. I keep hoping I'm wrong."

I held up my hands. "Whooooooa. Hold on there a minute, Kemosabe. You haven't even gone to the doctor? You're probably not even pregnant. You wouldn't be the first woman to miss a period, you know."

"But my breasts hurt, and I'm nauseated all the time."

I teased her, hoping to lighten the mood. "You know they sell these things called pregnancy tests."

"I know that," Rene snapped. "I'm not twelve. I took one. But they're not always accurate."

"Why don't you repeat it?"

"I did. Four times."

I already knew the answer, but I had to ask. "And?"

"I'm pregnant." Rene wailed. "How in this world did this happen?"

I didn't say anything, but I had a pretty good idea.

"And the whole thing gets worse and worse," she continued.

"How's that?"

"I've been looking on the Internet. All the sites say pregnant women shouldn't do Hot Yoga. The heat's bad for the baby."

"So?"

"My ass is going to get *huge.*"

I smiled. Finally. A glimpse of my friend underneath all of that drama. "Honey, I've got news for you. You're pregnant. Your butt won't be the only thing growing."

Rene punched me in the arm—hard.

"Ouch! That hurt!"

"I hate you." Rene smiled for the first time in days.

I wrapped her in my arms and hugged her fiercely. "I hate you, too, honey." We rocked back and forth, sobbing like fools. "Everything's going to turn out fine, I promise. You're going to be a great mother, and I'll be the world's best auntie."

Rene pulled back. "Kate, I need a huge favor."

"Anything. Name it." My mind spun through the possibilities. I wasn't ready to share "I dos" and have babies with Michael, but committing to Rene was a different matter entirely. She was family. If she and Sam split, Rene could move in with me. I'd give her my office and move the computer to the kitchen. I wasn't keen on the whole diaper changing business, but I'd be willing to take the 3:00 a.m. feedings.

And of course I'd be Rene's labor coach. I'd sign up for doula training tomorrow and look into Lamaze classes next week. Rene had always been there for me. I would do *anything* for her.

"I need you to tell Sam about the baby."

Except that.

"Are you crazy?"

"Please, Kate? I know I can't keep this from him much longer, but I can't face him, either."

I stepped back and crossed my arms. "No way, Rene. Not on your life. *You* have to tell Sam, and you have to do it soon. He's beside himself. He thinks you're having an affair."

Rene's expression changed from heartbreaking angst to aneurism-blowing anger in two seconds flat. Her face turned so red it was practically purple. Her skin seemed to throb. I was surprised her scalp didn't ignite.

"An *affair*! That lame-brained idiot thinks I'm having an *affair*? Cheating on him like some two-timing tramp?" Bella, the fearless guard dog, bolted away from the impending explosion and cowered behind me. "I'd never betray Sam!"

"Tone it down, Rene. You're scaring the dog."

Rene stopped shouting, but her perfectly plucked eyebrows still twitched with annoyance.

"Besides," I continued, "you're wrong. You may not be sleeping around, but you're still betraying Sam. He's not stupid. He knows you've been hiding something, and it's killing him."

Rene's shoulders sagged. "He said that?"

"Not in those exact words, but yes. Whatever you decide about this pregnancy, Sam needs to know about it, and soon. He should have known before me."

Rene stared off into the distance for several—pardon the pun—pregnant moments. She took a deep breath and squared her shoulders. "You're right. Now's not the time to be selfish. I'll tell Sam. I just need to figure out how."

"OK sweetie, but don't take too long."

"I won't. And Kate, don't tell Michael. Not until Sam knows."

Agreeing wasn't difficult, at least not in that moment. Michael probably wasn't speaking to me anyway. I pulled a tissue out of my pocket. "Now wipe that mascara off your face, or you'll really freak out Sam."

The three of us walked quietly for about ten more minutes. As we moved deeper into the forest, Rene's energy shifted. Her step became lighter. The color returned to her cheeks.

Bella sniffed the ground and munched on tall blades of grass. Rene rooted around in her jacket and pulled out a bar of organic dark chocolate. She broke off large pieces and shoveled them into her mouth.

"Looks like you got your appetite back."

"You know, I did. I feel a lot better. I'm not even nauseated anymore." She licked the last crumbs of candy off the wrapper, crumpled it into a ball, and shoved it back into her pocket. "Keeping the pregnancy a secret must have been bothering me more than I realized. I think it was literally eating a hole in my stomach. Talking to you totally helped."

We walked several more steps before Rene spoke again. "You're such a good friend."

ESP-like suspicion tingled the base of my skull. She was up to something.

"And?"

Rene stopped walking and looked at me through wide, child-like eyes. "And I need one more favor."

I took a step back and frowned at her suspiciously. "What kind of favor?"

"I need a distraction—something to keep me from freaking out until I tell Sam."

Rene flashed me an affected smile. It exposed sharp, pointy, chocolate-covered teeth. An evil spark flashed through her not-at-all-innocent eyes.

Ah, crap.

I'd obviously made some kind of fatal mistake. Perhaps I shouldn't have chastised Rene for hiding her pregnancy from Sam. Perhaps I should have promised her that her butt would stay small. Perhaps I should have avoided the whole conversation, turned tail, and run. Regardless, it was too late. Rene's inner devil had returned.

And it was eyeballing me.

I tried to back away, but a traitorous aspen tree blocked my escape. "What kind of distraction?"

"A puzzle. Something to keep my mind off my problems." She leaned forward and whispered. "You know, like a murder investigation." Rene crowded in close. I could have sworn that she flicked a pointed red tail. "You might be able to fool the boys, but you'll never fool me. I know why you were so late this morning. You're working the case."

"What if I am?"

"Then I'll help you, like I did last time."

I pushed away from her, waving my hands in the air. "Uh uh, Rene. No way." I'd learned my lesson about teaming up with Rene.

The last time we had sleuthed together, she'd promised to go out with one of the witnesses. When she stood him up, he retaliated. Against me. He printed my photograph on the front page of the local newspaper, complete with a caption that referred to me only as a "mentally ill woman."

"Come on," she implored. "It will be so much fun! We'll be like female Hardy Boys." Her face brightened. "We'll be the Hardy Girls!"

Hardy Girls indeed. I'd be Laurel; she'd be Hardy.

She bounced up and down like a golden retriever begging for someone to throw her a bright yellow tennis ball. "Please, Kate, please? It will distract me until I figure out how to tell Sam."

"Rene, I don't think—"

"Come on, you owe me that much."

I frowned. Why did I always let her talk me into things like this?

Maybe it wasn't such a bad idea after all. I'd never put an expecting woman in danger, but surely I could find *some* safe way to keep her occupied. Having a sounding board that wasn't also a suspect certainly couldn't hurt.

"OK, Rene. Fine. You can help."

"Awesome. Where do we start?"

———

Rene and I meandered along the trail for another half hour while I filled her in on my plans.

"Remember, keep all of this between us for now. The less Michael knows, the better. He'll just get pi—"

A hundred-pound anchor jerked me to a stop. "Bella, knock it off! You're going to dislocate my shoulder!"

Rene looked concerned, but not about me. "Is she eating grass again?"

It was the third patch of grass Bella had inhaled in the past fifteen minutes.

"Yes, and that's not normal for her. I don't think she feels well."

Bella snacked on grass all the time, but not like this. Grass hunting for Bella was a delicate, painstaking task. She searched through each clump like a master chef culling through produce, abandoning all but the youngest, most tender of blades. Today she acted more a lawnmower, shredding all plant life in sight.

I knelt down beside her. "Are you feeling OK, sweetie?" A low, gurgling noise rumbled from deep in her belly. Drool dripped from her lower lip, leaving dark mud splotches in the dirt.

Bella's wilted ears were trying to tell me something—something my subconscious mind knew I'd forgotten. But no matter how deeply I searched, my conscious mind refused to remember. I told myself not to worry; that everyone got an upset stomach now and then, especially scavenger-dogs like Bella. Bella's digestive system was fragile; it wouldn't take much to knock it off balance. Maybe the answer was simple. Maybe I'd given her too many treats. Maybe her belly reacted to my own internal stress. Maybe if I stopped worrying, we'd both feel better.

Bella stopped grazing to take care of her morning business.

Rene frowned in disgust. "That can't be good."

She was right.

One look at Bella's output, and I knew she was in trouble. Flare-ups of Bella's digestive disease weren't uncommon, and when they happened, the symptoms were obvious. Without going into the disgusting details, let's just say that the proof of an EPI setback was in the pudding. Bella's was of the butterscotch variety.

I looked at Rene, panicked. "Her autoimmune disease is flaring up."

After six months of experience, I knew more about Bella's rare disease than most veterinarians. EPI exacerbations were often hard to get under control. There were too many potential causes. Sometimes they were due to a vitamin B_{12} deficiency, sometimes to emerging food sensitivities. Sometimes the dog developed an infection that could be cured, but only with thirty-day course of special antibiotics.

I doubted that either of the two veterinarians on Orcas had ever heard of Bella's disease, much less knew how to treat it. Dogs with EPI could easily lose ten pounds or more in a week. What if Bella lost all of her hard-earned weight? What if she started starving to death again?

"Bella needs to see her vet. The police won't let me leave the island, so Michael will have to take her back to Seattle."

Rene looked concerned. "Will she be OK?"

"I think so, but I don't want to risk it."

I pulled out several extra-large dog waste bags. "I'm not sure what's wrong with her. She was fine back home. This is as bad as when I adopted her. It's almost like she's not getting her medicine..."

My stomach dropped to my toes.

Oh no.

I couldn't possibly have been that stupid, could I? Was I as addle-brained as Emmy's mother, leaving essential prescriptions at home on the kitchen counter? I tossed the bags to Rene and yelled, "Clean this up and meet me at the cabin. I have to go. Now!"

I sprinted back to the cabin as fast as my stubby legs would go, dragging a bewildered Bella behind me. I crashed into the cabin, ignored Michael's and Sam's confused looks, and frantically pawed through the refrigerator. Bella huddled close behind me.

I started on the top shelf, where I found three bottles of wine, a plate of fossilized cinnamon rolls, and two jars of eye cream. I'd ask Rene about those later.

The second shelf held two six packs of Guinness, several containers of leftover Chinese food, and an empty carton of orange juice. Michael's handiwork, I assumed. I pulled it out to toss in the trash.

Oh thank God.

Bella's bottle of enzymes sat safe and secure, pushed to the back of the shelf. *Get a grip, Kate.* I picked up the bottle and held it against my chest. *Of course you didn't forget Bella's medicine. You checked that cooler at least a thousand times.* I rubbed my thumb over the top of the bottle. *Only a truly negligent dog owner would forget—*

Wait a minute...

Why was the bottle still taped shut?

My conscious and unconscious minds finally connected. No wonder the consistency of Bella's food had been off. I'd remembered to bring Bella's medicine, all right, but I'd forgotten to add it to her food. My obsessive-compulsive organization had been my undoing. The piles of medicines I'd added to the containers at home had fooled me.

Part of me wanted to laugh. Bella would be fine. A bigger part of me felt like crying. She wasn't fine now, and it was all my fault. She'd be sick for at least twenty-four hours, maybe longer, until the unmedicated food made its way out of her system.

I sank down to the floor and hugged Bella in close. "I'm so sorry, sweetie. It's going to be a very long night."

FOURTEEN

"Don't look so worried. I promise, Kate, everything's going to be fine."

Easy for Michael to say. *I* was the one about to die.

If I was lucky.

Two hours after I discovered the sealed bottle of enzymes, I trudged, not toward the death chamber, but to a place much worse: my own private hellhole of mortal embarrassment. I'd avoided accompanying Michael to the Elysian Springs spa for two days, but frankly, I'd run out of excuses.

The private yoga class with Emmy's family wasn't scheduled until eleven the next morning, and my next public class was still four hours away. Michael had been a complete sweetheart the entire trip, in spite of my erratic behavior. Once I came back from Bella's three hundredth bathroom break, even I had to admit: I owed him some couples' time.

So I agreed to go to the reopened hot tubs.

It seemed like a good idea at the time.

The thought of hanging out in the buff—in public no less—made the roots of my hair turn purple, but it was safer than going anywhere else. Surely Michael wouldn't discuss our future in a gurgling bathtub full of naked strangers.

Would he?

I pulled Rene aside before leaving. "Talk to Sam while we're gone. That's an order."

She smiled insincerely and wiggled her fingers goodbye as she ushered Michael and me out the door. "Have a good time, you two." I had a feeling discussing babies-to-be wouldn't be on her agenda anytime soon.

I tried to postpone the inevitable by walking as slowly as possible, but we still ended up at the spa long before I was ready. I paused at the entrance and took a deep breath. Ganesh seemed to warn me away from the stairwell. I told myself that I was nervous about being nude in public, but that wasn't the real issue. Flashing my pasty-white bottom at strangers was the least of my worries. I was afraid of Technicolor flashes of memory. Freeze-frame images of floating blonde hair, rhinestone-studded dog leashes, and purple-blue lips. Coming back to this place so soon after Monica's death had obviously been a *very bad idea*.

I tried to distract myself by examining my surroundings, but I couldn't find a single place that was safe to look. People were everywhere. Naked people. They padded between hot tubs and rinsed off in showers. They sat on top of the very same towels they used to dry between their toes. A few of them leaned over the balcony, simultaneously enjoying the view and providing one of their own.

Michael slipped off his sandals and unbuttoned his shirt. I grimaced and hugged a folded towel to my chest. He pointed to an empty-looking building. "There's a changing room over there if you want. Most people get undressed here."

I would rather have died.

I undressed in the women's changing area and stalled for time by neatly folding and refolding my clothes. After the fourth permutation, I covered every inch of my skin from my throat to my knees in a bath sheet and hesitantly walked out onto the deck. A friendly-looking woman gestured with her eyes toward my white-knuckled grip. "This must be your first time."

You think?

I tried to find Michael, but no matter where my eyes pointed, they landed on something taboo. Hairy shoulders, suspicious-looking moles, strange scars, private body piercings. One ancient woman sported a multicolored chakra tattoo that started at her throat and extended down to her root—chakra, that is.

I found Michael submerged in the second tub, looking completely relaxed and chatting with several newfound friends. Maybe hanging out naked with strangers was easier once you got in the water. I knelt at the edge of the tub—towel still securely in place—and ran my fingers through the hot water.

Michael shifted to make space beside him. "Come on in. The water's great."

I stood up and placed my hands on the ladder. I even started to undo my towel. But I couldn't go any further. Intellectually, I knew the pool was nothing more than a man-made container of gurgling, chemically treated water, but that's not how I saw it. To me, it looked like a boiling, rectangular cauldron, waiting to swallow its next female body.

I had to get out of there.

I made a lame excuse about a contagious rash, ignored Michael's annoyed expression, and scooted to the sauna, where I hoped I could hide alone. For once, the universe was on my side. The sauna was completely empty. I turned off the lights, claimed a corner on the top level, and closed my eyes.

Before long, I began to relax. My breath lengthened. The knots in my shoulders loosened. The hot tubs obviously weren't for me, but perhaps Michael was right about the rest of the spa. Perhaps all I needed was some alone time, completely enveloped in warmth.

I mentally coached myself through a "safe place" meditation. A guided visualization designed to make the practitioner—me in this case—feel peaceful and safe.

Imagine that you're alone on a warm, sandy beach. Feel the sun bake your shoulders as your feet sink into the white sand. I sighed and snuggled deeper into my towel. *Wiggle your toes and feel the texture of—*

The door slammed open and two loudly chattering women entered the space.

"Getting off mid-afternoon is the only thing good about this job. I thought this day would never end."

I recognized them both. The first, a twenty-something blonde, was one of the center's cleaning staff. She would have been cute—in a perky, cheerleader sort of way—if she ever stopped scowling. The second, a mid-thirties Hispanic woman with a long dark braid, was the waitress I'd seen serving breakfast at Eden that morning.

I scrunched down in my dark corner and hid my face, but I needn't have bothered. Either the two friends didn't see me in the dark room, or they didn't care that they had an audience.

Maidzilla—my new nickname for the blonde—continued. "I don't know about you, but I'm ready to get out of here. This crappy job isn't worth risking my life over."

"You don't really think we're in danger, do you?" the waitress asked. "Kyle called a staff meeting after breakfast. He told us not to worry. He said the yoga teacher didn't do it, but the police had all but arrested the real killer."

"Yeah, Emmy fed me that load of crap, too. They're just trying to keep us all from freaking out and quitting."

Emmy and Kyle had followed through on their promises to talk to the staff, after all. Good for them.

Maidzilla continued. "What's going on between those two, anyway?"

"Emmy and Kyle?"

"Yeah. They've seemed awfully chummy lately." I didn't have to see her face to read her expression. The sneer was written all over her voice.

"Oh, come on. Emmy's getting married in a few days."

"When has a wedding ring ever stopped Kyle? If you ask me, those two spend waaaaay too much time together."

I wrapped my arms around my shins and cradled my knees to my chest. Emmy and Kyle? A couple? Granted, I hadn't spent much time with them, but they didn't seem like lovers to me. Not even friends. Could I have missed something?

After a brief moment of silence, the waitress replied. "You're just jealous because Kyle isn't interested in you. Why would Emmy have an affair? She and Josh seem great together."

Maidzilla's voice got lower. She leaned toward her friend and spoke in a conspiratorial whisper. "So you think. Those two fight all the time. If Josh had an IQ higher than an eggplant, he'd have dumped Emmy a long time ago. She's managing this place into the ground. If her father doesn't cough up some money soon, they'll be out of business before Christmas."

Bruce was Emmy's new investor? That was one interesting tidbit she failed to mention. A tidbit that gave her a whole new motive for wanting Monica out of the picture.

"I'm telling you, something is going on between Emmy and Kyle. All you have to do is look at them. They're doing it."

I was beginning to wonder if Maidzilla was right. Emmy and Josh seemed to truly be in love, but appearances—especially of relationships—could be deceiving. Emmy herself said that she and Josh and been fighting lately, and she opted to include Kyle, not Josh, in our plans. Could Emmy be fooling me after all?

Before the two women could finish their gossipy conversation, the lights turned on, the sauna's door opened, and three boisterous teenagers invaded the space. My newfound sources became suddenly mute. If I wanted more details, I'd have to find an excuse to talk to them later.

I leaned back and rested my head against the sauna's warm cedar planking, discouraged about more than Monica's murder. Why were relationships always so hard? Emmy and Josh, Rene and Sam, Michael and me: all of us struggled.

Rene and Sam were the one happily married couple I knew, and they might not make it until Monday. How could I expect anything different from Michael and me?

Beads of sweat dotted my body, and not from the sauna's dry heat. The air felt stiflingly thick—too thick to breathe. I had to get out of there.

"Excuse me. Sorry. Pardon me." I stumbled over three pairs of unclothed legs, threw open the door, and took deep, desperate gulps of fresh air. After a quick stop at the changing area to pull on my sweats, I ran for the stairs. I didn't even take the time to put on my shoes.

"Kate, wait!"

Michael jumped out of the tub. "Where are you going?"

"I'm sorry Michael, I can't stay. I have to get out of here."

"OK. Let me grab my pants."

I hated to risk hurting his feelings again, but I couldn't be with him right then. I needed to think. "It's okay, hon. I know you'd rather stay here."

He didn't disagree.

I gave him my best impersonation of a smile. "I"ll meet you back at the cabin later." I ran down the stairs, putting as much distance between me and the spa area as possible.

FIFTEEN

I RAN STRAIGHT BACK to the cabin. I wanted to be alone, but not by myself. I needed Bella.

The scene at the cabin was much as I left it. Sam brooded on the couch while Rene hid in the kitchen, washing already-clean dishes. I clipped on Bella's harness before accosting Rene. "You haven't talked to him yet?"

"Not yet. I'm still working up to it." She scanned the area behind me. "Where's Michael?"

"I left him back at the hot tubs."

Rene raised her eyebrows and tilted her head. "Left him?"

I sighed. "Don't ask. I wouldn't even know how to answer." I held up the leash. "I came back to grab Bella in case she needs another walk."

Rene dried her hands and draped the towel across the faucet. "I'll come with you. Let me grab my jacket."

"Sorry, Rene. Not this time."

She didn't argue. She picked up a magazine and sat on the couch next to Sam, studiously ignoring him. Bella looked from Sam, to Rene, then back to Sam again. To my horror, she lifted her upper lip and clearly exposed her canines.

"Bella! Stop that!" Bella responded to my admonishment by nudging my hand, as if expecting me to give her a cookie. Sam squeezed deeper into the corner and visibly shuddered. Rene giggled.

I apologized to Sam and pulled Bella out the door. Once it was securely closed behind us, I knelt on the deck, gently placed my hands on either side of Bella's face, and touched her nose with my own—a move that, done by anyone else, might well have resulted in a nose-ectomy.

"What's going on with you, girl? Sam is our friend."

Bella responded by licking my face and gently swishing her tail.

"OK, sweetie, we'll walk."

I wasn't ready to see Michael, so I avoided the path that went past the spa and guided Bella toward the upper campsites, where I hoped we would be alone. As we meandered along the desolate trail, I was struck once again by Elysian Springs' silence. You'd think I'd be used to tranquility in the yoga business. After all, that was the whole point: to find moments—no matter how fleeting— of inner calm.

I went to great lengths to create Serenity Yoga's peaceful environment. Multiple water fountains, live plants, soft music. I even hung signs at each doorway that reminded students to speak softly and turn off their cell phones.

None of it made much of a difference. Even inside the practice room, my so-called silent meditations were often dotted with sound. Echoes from the apartments above; traffic noise from busy Greenwood Avenue; the steady beep, beep, beep of delivery trucks backing into the alley.

But not here.

Here, I heard only rustling leaves and the subtle, breath-like sounds of the ocean. I tried to merge with that silence in a moving meditation, carefully treading heel to toe in the gentlest, quietest way possible.

Perhaps if I fully connected with this tranquil space, I would experience nirodha—the state of mental clarity the yoga teachings promised. Perhaps I would decipher the committed-relationship code. Perhaps I would solve Monica's murder. Heck, I would have settled for figuring out how to cure Bella's bellyache. I communed with nature for a good twenty minutes before the universe replied.

Good luck with all that.

I gave up and tried to simply enjoy the day. The sun had burned through the morning's fog and left the sky powder blue. An angry jay scolded from above. Dew drops fell from the branches of a Madrona tree and splashed on my shoulder.

I looked down at my jacket. *Seriously?*

Make that doo drops.

I bent down and picked up an oak leaf to wipe the bird waste off my jacket. Two teardrop-shaped indentations blinked back at me.

"Look Bella," I said, pointing down at the ground. "A deer's been here."

Bella's gaze followed my fingertips, then stopped. Her eyes widened; her ears pricked forward; the hair on her shoulders stood up. She thrust her nose to the ground, took two quick sniffs, then jumped back, as if the scent had scalded her nose. Her wide-eyed expression telegraphed her thoughts.

Monster tracks!

She glued her nose to the ground and launched forward, zooming after the scent like a low-flying rocket. I stumbled behind her.

"Bella, slow down, it's okay!"

My words had zero effect.

We zigged and we zagged. We dodged fallen branches and barreled between trees. I tried to stay upright behind her, unsure whether we were fleeing the perceived menace or chasing it.

The pursuit ended as quickly as it began. After several hundred feet, Bella stopped running, lifted her nose to the sky, and sniffed. She circled the area a few times, then sat down and furrowed her brow, as if considering her options.

"Did you lose the scent, sweetie?"

She gazed at me through wide, silent eyes.

I smiled and ruffled her ears. "C'mon Tracker Dog. Let's head back."

We followed the narrow, winding footpath back toward the cabin. Bella buried her nose in the leaves again, as intent on the scents of this new trail as she'd been on the one that she'd lost.

A good yogi would have tried to stay present and fully embrace that beautiful moment. A good girlfriend would have spent the walk figuring out how to salvage her relationship.

I contemplated murder.

Or at least how to solve it. I certainly had no shortage of suspects. To know Monica was to dislike her. Since we all had access to Bandit and his rhinestone-studded leash, I focused on motive and opportunity.

Dad used to say that nine times out of ten, the killer was a family member—usually the spouse. (Yet another stellar recommendation for marriage.) Not only was Monica a witch with a capital B, but I strongly suspected that Bruce's back wasn't the only one she'd scratched with those burgundy claws. If *I* could tell Monica was cheating, Bruce probably knew it too.

Infidelity and mortal irritation. Excellent reasons for divorce. But murder? Murder might be cheaper than alimony, but it seemed a little extreme, especially for Bruce. I couldn't articulate why, but Bruce didn't feel like a killer to me. Dad would have mocked using intuition to rule out a suspect, but Dad didn't teach yoga. The practice had sensitized me to energy. Bruce's energy seemed tamasic—dull and depressed—not angry. It certainly wasn't murderous.

Bella lunged toward a squirrel. I barely noticed. "Leave it," I said absently.

The timing wasn't right, either. Bruce couldn't have murdered Monica after I dropped off Bandit, at least not before I found her body.

I stopped walking, suddenly sick to my stomach.

How long had Monica been floating in that hot tub when I started CPR? At the time, I assumed that she was still alive—or at least close enough to try to resuscitate—but she could have been dead for hours. Partially digested pancakes gurgled up from my belly.

Best not to think about that, at least not after eating two breakfasts.

I made two mental notes: first, find out if the coroner had determined Monica's time of death; second, ask the hostess what time she spoke with Monica that morning.

Bella stopped to relieve herself—again. I cleaned it up and moved on to the next suspect.

Helen was another viable suspect, with more than one motive. Monica destroyed her marriage and was threatening to ruin her daughter's wedding. I may have been the only one who heard Helen and Monica argue, but that didn't make Helen's threats any less real.

As for opportunity, I assumed she had plenty. Helen hadn't been in yoga class that morning. Was she in bed, sleeping off a hangover, or at the spa, ridding herself of a whole different kind of headache? I'd have to ask Emmy where her mother was the morning of Monica's death.

Thinking of Emmy sent an ache from the base of my sternum to the pit of my throat. Lord, how I didn't want Emmy to be the killer. But as much as I liked the small, unassuming woman, I had to admit, she had motive galore, especially given the conversation I'd just overheard. Monica had destroyed her parents' marriage and threatened Elysian Springs. Emmy gave Monica the keys to the spa and suggested that she use it alone. She practically set Monica up for the kill.

Bella stopped to snack on yet another patch of tall grass. I sat on a moss-covered tree stump and played with her leash, wrapping and unwrapping it from around my fingers. If Emmy and Kyle were having an affair, they could have murdered Monica together. Kyle wasn't nearly as mellow as his dreadlocks and stoner hat would imply. He almost decked Monica that night at the party. But I, of all people, knew that having a bad temper didn't make you a killer. Besides, what was his motive? Killing off disgruntled diners didn't seem like the smartest way to build a clientele.

A loud crash startled me upright and jerked me out of my trance.

"What is it, girl?"

Bella froze at attention, staring off-trail at a brown shape barely visible through the thick undergrowth. I gripped both sides of her harness.

"Easy girl, don't frighten her."

A young doe stared back, deep brown eyes unblinking, as if daring me to make the first move. Light puffs of steam billowed from her nostrils.

I smiled, hoping to let the doe know I meant her no harm. "Hey there, lady. Don't worry. We won't hurt you." I whispered to Bella, "Easy, now. Sit. Stay."

Bella miraculously complied. Her body remained as still as a doggie statue, but her ears, brow, and eyes morphed through multiple expressions. From terror, to wariness, to curiosity, to confidence.

I amused myself by imagining her internal conversation. *Hmmf. You're not so scary.* She cocked her head to the side. *But what manner of beast are you?* Her brow furrowed as she sniffed the air. *Wide set eyes. Definitely not a hunter. Long, skinny legs, good for running. Pointy ears like a bunny rab—*

Bella's eyes grew huge. She stood up, tensed every muscle, and shifted her weight forward. *It's a huge bunny rabbit!*

She looked back at me beseechingly, begging me to let her chase the delightful new prey. Her ears twitched with anticipation; a long line of drool oozed from her lower lip; her tail whipped back and forth in a deer-induced frenzy.

I pulled some treats out of my pocket. "Bella, I said stay."

All of that time-intensive training must have paid off. Either that or Bella was too busy scarfing down lamb lung to chase after buckskin. Bella and I spent less than a minute with that graceful creature, but our friendship's short duration didn't make it any less powerful.

It was as if the universe had sent me a sign. A symbol of my dilemma with Michael. A preview of my upcoming choice. Ambivalence quivered through the doe's muscles. Indecision twitched her nose. She suspected I wouldn't hurt her, but she wouldn't give me the chance. One wrong move and she'd be gone. She leaned over and nibbled at a branch, never taking her eyes off mine.

Stay or flee? Stay or flee?

Which would it be?

A frustrated female voice whispered behind me. "I'm telling you, we can't do this here. If Monica figured it out, someone else will, too."

I gasped and the doe bolted, gone so quickly she might have been an apparition.

I scooted off the trail and crouched in the underbrush, hoping to hear more.

Toni's voice replied. "I'm tired of all of this sneaking around. Make up your mind. Either you're in, or you're out."

Who was Toni talking to, and what were they hiding? I peeked through the leaves, but I couldn't see them clearly.

A rumble vibrated deep in Bella's throat.

The hair on the back of my arms stood up. Bella never growled without reason. She only made that low, threatening sound when she sensed danger: footsteps outside our home late at night; a stranger peeking through my bedroom window; a brown-suited psycho-killer delivering packages …

I wrapped my hand around her muzzle. "Quiet," I whispered. I shifted position, but I still couldn't see who Toni was talking to. I grabbed onto a low branch. If I could contort my neck around this trunk …

My hand slipped and I fell to the ground with an undignified whumpf.

"Someone's coming. We can talk about this later."

Toni replied. "Who cares if someone's coming? I mean it, Helen, I'm sick of all this hiding."

Helen. The second woman was Helen.

Toni moved into view. Her face glowed bright red, but her eyes seemed more hurt than angry. "I understood why you wanted to keep our relationship a secret until after the divorce was final. I even put up with your paranoia while Monica was alive. That witch probably *would* have found some way to use it against us. But what's your excuse now?"

"Emmy and Bruce—"

Toni cut off her reply. "Emmy's a big girl. She can take it. And if Bruce blows a gasket and stops the alimony payments, so what? We can support ourselves. Admit it. You're afraid to come out of the closet."

Helen didn't reply.

"It's time to decide: either you're committed to this relationship, or you're not. I've waited too long already. I'm not waiting a day more." Toni turned and started to march away.

"Toni, wait!" Helen cried. She grabbed Toni's hands. "Please, wait for a minute, and listen. You're right. I'm not ready to come out. Not here. Not now."

"We don't have anything to be ashamed of."

"I know that. But how can I tell Bruce—how can I tell Emmy, for that matter—that our marriage was a sham."

"You didn't do anything wrong, Helen. You never cheated on Bruce. Not once."

"Maybe not, but our marriage was a sham all the same. I simply didn't realize it until I fell in love with you." Her smile looked more beseeching than amorous. "I still haven't figured out what all of this means myself. I'm not ready to bring in anyone else. Please, let's just get through this week."

Toni dropped Helen's hands and took several steps back. "You don't know what this means? We've been together almost two years. How can you not know what we mean?"

"Honey, I'm sorry. I didn't mean that the way it sounded." Helen reached toward her again.

"Don't touch me," Toni snapped. "Don't even come near me." She walked several feet away, then turned back. "I love you. But I won't be in a relationship with someone who's ashamed of me."

Toni marched away, alone this time. Helen watched until she disappeared, then turned and trudged in the opposite direction.

I leaned against the tree, kicking myself. Toni and Helen weren't just long-term friends. They were lovers. How did I not realize that before?

I hadn't even considered Toni as a suspect—not until now. She obviously had reason to want Monica gone. Where was Toni when Monica was murdered? She took my yoga class that morning, but she disappeared while the rest of us were trying to trap Bandit. Had she gone back to the hot tubs? I banged the back of my head against the rough bark. How would I ever solve this case if my suspect list kept growing?

Even worse, now I faced a different dilemma. What was I supposed to do with this new information? Should I tell Emmy? Helen obviously wanted her and Toni's relationship kept secret, but what if it was somehow related to Monica's murder? What if discussing it with Emmy helped me piece the puzzle together?

And what if it didn't?

Then I would have divulged a secret I had no right to know and hurt two innocent people—maybe more—in the process. After ten minutes of circular thinking, I still couldn't make up my mind. Ultimately, I decided not to decide, at least not until after I taught the private yoga class to Emmy's family tomorrow.

I stood up, brushed off my pants, and led Bella back to the cabin. If I was lucky, I'd learn something at my evening class that would render the whole point moot.

SIXTEEN

FOR THE RECORD, DISCUSSING murder during Yoga for Relaxation is counterproductive.

I taught the evening workshop to a handful of students, most of whom I'd never seen before, and all of whom seemed to know nothing about Monica's murder. Each student readily agreed that having a killer loose on the premises was terrifying, but not one of them provided any useful information.

When everyone left Shanti House, they seemed significantly more stressed out than when they arrived. They pointed their flashlights in all directions, fearfully glanced over their shoulders, and scurried across the field in a single group, like a herd of antelope fending off a predator. Obviously, I should have called the class Yoga for Anxiety.

Maidzilla and her waitress friend didn't attend, so I decided to eat breakfast at Eden the following morning. Hopefully I'd be able to question both the waitress and Jennifer, the morning hostess who had spoken to Monica shortly before her death. Kyle was officially in charge of interviewing the restaurant staff, but I needed information he might choose to omit. Like the truth about him and Emmy. I'd figure out how to corner Maidzilla later.

Plans in place, I went back to the cabin.

The rest of the evening passed in a thick fog of wary discomfiture and avoided conversations. Sam and Rene refused to look at each other, each terrified of what the other might say. Michael made plenty of eye contact—most of it angry and wounded. I apologized for running out on him at the spa, but he wasn't ready to forgive me. Frankly, I didn't blame him.

We went to bed early, more to avoid the heartbreaking silence than because we were actually tired. The inches of mattress space between Michael and me felt like a minefield, much too dangerous to cross, so I stuck to my side of the bed, stared at the ceiling, and listened to rain patter the roof.

Four hours later, Bella nudged my hand and let out a low, tortured moan.

"Seriously, Bella? Again?"

Bella suffered from a severe case of Restless Dog Syndrome. She panted, she paced, she scratched, she whined. She asked to go outside every two hours. I couldn't blame her. After all, she still had a day's worth of undigested food in her system. The poor creature was obviously miserable.

Still, it was after two in the morning, and I'd already gotten up to take Bella out twice. Michael—obviously still cross with me—hadn't volunteered to get up either time.

"Ask Michael this time, sweetie. I have to get up in four hours."

My words were more than loud enough to wake him. In fact, I might have even leaned over and spoken directly into his ear.

He didn't move.

I narrowed my eyes and glared at his back with laser-like focus, hoping to pierce his protective armor with bad-boyfriend guilt rays.

Nothing.

I nudged him under the covers. That, at least, earned me a response.

"She's your dog, Kate."

Bella moaned again, louder and more insistent this time.

I sighed. "Hang on, sweetie, let me get my shoes."

I stumbled behind Bella through a dark field of tall, muddy grass for ten minutes while she searched for the perfect place to do her business. After what felt like ten hours, I staggered back into the cabin, hung up my sopping jacket, and unhooked Bella's collar.

Bella looked at the towel in my hands, gave me a don't-you-dare-touch-my-feet look, and padded off to join Michael in the bedroom, leaving a trail of muddy paw prints behind her.

Et tu, Bella? Et tu?

I staggered into the bathroom and leaned against the counter, practically weeping. When I looked up, a drenched zombie woman stared back at me. Spending life behind bars didn't seem all that bad anymore. At least in prison I might be able to get some sleep.

I turned off the bathroom light, tiptoed down the hallway, and cracked open the door. The bedroom was as dark as Bella's muddy black coat. I considered turning on the lights, but that would have disturbed Michael, so I opted to work my way to the bed by Braille. I slipped on one of Michael's socks and tripped on a shoe, but my fingers eventually found the edge of the mattress, and the mound of wet, warm fur draped across it.

One hundred pounds of fur, to be precise.

Snoring on my side of the bed.

On a typical night, I would have asked Bella to move. She was hogging the entire area my legs would normally occupy. But this wasn't a typical night. Bella finally seemed comfortable after a day of misery. She deserved at least a few hours of sleep, didn't she? After all, she was only sick because I had forgotten her medicine.

Ultimately, I decided to sleep curled up in a side-lying Child's Pose.

I sat on the edge of the bed and pulled my knees up to my chest, creating a human cannonball. Then I placed my feet on the sheet behind Bella's shoulders, closed my eyes, and leaned back to rest my head on the pillow.

I completely forgot that Michael had pulled the bed away from the wall.

"What the—Whoa!"

Rather than floating back to rest on a soft, comfy pillow, my upper body fell through the air. My butt and my chunky thighs tumbled behind it.

I flailed arms and legs in a desperate attempt to stay upright, but the action did nothing to prevent my inevitable descent. Bella let out a loud yelp as my right foot connected solidly with her jaw. My left foot connected with something significantly softer.

My body kept falling.

I heard a terrifying crunch as my head connected with hard-wood. Sharp pain jolted down my left arm.

Michael's surprised voice yelled from above. "What the hell, Kate! Why'd you poke me in the eye?"

On a different night, I would have argued that Michael had nothing to complain about; he was, after all, still resting comfortably on top of the cushy, warm bed. On a different night, I would have apologized to both Michael and Bella for my unintentional acts of violence. On a different night, I might even have laughed at the sheer ludicrousness of the whole situation.

But not tonight.

Tonight, I was stuck between a mattress and a hard place. Literally. My torso was wedged between the bed and the wall. My feet pointed straight in the air. Only my head, neck, and shoulders connected with the wood floor.

At first, only one insane thought zipped through my mind. *This is the worst Shoulder Stand ever.* Then my rational mind took over and my entire body flashed cold. *What made that crunching noise when my head hit the floor?*

Visions of wheelchairs, feeding tubes, and a lifetime of dependency paralyzed me. For a few terrified instants, I didn't try to move, afraid—no, petrified—that I might not be able to.

Michael's shocked face peered over the edge of the bed. "What happened? Are you OK?"

Good question.

"I'm not sure. Give me a second." I summoned enough courage to wiggle my fingers, then my toes. Thank God. Everything moved.

"I think I'm OK. Help me up."

Michael grabbed my arms and pulled me back onto the bed. "How did you get down there, anyway?"

"Not so carefully."

He didn't laugh at my joke.

Rene knocked on the bedroom door. "What's going on in there?"

"You wouldn't believe me if I told you," Michael replied. "Come on in."

Great. May as well make it a party.

Rene turned on the lights. She, Sam, and Michael all watched with concerned expressions as I explored my neck's new range of motion. I started with several of the exercises typically done at the beginning of yoga class. I carefully lowered my chin to my chest, then lifted it up toward the ceiling. So far so good.

I turned my head to the right. *Maybe I got lucky.* I turned it to the left. A lightning bolt shot down my arm and out my pinky finger.

Then again, maybe not.

"Rene, do me a favor," I said. "There are some plastic bags next to the refrigerator. Would you please fill one with ice and bring it to me?" I glanced around the room. "Where's Bella?"

Michael pointed toward the window "Over there. Don't worry about her. She's fine."

Bella certainly didn't *look* fine. She cowered in the corner and stared at me with a hurt expression, obviously wondering why I'd kicked her. Any dog—any sentient being, really—would be frightened if woken by a blow to the jaw. But for Bella, it had to be especially traumatic. Bella had been abused as a puppy by a cretin who enjoyed using his boots. She had to wonder if her past was about to repeat itself.

Remorse, shock, and what was probably a minor concussion overwhelmed me. I ignored the lightning storm raging in my arm, staggered over to Bella, and wrapped my arms around her neck. I sobbed into her soft, still-damp fur. "Please forgive me, sweetie. I'm so sorry. I never meant to hurt you."

Bella sighed and leaned into my embrace. I held her tight and rocked back and forth for several long moments, before looking up to meet Michael's gaze. "I never meant to hurt anyone."

It wasn't the apology I owed him, but it was a start.

He replied with a single nod.

Rene returned with Ziplok full of ice and a look that invited no discussion. "Sam, go find Emmy and Josh. We might need an ambulance."

I stood up. "Rene, seriously, I'm fine I don't want an ambula—"

She shushed me with her index finger. "Kate, don't be stupid. A neck injury is nothing to mess with, and you know it. Sit back on the bed now."

I sat.

She turned toward Michael. "Get Bruce. There's a doctor in this place, and we're damned well going to use him."

The boys each ran off on their separate errands. Bella jumped on the bed and cuddled next to me, while Rene pressed the bag of ice cold pain relief against my neck. Head trauma combined with the mental image of my butt suspended in air made me feel giddy. I couldn't stop giggling.

"What's so funny?" Rene asked.

"You should have seen the look on Michael's face when he found me trapped behind the bed." I imagined the scene through Michael's eyes and snorted.

"What now?"

"I think I invented a new yoga pose! Capsized Turtle!"

Rene rolled her eyes. "More like Broken Neckasana." She sobered. "Don't joke around about this. You might still be hurt."

"Come on, Rene, lighten up. I'm fine. Besides, you have to admit, this gives me the perfect opportunity to talk to Bruce."

Rene pinched my arm. Hard.

"Ouch!"

She widened her eyes in mock innocence. "Oh, I'm sorry. Did that hurt? Well, now we know your neck isn't broken." She paused, as if thinking. "At least I don't think so. I'm not a doctor, after all." She walked away, waving her hands through the air. "No worries. If I'm wrong, you'll only end up in a wheelchair." She gave me a look that would have melted a glacier. "Now, are you going to take this seriously, or do I have to pinch you again?"

I was pretty sure any answer other than "Yes ma'am, absolutely, ma'am," would have netted me a matching bruise on the other arm. I stayed silent.

"Get this straight, Kate. Right now Bruce is a *doctor*, not a murder suspect. You're his patient. Interview him later."

I heard the cabin door open. I could make out Emmy's and Sam's voices, but they didn't join us in the bedroom. If they meant to keep me from panicking, they should have talked significantly more softly, or at least spoken in code. The phrases I could make out were "head injury," "no hospital," and "on-call doctor." Bruce and Michael arrived next and added words like "MRI," "not a neurologist," and "helicopter off the island."

I'd heard enough. I pushed Rene's ice-pack-holding hand off my neck and quickly stood up.

Uh oh. Maybe that was a bad idea.

The ground shifted. Warm saliva pooled under my tongue. A wave of nausea crashed through my belly.

A really bad idea.

I grabbed the nightstand to steady myself. Starbursts of pain exploded behind my eyes and shot down my arm.

Even worse idea.

I ignored it all and yelled, "Hold on, you guys. Get in here and talk to me. No one's flying me anywhere."

The four of them crowded into the room.

"I'm fine, guys. Just horrifically embarrassed."

Rene disagreed. "Kate, you need to get checked out by a doctor."

Emmy looked uncertainly at Bruce. "Dad, can you take a look at her?"

"I'm not qualified, honey. I'm a pediatrician, not an ER doc."

"Please?" Michael replied. "We'd really appreciate it."

I looked around the room at four unanimously nodding heads. Michael, Sam, Emmy, and Rene: everyone was in agreement. Everyone, that is, except Bruce and me, and no one seemed interested in our opinions.

Frankly, if someone had lined up the ten worst physicians in America and asked me to pick one as my doctor, Bruce wouldn't have been in the top nine.

First, he looked awful. He'd aged at least a decade in the past two days. His cheekbones were covered in yellowish-gray skin that sagged loosely underneath tired-looking eyes, and his limp, greasy hair no longer came close to covering his prominent bald spot. He looked less like a doctor and more like an overaged medical student at the end of a twenty-four hour shift. If said student had a five-martini hangover.

Second, I was the prime suspect in his wife's murder. Even if Bruce *was* more competent than he appeared, he probably had no desire to help me. He might even wrap me in a full body cast, just for the sport of it.

"Thanks, Bruce, but—"

Rene yelled through clenched teeth. "Kate! What. Did. I. Say?" She pursed her lips, narrowed her eyebrows, and glared.

When Rene wore that pigheaded expression, resistance wasn't just futile; it was catastrophic. I had two options: let Bruce play doctor or go for a whirlybird ride to Anacortes. I wanted off the island, but not that way.

I submitted and did my best impersonation of a cooperative patient. I allowed Bruce to shine a blinding light in each of my eyes. I followed his fingers, told him what day it was, and named the current president. I turned my head left and right, making a concerted effort not to wince. I allowed him to palpate my neck and tolerated his fingertips pressing up and down my spine. I was basically truthful when I answered his questions, though I might have left out a detail or two about dizziness, nausea, and the electrical storm raging down my arm. What were a couple of missing details between friends?

Bruce finished his examination, leaned back, and looked at me uncertainly. "I'm a pediatrician, not a neurologist or a spine specialist." He frowned. "If we were in Seattle, I'd suggest you go to a hospital."

"I really don't think I need—"

He held up his hand. "I know. You've made it abundantly clear. You don't want to go to the hospital." He sighed. "Honestly, an ER doc would probably send you home, anyway." He stood up. "I seriously doubt anything's broken, though you certainly have some strained muscles. You might have a minor concussion, but the fall was pretty short, and you seem lucid."

"I don't know," Rene said. "Lucid might be stretching it for Kate, even on a good day."

Bruce smiled—the first smile I'd seen from him since the night before Monica's death. "I think we can hold off on anything drastic for now. Your friends can take you to the clinic in Eastsound tomorrow if you feel worse." He pulled a notebook out of his pocket. "I'm going to write down a list of danger signs. If you start vomiting, have trouble staying conscious, or start having balance issues, we're calling that helicopter." He looked at me through raised eyebrows. "Agreed?"

Rene and I spoke at the same time.

"Absolutely," she replied.

I smiled. "Agreed. Thank you."

Bruce shook his head. "Don't thank me yet. This may be a huge mistake." He jotted down some notes and handed the paper to Michael. "Make sure she wakes up every few hours. I'll phone in a painkiller prescription tomorrow." To me, he said, "Any allergies I need to know about?"

"No."

He reached into his pocket again and pulled out a brown vial. "If you promise not to tell anyone, I'll give you a couple of Vicodin to get through the night. Ice your neck every couple of hours, and we'll see how you do." He looked at Emmy. "Honey, would you please get Kate a glass of water?" He shook two white, oblong pills into my hand. "Take these and try to get some sleep."

I only got a quick glance at the label, and my vision was undeniably blurry from head trauma. But the name I saw printed on top clearly wasn't Bruce. It wasn't Monica, either. It certainly wasn't she-who-will-soon-fall-on-her-head. If I had to guess, I'd have said that the name on that bottle looked a lot like Helen.

Was Bruce the mysterious drug thief?

I knew Vicodin could be addictive, but pilfering a few pills from his ex-wife seemed like an odd way to obtain it, considering Bruce had a prescription pad of his very own.

I should have quizzed Bruce about Helen's medicine or at least puzzled through some scenarios with Rene, but I didn't have a single brain cell to spare. My head pounded, my back ached, and what little was left of my brainpower was foggy and dull. Solving this particular riddle would have to wait until tomorrow. I took the water from Emmy and gratefully swallowed the bitter pills.

Michael and Sam walked Bruce to the door while Emmy and Rene stayed behind with me.

"See, just like I told you. I'm fine. You were all worried for nothing."

Emmy's expression remained concerned. "Maybe, but be careful. I'm beginning to think this place is cursed." She walked to the door but stopped with her hand on the doorknob. "Don't worry about teaching tomorrow. I'll put up a sign at Shanti House saying that classes have been cancelled for the rest of the week."

"Not on your life," I replied emphatically. "Those yoga classes are the only way I'll get people to talk to me. I'll be there—early even—for the morning class. You'd better con some people into attending. And I'll still teach the private class to your family at eleven. I might be looped-up on pain killers, but I'll be there."

It took some convincing, but Emmy eventually agreed. The Vicodin had begun to kick in, coating my brain in a warm, mellow haze, so I opted to wait and grill Emmy about her supposed relationship with Kyle the following morning. I told her good night and thanked her for her help.

A few minutes later, we all went back to bed. Rene and Sam retired to the living room. Michael lay next to me; Bella curled up at my feet. I couldn't turn my head left to face Michael, so I stared at the ceiling as I whispered the words.

"I *do* love you, you know."

Michael didn't reply, but he reached across that cold, empty minefield and took my hand. When Bella asked to go outside again two hours later, he whispered the three most beautiful words this girl had ever heard.

"I'll take her."

SEVENTEEN

DYING WASN'T ALL IT was cracked up to be. There were no white lights, no long tunnels. No coaxing voices beckoning me to the other side. Just impenetrable darkness and a shrill, beeping noise that pierced my head like the repeated thrusts of an ice pick.

I'd died and gone straight to Hell.

My neck had fused into one solid block of cement. Muscles up and down my spine—some I didn't even know existed—screamed. Fists gripped my lower back and pounded my skull.

And it was time to get up and teach yoga.

I looked at the clock and groaned. Only fifty-eight minutes left until my seven o'clock class. The way I felt, I'd need every one of them. I shut off the alarm, inched to the side of the bed, and placed my feet on the floor. *OK, Kate. You can do this.* I took a deep breath and stood up.

Ouch!

Make that *tried* to stand up.

I froze, immobilized by an excruciating back spasm.

Come on, Kate. Move!

I slowly lowered my knees to the floor, turned on the table lamp, and looked around the room. Extricating my yoga mat from the top shelf of the closet was out of the question, so I crawled, inch by painful inch, to Bella's dog blanket. It wasn't a yoga mat, but it would have to do.

I knew enough about yoga to not have any misplaced delusions. Unlike the Vicodin Bruce had given me last night, yoga didn't provide a quick fix. In cases of acute injury like mine, rest and ice were often more effective. Rest wasn't an option this morning, so I hoped an extra-gentle movement practice would ease my battered body—at least enough for me to regain the will to live.

I started lying on my back in a pose called Apanasana, or Knees-to-Chest Pose. I placed my palms on my kneecaps. With each inhale, I rocked my knees away from my chest until my arms were straight. With each exhale, I drew my thighs toward my ribcage, gently stretching my lower back. Fingers of tension slowly released their grip on my lumbar spine. I wrapped my arms around my shins and rocked left and right, gently massaging my sacral area.

I lowered my feet to the floor and transitioned to hands and knees for a modified Cat Pose. The traction-like movement on inhale lengthened my spine. As I exhaled to Child's Pose, my upper back released in a soft snap, crackle, pop.

My neck was a completely different animal. A stubborn one. No matter what pose I tried, it refused to move. Having a cement block where my neck used to be was probably a blessing, since each time I tried to turn my head left, I received a uniquely exquisite form of shock treatment. But did my scalp need to shrink three hat sizes? I could barely think through the pressure building inside of my skull.

Teaching yoga wouldn't be a problem; I could do that on autopilot. Not a great class, mind you. Perhaps not even a good one. But I could do it. Investigating murder was a different story. How was I supposed to think up snappy, insightful interrogation questions when my head was about to explode?

I finished my short practice, iced my neck for ten minutes, and popped three Advil. Before I walked out the door, I checked to make sure the Yoga Chick was in my jacket pocket. I had no plans to stumble across any new bodies, but I wasn't willing to risk being phoneless again, either.

I shuffled my way to Shanti House, unlocked the door, and gingerly set up a mat at the front of the room. Pins and needles pierced my fingertips, but I pasted on a fake smile, greeted each student without turning my head, and prayed that the Advil would kick in soon.

No one appeared to notice my discomfort.

Pretending to be OK—even when you weren't—was a yoga teacher's core competency. Bad day or not, injured or not, even accused of murder or not, once a yoga teacher sat on her mat, she was expected to exude calm equanimity and easeful grace. Like an old woman trapped in a bad marriage, I'd learned to fake it.

It was a good thing.

Emmy had, indeed, worked her magic. Over a dozen people showed up for that morning class, including several people I recognized as Elysian Springs' employees, an elderly woman, and two chatty teenage boys who placed their mats in the front row.

As I slowly lowered my body to the floor, the fourteenth student—the Grumpy Yogini—sneaked in the door. I smiled to greet her. She glanced at the floor and pretended to flick dust bunnies off her mat.

Nice to see you, too.

I began class the way I always did.

"Hi everyone. Welcome to this morning's yoga class. Please turn off your cell phones." I smiled. "Though only a crazy person would call this early." Several people laughed at my joke, which was my first intention. The elderly woman stood up, fished around in her purse, and turned off her phone. That was my second.

I closed my eyes and silently begged the jackhammer pounding behind them to give it a rest.

"Be. Here. Now."

I spoke the three words to myself as much as my students.

"Leave your day outside the door. In this moment, everything is perfect. In this moment, you are at peace. Sit quietly and be with that peace."

What a load of crap.

I didn't *want* to be here now. Here now sucked.

My back ached, my head throbbed, and my mind wandered. I wanted to be somewhere else, at some other time. Preferably off this island, three days ago—when my body was uninjured, my relationship was healthy, and my future was more than a mental diorama of courtrooms and prison cells.

My thoughts rambled on in a monologue of unrelated questions: Who killed Monica? Why did the Grumpy Yogini keep attending my classes when she so obviously hated them? If I sliced my head off at the shoulders, would it finally stop pounding? Who invented yoga shoes and why?

I opened my eyes. Twenty-eight eyes stared back. How long had I been sitting there, silent?

Come on, Kate. You can get through this.

I picked up the Tibetan chimes I rang at the beginning of each class. No matter how scattered I felt when I arrived on my mat, their melodious, clear sound always centered me.

The first strike rang out clearly and vibrated soothingly across the space. I felt my shoulders drop down from my ears.

I could do this.

The second chime fell less precisely, but that was OK. I didn't think anyone but me noticed. I took another deep breath.

Evidently, the third chime's a charm.

As I lifted the two metal bells to ring them a final time, my neck spasmed and the leather string attaching them slipped through my fingers. They fell to the floor with a loud, metallic, inharmonious clank.

Fourteen bodies flinched. Fourteen pairs of eyes flew open. The two teenagers burst out laughing.

A smart yoga teacher would have admitted defeat, gathered her belongings, and headed on home.

I kept teaching.

The class went reasonably well until the fourth posture. "Cross your right ankle over your right knee, and hold it with your left elbow." Fourteen pairs of confused eyes looked anxiously around the room, obviously hoping someone—anyone—knew what I meant. I looked around, too. After all, I was as confused as they were. "Oh wait a minute. I mean *left* ankle over right knee."

"Wasn't that the side we just did?" asked the obnoxious teenager I now hated. His friend sniggered.

"You're right. I mean right ankle over right knee." The grumpy yogini furrowed her brow and frowned, then crossed her right ankle over her *left* knee, as I had intended. I threw my hands up in frustration. "Oh, you know what I mean."

Five minutes later, one of the teenagers released a very loud, very smelly, plume of intestinal gas. His friend poked him and yelled, "Gross!" The rest of the room pretended not to notice.

Class went downhill from there.

I stepped on the Grumpy Yogini's hand when I tried to adjust her in Cobra Pose and dropped a bamboo block on the elderly woman's foot. For everyone's safety, I moved to the front of the room, where I promptly kicked over the pillar candle. Words never before uttered in yoga class poured from my mouth as I slapped out the flames licking up my pant leg.

Meditation had to be safe, right?

I brought the class to sitting, leaned against the wall to support my back, and tried to block out the pain. I spoke in a low, hypnotic voice. "Notice the silence surrounding you. Drink in that silence. Allow it to nurture your soul. Allow it to—"

A loud, vibrating rumble—not unlike the jackhammer ripping apart my brain—drowned out the rest of my sentence.

What the heck?

I stood up and glanced out the window. One of the center's groundskeepers cheerfully waved back from his riding lawnmower. At first I tried to simply ignore the intrusive sound. If experienced meditators could focus in Grand Central Station, surely I could deal with the rumblings of the world's tiniest tractor.

I continued teaching. "Sound is simply another of life's many distractions. Use what you hear now to deepen your practice." My students shifted uncomfortably and glowered at the window.

I could take a hint.

I walked back to the window and nonverbally dialogued with the gardener. I started the conversation by waving. He waved back. I made a slashing move across my throat. He cocked his head curiously. I pretended to shoot myself in the head.

I wasn't going for subtlety.

It worked. He winced, turned off the machine, and mouthed the word "sorry."

Meditation was obviously a lost cause, but I still had one last, magic tool in my bag of yoga tricks. Nothing cured the hangover of a truly awful yoga class like an extra long period of Savasana—yoga's pose of quiet rest. If I played my cards right, after fifteen-minutes of deep relaxation, everyone—myself included—would have forgotten all about this horrible class.

I asked the students to lie down, covered them shoulders-to-toes in warm cotton blankets, and turned on the CD player. Melodic Sanskrit chanting filled the space with promises of peace.

I laid my aching body on my mat, covered my eyes with a lavender-scented eye pillow, and tried to regain my composure.

I was five breaths into a gentle pranayama practice when a metallic rendition of "Who Let the Dogs Out?" shattered the atmosphere. Annoyed-looking students opened their eyes, shifted under their blankets, and surreptitiously glared at their neighbors.

At first I was mildly amused. *Only in Washington.* Next to "Louie Louie," "Who Let the Dogs Out?" was practically the state theme song.

Then I was irritated. *How rude.* I'd clearly asked everyone to turn off their cell phones. It had to be that obnoxious teenager. I was about to order him to get off of his gas-producing behind and turn it off, when the phone stopped ringing.

Five minutes later, it rang again.

The snarky teenager replied. "Someone should let them back in." His friend guffawed. The Grumpy Yogini buried her head underneath her blanket. The elderly woman tsk-tsked through her dentures.

And that's when my head exploded.

Or at least that's what it felt like. My upper lip twitched; my hands formed tight fists; my teeth ground together. I marched to the shelves by the door, determined to find the offending device and stomp it to death with my candle-wax-encrusted foot. The phone rang again, inquiring over and over again about those exasperating, free-running canines.

I ignored all rules of etiquette and pawed through the pile of other people's belongings. I was going to find that phone and destroy it. It was right there. Right under that purse in ...

My jacket pocket.

Oh good lord, it's mine.

In my haze of narcotics-dulled pain, I'd forgotten to turn off my *own* cell phone. I didn't recognize the ringtone because that damned prankster Rene had changed it again. An image of the headline of today's *Orcas Islander* flashed through my mind: "Yoga Teacher Dies Shoving Phone Down Own Throat."

Make that tomorrow's headline.

Before I euthanized myself with the infernal device, I was going to use it to beat Rene senseless.

The Yoga Chick mocked me with a feather-faced grin. *Don't look so smug*, I thought. *You're about to end up in landfill.* I quickly glanced down at the missed calls indicator. Three messages, all from Serenity Yoga. All before eight in the morning. That couldn't be good.

I turned off the phone, put it back in my jacket, and counted the minutes until I could end this disastrous class. I'm pretty sure my students were counting, too. As soon as I sounded the chimes, they popped up like Pop Tarts, quickly gathered their belongings, and darted out of the building without even saying Namaste. Detaining them to talk about Monica's murder was out of the question.

I scraped the dried wax off the floor, swept up the remnants, and prepared to slink home. When I opened the door, the Grumpy Yogini waited outside, frowning and pacing back and forth on the lawn.

Seriously? She stayed after class today?

I considered waiting her out under a pile of yoga props, but my red-hot face and inflamed nerve endings would have melted the mats. I rubbed my aching shoulders and steeled myself for some unpleasant student feedback.

"Do you have a question?"

She didn't make eye contact. "No … not really. I mean …" Her voice, barely audible to begin with, drifted off. She glanced up, flashed a wan smile, and quickly looked away again. "I wanted … um … I wanted to talk to you for a minute. To thank you for the yoga classes." She twirled a strand of hair around her index finger. "You're an amazing teacher."

Huh?

I expected to hear any number of words, but none of them those. Not thank you. And frankly, the only thing "amazing" about my teaching that morning was the lack of significant casualties. I took a step back and glanced around, looking for a hidden camera. Was this some kind of practical joke?

I narrowed my eyes. "Did Rene put you up to this?"

She looked confused. "Rene? Oh, you must mean Emmy!"

I didn't, of course, but I shook my head yes, anyway.

"Sort of... I mean... Emmy asked me to talk to you, but not about yoga. She told me to tell you that she and Kyle can't make your meeting."

"Why not?"

"There's no water at Eden, so we can't open for breakfast, and Kyle's about to blow an aneurism. Emmy says they need to deal with that first. She'll call you after they figure out what's wrong."

There went my plans for the morning. No gossiping with restaurant employees, no grilling would-be lovers. But on the bright side, I'd have plenty of time to talk to Bruce before my private class.

"Thanks for telling me." I started to walk away.

"That's not all. I mean..." She looked down at her feet. "I wanted to talk to you about something else." Her face turned bright red, but her words became less hesitant, as if by uttering the first phrases, she had opened the floodgates of communication. "It's been great to practice yoga again. I haven't been able to afford classes since Emmy talked me into moving here a few weeks ago."

"Do you work at Elysian Springs?"

"Yes, at Eden, but that's not how I know Emmy. Emmy and I went to high school together, back in New York. I ran away from there, really. My ex-boyfriend…" She shuddered and briefly—so very briefly—made eye contact. "He wasn't a nice man. I had to get away from him." Her eyes filled with tears. "The only time I feel completely safe is when I'm practicing yoga." She paused. "I don't know why I'm telling you all of this."

I did. Emmy was right. For better or worse, students inherently trusted their yoga teacher. I tried to always deserve that trust. I smiled, hoping to encourage her. She nudged the grass with her foot.

"All I really wanted to tell you is that I love this style of yoga. All of the breathing… It makes me feel whole again." The tears that had been building in her eyes cascaded down her cheeks.

I felt like an idiot. I had obviously misread this woman. She wasn't the Grumpy Yogini at all. She was a female yogi, that much was certain. But she wasn't irritable. She was shy, scared, and recovering from what was likely more than one form of abuse.

The more she spoke, the more her confidence seemed to build.

"I also want to apologize," she said.

"For what?"

"For cutting class early every morning. I know it's terribly rude, but I can't afford to be late for work. I showed up ten minutes late after our first class, and Kyle almost bit my head off."

All of the pieces finally clicked into place. *Not everything's about you, Kate.* This lovely woman didn't *want* to leave class early every morning; she was afraid not to. This was Jennifer, the hostess at Kyle's restaurant. One of the last people to see Monica alive.

I wanted to ask her about that morning, but if I questioned her too aggressively, she might bolt. I worked on building our rapport instead.

"You're the hostess, aren't you?"

"Yes, at least one of them. I cover breakfast and lunch." She frowned. "God, I hate that job. I don't like talking to strangers."

"Why don't you work somewhere else, then? There must be a lot of different jobs you could do here at the center."

"Emmy needs some more maids, but I'd rather work at Eden. I'm trying to get restaurant experience. I'd like to work my way up to assistant chef someday. I took culinary training in New York and everything." She shrugged. "But Kyle doesn't need any help in the kitchen right now, so I'm stuck at that hostess desk."

I hated to push her, but it was a natural opening. "Were you at the desk the morning Monica was killed?"

She swallowed hard. "Unfortunately, yes."

"Kyle told me that you talked to her."

"Yes, but I sure wish I hadn't. She was so mad. It wasn't my fault she got sick at dinner the night before. I wasn't even on shift. But she wouldn't stop yelling. She was just so ..."

Awful.

"Jennifer, this is important. What time did you see her?"

She thought for a moment. "I didn't look at my watch, but it wasn't long after I got to work. Maybe five or ten minutes? So I guess that makes it around eight-fifteen."

I puzzled through the timeline. If Jennifer's estimate was right, I'd found Monica's body about forty-five minutes after she left the restaurant. It took me about fifteen minutes to talk to Bruce and walk to the hot tubs. That left thirty minutes for Bruce to follow Monica from Eden to the spa, wait for her to get undressed, kill her, and hustle back to his cabin.

It was certainly possible.

"Did she say if she was planning to meet anyone?"

"No, but we weren't exactly making small talk. I just wanted to get rid of her." Jennifer's cheeks turned pink. "I sent her after Kyle. I told her that he had already left, but if she hurried, she might be able to catch him. Thank goodness she didn't run into him. He'd have served my head on a platter for sure."

"Anything else you can remember?"

Jennifer shook her head. "Not really. She was carrying a towel, so I assumed she was on her way to the spa. I almost told her not to go. You're not supposed to use the sauna or hot tubs when you're sick, and I was afraid she might pass out." Her lower lip trembled. "I haven't told anyone else this, but I feel kind of guilty. Like maybe Monica died because I didn't warn her." Her eyes met mine. "You don't think that's possible, do you?"

I shook my head emphatically. "Absolutely not. Zero percent chance. Monica didn't pass out and drown; she was strangled."

Jennifer's whole body seemed to relax. "Thank you. I knew that, but I needed to hear someone say it out loud. But I still should have said something. I mean, she didn't seem a little under the weather. She looked like she had the plague."

Bruce had mentioned that Monica was sick the night before her death, but this sounded more serious than a bout of the stomach flu. Why did he let her wander off to go hot tubbing alone? I didn't see how an upset stomach could be related to Monica's strangulation, but I made a mental note to ask Bruce about it, nonetheless.

Jennifer and I spoke for several more minutes, but she didn't remember anything else helpful. We said our goodbyes and promised to see each other in class the next morning.

As I limped back to the cabin, I listened to my messages. All three were from Mandy, who grew progressively more desperate-sounding with each recording.

First message: "Kate, it's Mandy. I'm here at the studio. I got a call at home early this morning. The Power Yoga teacher put her back out changing the bottle on the water cooler. She can't get up. I called 911, and the paramedics are on their way. Call me back as soon as you get this."

I closed my eyes. The pounding in my head grew louder.

Second Message: "Hi Kate, it's Mandy again. The ambulance just left. Call me right away. We need to talk."

Third message: "Kate, I looked at the schedule. The Power Yoga teacher was signed up to cover most of your classes. She's supposed to teach two more today, and the students for your Morning Flow class will start arriving any minute. I'll teach this one, but I'm not doing the rest. When you asked me to look after the studio, you said I'd only have to answer the phone and bring in the mail. I didn't sign up for this crap."

Welcome to my world. I turned off the phone and shoved it back into my jacket, accidentally turning my head in the process. A white-hot spasm zapped down my arm.

Confessing to murder was starting to sound pretty darned attractive. Prison would offer free healthcare, a bed that was securely bolted to the side of the wall, and a drill-sergeant-like warden responsible for recalcitrant employees. I'd miss Michael, but perhaps I could arrange for a few conjugal visits. Prison would have everything I needed.

Except Bella.

My mouth went dry. Bella would survive just fine if I was arrested. Michael and Rene would make sure she found a good home. But how would I survive without her?

I steeled my shoulders, pulled the phone back out of my pocket, and started dialing.

EIGHTEEN

My call to Serenity Yoga went straight to voice mail. I was scheduled to teach most of the morning and Rene claimed she still didn't feel well, so Michael, Sam, and a newly reenergized Bella headed off for a day hike on Mount Constitution. Sam—still convinced that Bella was planning to eat him—insisted on driving both vehicles. As soon as the door closed behind them, Rene leaped up from the couch.

"Thank God they're finally gone." Her eyes sparkled with mischief. She rubbed her palms briskly together, ready to pounce, like a feral cat lurking outside of a mouse hole. "What are we going to do now?"

I massaged the back of my neck and scowled. "Don't look so pleased with yourself. I'm still mad at you."

"It's not my fault you forgot to turn off your cell phone!" Rene didn't even pretend to look guilty. "Now, my gimpy Sherlock, what's our crime fighting strategy for the day?"

I couldn't speak for Rene, but *my* strategy was simple. Ditch my evil friend, ice my neck, and sleuth on my own. I simply had to figure out a way to get rid of her that didn't involve driving. Fortunately, I had an idea.

The only thing bigger than Rene's heart was her ego. I'd never *fool* her, but I might manage to trick her. I crossed my arms, looked to the side and frowned, pretending to sort through various options. After enough time had passed to hopefully be convincing, I snapped my fingers.

"I have an idea."

I moved Michael's dirty breakfast dishes to the side and dug through the flyers he'd haphazardly scattered across the table. I eventually found the one with a blue heron on the front. "We should divide and conquer."

"What do you mean?" Rene cocked her head and peered at me suspiciously.

"Teaching Emmy's family gives me the perfect excuse to interview them. You should focus on everyone else." I handed her the flyer. "This nature hike will be perfect. You can eavesdrop on the other guests and work your charms on the trail guide. You're great at getting men to open up."

I didn't lie. Rene *was* good at getting men to talk—or do just about anything else, for that matter. Was it my fault that the trail guide was female?

Rene read the flyer. "*Four hours?* You expect me to tramp around in some muddy, mosquito-infested swampland for *four hours?*" She shuddered.

Technically, she'd be hiking through a forest, but I knew what she meant. Rene considered watching the Discovery Channel bonding with nature. Four hours hiking off-trail wasn't exactly her cup of chai.

I took the flyer back and pretended to read it. Ten to two, exactly as I remembered. I mentally crossed my fingers, hoping my plan would work. "Gee, Rene, I didn't realize it was that long." I shook my head in mock agreement. "You're right, four hours is too much for a woman in your condition. Between the vomiting and the lack of exercise, you're pretty out of shape. I'll have to do it myself tomorrow."

She snatched the flyer back from me. "Out of shape, my a—"

She stopped mid-sentence and furrowed her eyebrows. "Wait a minute. I know what you're doing."

Yes, but would it work?

I assumed my most innocent expression. Rene glared at me for several seconds, eyes mere inches away from my pupils. She opened her mouth as if to argue, but stopped short. A final, under-her-breath grumble later, she swatted her hand through the air. "Fine. Whatever. You win." She sat down on the couch with a heavy thud and pulled on her pink suede boots. "But I'd better not get any mud on my UGGs."

I bit the inside of my lip to keep from smirking. Rene could never say no to a challenge, even when she knew she was being hoodwinked. I'd deal with the fallout over her soon-to-be-ruined boots later, but at least for now she'd be safe and out of the way.

I closed the door behind her at nine forty-five. Seventy-five minutes until my class started. Plenty of time to ice my neck, come up with a story that would entice Bruce to spill his guts, then hop on over to the Retreat House for my combination yoga class/interrogation session. With any luck, I'd have the case solved by noon.

But first, I had to call Serenity Yoga again. Mandy had likely been teaching the first time I called, but she should be done by now.

High-pitched wails howled through the phone line.

"Serenity Yoga, how can I..." Mandy's flustered voice trailed off. "Honey, untie your brother. Those yoga straps aren't toys." I heard a frustrated sigh. "How can I help... Oh crap. Hang on a minute."

The phone clanked on the counter. Mandy yelled, "Put that candle down this instant, missy! You're spilling wax all over the carpet!" Frantic yelling turned into tortured pleading. "Please, honey. Please be a good girl. If you behave for just a few minutes, Mommy will buy you a cookie."

I considered hanging up and flushing my cell phone. Whatever was happening back at the studio, I obviously didn't want to know about it. When Mandy picked up the phone again, I tried to make my voice sound confident, yet soothing. "Hi Mandy, it's Kate. How are things going?"

"What do you mean, how are things going? How do you think they're going? Didn't you get my messages?"

"Yes, and—"

"Well, it sure took you long enough to call back. I started calling you over two hours ago!"

I tried to tell her that I had, indeed, phoned earlier, but she didn't give me a chance.

"This is the last class I'm covering for you. I have kids, you know."

Gee, and I almost forgot.

She continued. "My sitter couldn't come on such short notice, so I had to bring my kids to the studio. Do you have any idea how hard it is to teach with a baby on your hip and two three-year-olds throwing temper tantrums in the background?" I didn't, but I had a feeling I was about to find out.

"Four students left fifteen minutes into class, the ingrates."

I made a mental note to call them and apologize as soon as I got back to Seattle. "I'm sure it went better than you think."

"Easy for you to say. You're off relaxing on some island vacation. I'm stuck here in the disaster zone. You promised me that filling in for you would be cake."

"It is," I replied, trying to lighten the mood. "I just didn't tell you it was Devils food."

She didn't appreciate the joke.

"Nothing about this is funny, Kate. I've got my own life, and it includes three children. Classes are covered through six, but if the Power Yoga teacher can't come back by then, you're on your own."

I spent the next hour trying to bring order to the den of chaos formerly known as Serenity Yoga. As soon as I got off the phone with Mandy, I called the Power Yoga instructor. The doctor had sent her home with a lumbar support brace, two painkiller prescriptions, and orders not to teach for at least two weeks.

That left me forty-five minutes to find coverage for the ten classes she was supposed to teach before I got back. I started with polite requests for help from my five most senior instructors. After five equally polite answers of "no," I changed tactics. For the next five stern conversations, I reminded the now-grumpy teachers that *I* was the boss. No better. I ultimately resorted to the only two management tactics that always worked: groveling and bribing.

Three hundred phone calls later, I hung up the phone, victorious. I now had coverage for all the Power Yoga teacher's classes—at least until the beginning of next week. Hopefully by then I'd be cleared of all murder charges, my own neck would be healed, and I'd be able to teach her classes myself. If not, well, I didn't even want to think about the alternative.

I looked down at my watch. Ten-fifty. Only ten minutes until I had to be at the Retreat House. So much for that ice pack.

I grabbed my yoga bag and slipped on my favorite fall footwear: thick cotton socks and Birkenstocks. As I painfully rushed toward the Retreat House, I mentally rehearsed the upcoming ninety minutes.

No, my mind wasn't filled with visions of bendy postures, deep breaths, and blissful meditations. I imagined pointed questions, piercing glares, and insightful deductions. In my mental motion picture, my mind was razor sharp; my focus, unbreakable. Squirming suspects froze on their yoga mats in guilt-filled terror. I asked just the right questions at exactly the right time. The guilty party squirmed in discomfort under the intense focus of imaginary Kate's withering gaze.

In a scene worthy of a *Perry Mason* finale, imaginary Kate pointed her finger at the guilty party. She was about to yell, "Admit it. You did it! You killed her!" when an angry male voice interrupted.

"What in the hell makes *you* qualified?"

I stopped walking and warily glanced around me. Now I was hearing voices? Was that God admonishing me, or was my head injury worse than I thought?

Whoever it belonged to, I had to admit: the voice in my brain-damaged skull had a point.

I almost answered. I almost told him that he was right—that I had no business getting involved in murder. Heck, I couldn't even solve my own problems. I opened my mouth to promise the intruding wise man that I'd learned my lesson. To assure him that if he let me, I'd be on my way back to Seattle, where the only corpses posing would be those of my grateful yoga students.

But before I could speak, the voice interrupted again. "You need to call a plumber."

Huh?

Why would God—or a misfiring synapse in my brain, for that matter—chastise me about broken toilets? And why did God's voice sound suspiciously like Kyle's?

I tiptoed off the path and peered through the bushes toward the sound. Kyle and Josh stood near the animal enclosures next to a car-sized, water-filled sinkhole. Somehow I didn't think they were putting in a new swimming pool. Josh leaned on a backhoe. Kyle stood ominously over him.

"Damn it, Josh! I told you all those shortcuts were a mistake! How am I supposed to run a restaurant without water?"

Josh leaned down, broke off a long blade of grass, and absently chewed at its end. "Calm down, Kyle. You're getting all worked up over nothing. I told you, I can fix this. Emmy will be back with the parts in no time. We'll have you up and running again in a few hours."

"That's not the point, and you know it. You'll patch this section up today, and we'll spring a new leak tomorrow. Who knows how many more of these old pipes are about to burst? How could you have spent all that money on designer rugs and bamboo flooring without upgrading the plumbing? I'm beginning to think that your mother-in-law was right. This place is nothing but a rat trap." His voice grew louder. "You and your dimwit fiancé are going to ruin me!"

Josh flipped in an instant. He removed the blade of grass from his mouth and threw it to the ground. His face turned so red I was surprised his beard didn't spontaneously ignite. He leaned forward, grabbed the front of Kyle's shirt, and pulled Kyle's face to within an inch of his own. "Lower your voice," he growled. "And be *very* careful how you refer to my future wife."

The two men didn't move for several seconds. Josh's white-fisted, black-bearded body was rigid; his arms trembled. Kyle gaped at him through wide, surprised-looking eyes. I had a sudden vision of Kyle being drowned in a three-foot-deep puddle of waterlogged mud.

Should I say something? This was a side of Josh I'd never seen before, and I had no desire to witness more violence. Then again, I wanted to see how the scene would play out.

In the end, I decided to wait.

The moment passed almost as quickly as it began. Josh opened his hands and roughly released Kyle's lapels. Kyle stumbled a step, then righted himself and yanked the wrinkles out of his shirt. Josh leaned on the tractor and smiled. The expression never quite reached his eyes.

When Josh spoke, the friendliness in his voice sounded forced. "I already told you. The remodels are part of Emmy's plan. We've had a few stumbles, but it will all work out. Emmy's father is loaded. She just has to convince him that this place is a good investment. Believe me, she knows what she's doing."

Kyle's upper lip twitched. "I sure as hell hope so. For all of us." He gestured toward the sinkhole. "This had better be fixed before I have to start dinner prep. And if you think I'm paying a penny for it, you're wrong!" Kyle stomped away, dreadlocks bouncing with every step. He slammed his hand into the side of the chicken coop, startling the hens into a squawking eruption of feathers, dust, birdfeed, and chicken droppings.

Josh watched Kyle storm off, then knelt next to the coop. "Easy there now girls," he said to the still-worked-up hens. "Mellow out. That old fox isn't nearly as smart as he thinks." He picked up a rock, tossed it into the water-filled hole, and watched it sink to the bottom. "Not so smart at all." A shiver ran down my spine.

The Josh I had just witnessed wasn't nearly as mellow—or as oblivious to money—as the one Emmy had described. Was he fooling her?

Or was Emmy fooling me?

I thought back to our conversation the morning after Monica's death. I'd just finished teaching my class when—

Oh, no! Class! I'd forgotten all about class! I glanced at my watch. Eleven-ten. My private class was supposed to start ten minutes ago. I picked up my yoga mat and rushed across the field, hoping I wasn't already too late.

NINETEEN

"You're late." Helen's pinched face scolded me through the Retreat House's doorway. "Class was supposed to start fifteen minutes ago." Her breath—which smelled like fruity gym socks—packed a bigger punch than her words.

I flinched and took several steps back.

Who was this woman?

Physically, she was the same anxious but friendly woman I had traded jokes with two nights before, but energetically, she was different. She was obviously agitated about my tardiness, but it was more than that. She seemed sharp, almost bitter, and she gave me the same don't-mess-with-me glare she'd used when confronting Monica.

This was a woman I didn't want to cross.

"I'm so sorry. I got tied up in some personal business." I opted not to tell her that said business was eavesdropping on her future son-in-law. I smiled, hoping to mollify her. "But I'm glad to be here now."

Her brows knit together irritably. "I was about to send everyone home. We were supposed to be done here at twelve-fifteen. Now we'll be late, you know."

Fifteen minutes hardly seemed earth shattering, but I played along. I stared at my feet, doing my best impersonation of a repentant yoga teacher. "You're right, Helen, and it's all my fault. There's no good excuse. I won't charge for the session."

I waited through several infinite seconds of silence before she replied. "Well, I suppose you're here now. We may as well get started." She opened the door wider and gestured with a half-empty champagne glass for me to come inside. Sparkling fluid splashed over the rim, creating a spatter of effervescent droplets across the hardwood floor.

I looked around the empty hallway, hoping to see Emmy—or any other friendly face, for that matter. "Where is everyone?"

"They're all waiting for you in the living room. Emmy set everything up this morning." She staggered slightly as she walked down the hall. "Follow me."

I followed.

I paused at the room's entrance, surprised. The living room, though gorgeous before, had been completely transformed since the night of the reception. The serving tables had been removed, but that was far from the only change. The furniture—couches, chairs, and end tables included—had either been moved out of the room or pushed against the walls, and the colorful Gabbeh area rug had been rolled up near the door. In the rug's place were twelve staggered yoga mats. A large ceramic vase containing purple dendrobium orchids, orange birds of paradise, and tall sprigs of red ginger decorated an altar in front of the fireplace; several lit candles flickered from the mantle. Strands of white Christmas lights bathed the room in a warm, inviting glow.

"Wow! You and Emmy did a fabulous job! This looks better than my yoga studio."

"Don't look at me," Helen replied. "It's all Emmy's doing. She wanted the space to look perfect for you, since Shanti House wasn't available. Too bad she's not here to enjoy it."

"Not here?"

I peered around the room, looking for familiar faces. Women of all ages chatted in small groups, most of them sipping light orange liquid from crystal champagne flutes. Emmy wasn't among them, nor was Bruce. In fact, the gathering was completely devoid of the male gender.

"Aren't Bruce and Emmy joining us?"

Helen waved her hand dismissively. "Lord only knows where Bruce is. That man is useless. Emmy's off dealing with the latest emergency, so I guess I'm in charge of entertaining everyone." She took a huge swig of champagne. "And this was supposed to be Emmy's bridal shower." She scowled. "What a disaster."

"What happened?"

"Would you believe it? The water line to the restaurant burst this morning."

That explained the center's new swimming pool. Monica's food poisoning and now a burst water line? Was Elysian Springs badly managed, or was it cursed? Or was the problem something more sinister entirely?

Helen kept talking. "We were supposed to have Emmy's bridal luncheon at Eden today, but now that's ruined, too. Josh says the restaurant probably won't even open today." She shrugged. "Not that it matters. Emmy wouldn't be able to attend anyway. She had to go to Anacortes to get parts."

Helen drained the rest of her glass. "But Emmy insisted that we still hold this harebrained yoga class." She walked—a little more unsteadily than I would have preferred—to a table containing several champagne bottles and a carton of orange juice. She filled her glass with champagne, topped it with a splash of orange juice, then waved her hands in the air. "So here we are."

I didn't dare risk replying. Helen was obviously feeling both tipsy *and* cranky. But did she have to call my life's work harebrained? Yoga might not be up there with brain surgery, but it wasn't exactly dog fighting, either. I took my work seriously. Any long-term practitioner would agree: yoga changed lives. My face must have betrayed my frustration, because Helen apologized.

Sort of.

"I'm sorry. That came out wrong. I'm sure your classes are lovely." She muttered under her breath. "Even if Emmy *did* have to browbeat everyone into coming." She leaned against the table to steady herself and took another long drink.

Perfect.

Rene once told me that yoga was the world's best hangover cure, but generally speaking, I preferred that my students be sober. Down Dogging under the influence might not be a felony, but that didn't make it a good idea. I looked pointedly at the almost-empty glass in Helen's hand. "Since you ladies have been drinking, maybe we should do a lovely visualization instead of a movement practice."

"Don't be ridiculous," Helen snapped. "I poured them each one glass. And I only did that because they were getting antsy waiting for you. Now let's get this over with."

She gave three sharp claps. "Ladies, set down your drinks and pick out a mat. The yoga teacher is finally here."

As the other women looked up from their conversations, Toni and Helen made eye contact. Toni frowned. Helen flinched. Helen thudded her glass on the table and turned toward me, lips pressed together so tightly they almost disappeared. "They're all yours."

I smiled at the fidgety crowd and pointed toward the blankets, blocks, straps, and bolsters stacked neatly against the wall. "Hi, everyone. Please grab a blanket and two blocks, and sit down on a mat. We'll get started in a minute."

I rolled out my own mat, set my chimes on the floor, and carefully watched my student suspects as they gathered yoga props and staked out their territories. No one acted unusual, except Helen and her would-be lover.

Toni and Helen didn't *seem* like lovers, or even friends, anymore. More like aging cheerleaders who'd just discovered that they were sleeping with the same quarterback. The two feuding women chose mats on opposite corners of the room. Toni studiously avoided looking at Helen; Helen stole quick glances at Toni. The tension between them was so sharp it could have cut glass. The rest of the guests obviously noticed; they glanced warily back and forth between the two women, as if wondering which would be their new alpha.

Time to shift focus.

I sat cross-legged on a blanket, smiled, and made eye contact with each of my new students. "Hi everyone. I understand most of

227

you were sentenced to be here today." A light twitter tinkled across the room. "That's OK. Hopefully by the end of class, you'll be glad you came."

I ignored my aching neck and told them about Viniyoga, the style of yoga I taught. "This type of yoga isn't about what the poses look like; it's about how they feel in your body. Your goal today is to walk out of the room feeling better than when you walked in— maybe even better than after your first mimosa."

They all laughed again. So far so good.

"Any requests today?"

Several hands lifted, asking for everything from low back stretches to poses that would help relieve stress. I shifted, almost automatically, into teacher mode. "Let's start by lying on our backs."

I asked everyone to stretch out on their mats and begin to lengthen their breath. After a few gentle movements designed start warming their bodies, I guided them into Bridge Pose.

"Place your feet flat on the floor, about four inches apart and six inches away from your hips."

Helen turned her head to look at Toni. My own neck spasmed in response.

"Please don't turn your head in this pose." Helen frowned at me, then looked up at the ceiling again. I continued. "Good. Now, as you inhale, press down on your feet and lift your hips up toward the sky." Everyone complied. Some of the women arched their backs deeply; others were only able to lift a few inches away from the floor. But they all seemed to be getting the desired effect: strengthening their legs, hips, and backs while stretching the fronts of their bodies. "Excellent. Now, pretend that your spine is a pearl necklace, and as you exhale, lower it to the floor a single pearl at a time."

A student in the middle of the room quipped, "My spine feels more like a two-by-four."

We all laughed.

Next I asked the class to come to hands and knees for a pose called Upward Facing Dog.

"Start resting in Child's Pose. With your next inhale, move forward past hands and knees until your back arches and the crown of your head reaches up to the sky. Relax your shoulders down from your ears and..."

The women kept moving, so I must have kept speaking, though I have no earthly idea what I said. My mouth was set firmly on auto pilot. My brain was otherwise occupied, scrutinizing each student and sorting them into groups: guilty, not guilty, and to-be-determined.

The preteen to the right belonged in the not guilty pile. Teenage hormones notwithstanding, she didn't look nearly strong enough to subdue Monica, even if Monica was sick at the time. Ditto the eighties-ish woman practicing beside her.

Helen and Toni, on the other hand, were to-be-determined. Both women were physically capable of the deed, and they both had reason to want Monica out of the way. The rest of the class—ranging in age from twenties to sixties—remained mysteries. None of them looked like female body builders, but they weren't exactly feeble, either.

That blonde in the second row, for example. The one glaring at me and gritting her teeth. I could easily imagine her wrapping a leash around someone's throat.

Mine, for instance.

I glanced around the room. The rest of the students wore similar expressions.

How long had I left them in Upward Facing Dog?

Pained-looking faces grimaced from every row. The elderly woman, who I suspected was Josh's grandmother, collapsed on the floor with an audible grunt. Sweat dripped off the preteen's collarbones and pooled on her mat.

"Oh my gosh, everyone. I'm so sorry. Let's rest in Child's Pose for a few breaths."

"Oh thank God," cried a voice from the back of the room.

I hadn't intended to beat the class into submission, but it worked. For the next forty-five minutes, they were focused; they moved in harmony; they even seemed to be enjoying themselves.

By the time we entered Savasana, I could tell from their expressions that I'd done exactly what I'd hoped. I'd helped each of these women find inner peace. More importantly than that, I'd built a bridge of trust between us. My heart swelled.

Then my stomach constricted.

I'd built that trust fully intending to abuse it. Gathering information to trap a killer wasn't exactly up there with seducing a student, but I still felt guilty. Just not guilty enough to change tactics.

I rang the chimes three times.

"Take as long as you need. Wiggle your fingers and toes and take a few deep breaths." I saw several small movements. A couple of students stretched and yawned. "Rest for a breath or two, then roll to your side and press yourself up to sitting."

I made eye contact with each student a final time, then touched my palms together at my heart. "Namaste. The light in me honors the light in you." I smiled across the room.

Eleven relaxed-looking women beamed back at me—and Helen, who looked like she had bitten into an under-ripe lemon.

"Any questions?" No one raised their hands, so I said, "I hope you'll all hang out and chat for awhile. I'd love to get to know you better."

The practice must have metabolized the alcohol in Helen's bloodstream, because when she spoke, she sounded surprisingly sober. "I'm sorry, Kate, but you'll have to catch up with everyone later." She stood and turned toward the rest of the room. "Ladies, head back to your rooms, change clothes, and meet me outside the office in ten minutes. Eden is closed, so we'll have lunch in Olga, a cute little town about thirty minutes from here."

That was okay, I could improvise. "That sounds like fun. I'll come with you."

Helen's look didn't invite discussion. "No, you won't. This party is for family only." She waved toward the door. "Go now ladies, scoot! We're late, as it is!"

The preteen knelt down to roll up her mat.

"Leave the yoga equipment here," Helen said. "Kate will put it away."

To my horror, all of my suspects stood up and slipped on their shoes. I stared at them, powerless, as they filed one-by-one out the door. Toni gave Helen a you-didn't-have-to-be-so-rude look before joining them. When the door closed behind the last student, Helen turned to face me.

"I'm sorry, Kate. I'm sure that seemed impolite." Her voice sounded more frustrated than apologetic. "If you hadn't arrived over fifteen minutes late, I would have told you before class. Emmy forced me to host this silly gathering, but I will *not* allow you to interrogate my friends and family. If you want to question someone, it will have to be me." She looked pointedly at her watch. "You have five minutes."

"Emmy *told* you?" That probably wasn't the most relevant question to start with, but it was the one that flew out of my mouth. How was I supposed to catch Monica's killer if Emmy forewarned all the suspects?

"Yes, she filled me in on your cockamamie scheme this morning."

I felt my face grow hot.

"Oh, don't look so upset," Helen chided. "She didn't tell everyone, just me." She paused. "And that chef." She looked off to the side, as if thinking. "And I'm sure she told Josh, but that's probably it."

In other words, Emmy likely told everyone.

I sighed. "How about you? Did you tell anyone?"

Helen wrinkled her lips in irritation. "Certainly not. This whole murder business is sordid enough. I made Emmy promise not to say anything to her father, either. He's already useless. The last thing we need is to get him *more* worked up."

"Well, you can't blame him for being upset. His wife *is* dead, after all."

Helen cringed, then visibly deflated. "You're right. I don't know what's gotten into me." She gestured toward a sofa pressed against the wall. "Please sit for a minute." I sat on the cushion next to her. "Talking about Monica always brings out the worst in me. But honestly, couldn't she at least manage to die without screwing me over?"

Now *I* was the one who cringed.

"That sounds terrible, I know." Helen stared at her hands and worried a thumb nail with her index finger. "I suppose I should feel bad that Monica was murdered, but I don't. Frankly, I'm relieved that she's finally gone."

Relieved enough to make her disappear permanently?

She looked up again. "You'd think after almost two years, I'd be over it."

I wasn't sure how long she'd keep talking, but I planned to take advantage of every second. "You and Bruce divorced two years ago?"

"Yes, though he started sleeping with that floozy almost a year before that. At first I ignored it. I assumed it was some sort of midlife crisis—that he'd eventually come back to his senses." She shook her head, as if she still couldn't believe it. "But he didn't. He fell in love with her."

"Did your marriage have troubles before?"

"Yes, but nothing serious. Certainly not an affair. After twenty-five years together, Bruce and I may not have been crazy in love anymore, but we *did* love each other, and we would have done anything for Emmy. But once she moved out on her own..." Her voice trailed off.

I filled in the blanks. "He started seeing Monica."

She grunted. "It was such a cliché. A blonde over twenty years younger than him and his receptionist to boot. I was a laughingstock." She shook her head. "And now she went and got murdered. People will never stop talking."

"Sounds like you really resented her."

Helen's eyebrows lifted. Hard lines creased her mouth. "You met Monica. Can you blame me?"

"Ever feel like strangling her?"

Helen sighed. "Honestly, the only person I feel like strangling is Emmy, for involving you in this foolish scheme." She placed her hands on her thighs and stood up. "If you think someone here for the wedding killed Monica, you're crazy. If I had the guts, I'd have strangled the tramp two years ago, before she ruined my family. It's too late now." She shrugged. "Why would anyone else care?"

"What about Bruce?"

"Are you kidding? That poor schmuck loved her. She made his life a living hell, but he can't stand being without her, either. He's completely fallen apart since her death."

I didn't want say it, but I had to. "How about Emmy, then? I understand she and Josh are having financial difficulties. Monica could have made it difficult for Bruce to give her money."

Helen laughed. "Emmy? That girl can't even hurt a fish. It broke her heart to buy that salmon for Monica. She told me she cried for days. All of this vegetarian nonsense is beyond me, but it proves that Emmy's not capable of hurting anyone." She picked up her jacket and keys. "It had to be some crazed local. Half of these people are barely better than glorified hermits."

She rechecked her watch. "Your five minutes are up."

"Just a few more questions, Helen, please."

She hesitated, but sat down again. "Make it quick. I still need to change clothes."

"Emmy told me that you lost some medicine."

"I didn't lose those prescriptions, they were stolen." Her tone grew irritated. "And I know who took them, too."

"Who?" I scooted to the edge of the couch, fully expecting to hear the name Bruce.

"That grumpy blonde maid, that's who."

Maidzilla?

"I noticed her snooping through my belongings a few days ago. I told Emmy about it, but she's blind when it comes to her staff. She claims the little blonde grump was simply straightening up." Helen grumbled under her breath. "I suppose she needed to vacuum my pants pockets, too."

That couldn't be right. "Did you actually see the maid steal your prescriptions?"

Helen hesitated. "Well, no, but it has to be her. I caught her again this morning, trying to snag a bottle of wine from the kitchen. Who else would it be?"

"This might sound crazy, so bear with me. Could it be Bruce?" I told her about my fall, Bruce's late night visit to the cabin, and what I'd seen written on the prescription vial.

Helen dismissed the idea with a flip of her hand. "Don't be daft. Bruce wouldn't steal drugs. Besides, I don't think I brought any Vicodin. I haven't used pain medication in years. You must have misread the bottle."

I supposed it was possible…

"And even if the prescription *was* mine, Bruce didn't steal it. He and I lived together for twenty-five years. Lord knows how many of each other's possessions we still have."

I couldn't imagine why Bruce would have carted a likely expired vial of his ex-wife's pain medication across the country, but I didn't have a better explanation, either.

"Now stop snooping around in my family's affairs and mind your own business. I have a luncheon to attend." Helen looked at her watch, jumped up and brushed off her slacks. "Oh, for goodness sake. And now you've made me too late to change." She took my arm and led me to the exit.

I stopped at the doorway. "Why don't you go on ahead? I still need to return the yoga equipment, and I don't want to make you any later than I already have." I flashed what I hoped was a sincere-looking smile.

Helen wasn't fooled. "Nice try. But if you want to snoop through my belongings, you'll have to come up with a better excuse than that." She grinned sardonically. "Maybe Emmy will hire you as a maid." She ushered me through the door. "I'll take everything back later."

As she placed the key in the lock, I played my one final card. "One more thing, Helen."

"I told you, I'm in a hurry. What now?"

"I overheard you and Toni on the upper trails yesterday."

Helen stood completely motionless for several seconds. Then she slowly, deliberately removed the key and placed it in her pocket. When she turned to face me, her eyes glittered like frozen glass. "I don't know what you think you overheard, but you'd better be *very* careful what you say and who you say it to." I felt, more than saw, a force field surround her. "That part of my life is no one's business but my own."

In spite of her armor—perhaps even because of it—my heart broke for her. Helen was trapped in a lie, too terrified to confront the truth.

She knew it.

I knew it.

The question was, did Monica?

I spoke in a soft voice, as if coaxing a frightened animal. "Helen, did Monica know about you and Toni?"

Helen bit her lower lip, but that didn't keep it from trembling. "Kate, let this go. Toni and I have nothing to do with Monica's death. Nothing at all. Please get on a ferry and go back to Seattle before you ruin everything."

She ran toward the parking lot before I could ask her any more questions.

TWENTY

THIRTY MINUTES AND SIX hundred milligrams of Advil later, the pounding in my head receded to a dull, aching throb. The pain in my neck, however, was more annoying than ever.

Her name was Rene.

She harassed me incessantly as we trudged toward Bruce's cabin. "You owe me, Miss Kate. And, believe me. You. Will. Pay." She punctuated each word with a thrust of her index finger. "Consider yourself lucky that they ended the hike two hours early."

She stopped and cocked her head to the side. "At least that's what they claimed. A few minutes after they dropped me off at the office, I saw that guide lead everyone else back to the trailhead." She shrugged. "No matter. I was all natured out, anyway."

She wagged her finger back and forth. "But that doesn't save your sorry butt, Missy Girl. No way. I'll get my revenge. When you least expect it…"

Rene's shrill chatter reverberated through my skull, bouncing back and forth like a lead-lined ping pong ball. I tried to focus my mind by mentally chanting the first chapter of *The Yoga Sutras*. When that didn't work, I tried a mental rendition of Katy Perry's greatest hits. That didn't help either. No matter what tune I played in my head, Rene's lips kept moving.

"Who ever heard of a female trail guide, anyway? All Dora the Explorer would talk about were birds, insects, and rotting tree stumps." She rolled her eyes. "Then everyone got all caught up in some debate about whether the dowatchamacallits we saw were short-billed or long-billed."

That caught my attention. "You saw some dowitchers? They're rare. How cool!"

Rene scowled. "Oh for goodness sake, Kate. Not you too."

She stomped several feet ahead, then turned around and re-commenced complaining. "Even worse, Miss Bird-on-the-Brain absolutely refused to share any good gossip with me. And those grumpy little old biddies from the Audubon Society kept shushing me whenever I tried to change the subject. I didn't have any fun at all." She pointed to her mud-ruined shoes. "I fully expect you to buy me a new pair of boots. I might even replace these UGGs with some Louis Vuittons. That will teach you to send me off on a fool's errand."

I sighed and kept trudging forward. Hoping—praying even—for the universe to strike me deaf.

"I didn't even get in any decent exercise. Every three minutes they wanted to stop and look at some stupid bird's nest and—"

"I know, Rene, I know. You've told me a dozen times already. There weren't any men to manipulate, you didn't have fun, and I owe you a new pair of shoes. Now would you please be quiet for five minutes and let me think?"

Rene flinched. "Good lord, Kate. You're as bad as those old bird biddies." She nudged the grass with her toe. "I was trying to help, you know."

I felt bad for snapping at her. I felt even worse when I saw the injured look on her face. But at least she stopped talking.

Don't get me wrong. I loved Rene. That was the problem. I loved her too much to put her in danger.

The last time I confronted a murderer, Bella and I *both* almost got killed. If Rene got hurt because of me, I would never forgive myself. I didn't think Bruce was the killer, but I was beginning to wonder. So if Rene was determined to come with me—which she was—I needed to figure out how to question Bruce without making him suspicious.

We walked in silence until we reached Bruce's cabin. Up close, the building was even more impressive than I remembered. Climbing roses and old-growth rhododendrons nestled up to impeccably stained siding; a steep staircase led to an expansive deck and a second story entrance that protected the inhabitants' privacy; floor-to-ceiling windows on the ocean side of the building overlooked a stunning Puget Sound view.

As we ascended the stairs, I reminded Rene of our agreed-upon strategy. "Okay Rene, remember what we decided. I'll take the lead. You're here for two reasons and two reasons only: moral support and to distract Bruce while I find an excuse to look around."

Rene grinned. "Oh, I'll distract Brucey all right. Miss Bird-on-the-Brain may have been immune to my charms, but Bruce will be a different story. Now that my morning sickness has started to subside, I'm back on my game. There hasn't been a man born yet who's able to resist me."

Unfortunately, she was right.

"Who knows?" she continued. "Maybe I'll even get a chance to do a little snooping myself."

I grabbed her arm and yanked her to a stop. "I mean it, Rene. You're nothing but window dressing." My voice sounded more irritable than I intended. I ratcheted my attitude back a notch. "Sam will have my head if he finds out that I got you involved in this."

Rene looked at me, askance. "Mellow out, Kate. I've told you before. What Sam doesn't know won't hurt him."

"Just stay quiet and let me do the talking, OK?"

Rene stopped at the door and gave me a chivalrous bow. "As you wish, m'lady." Then she stuck out her tongue. "But you're no fun at all."

I paused for a moment, held my breath, and lightly tapped on the door. A high pitched string of ear-piercing yelps responded.

I covered my ears and yelled over the din. "Sounds like Bandit's home."

Bruce was either off the premises or dead. No living being within a fifteen-mile radius could have ignored that infernal yapping.

"No one's here," I yelled. "I'll have to come back later."

"Don't give up so quickly," Rene replied. She pounded on the door with her fist. "Yoo hoo! Anybody home?" Bandit's yips turned into wailing screams.

We waited another full minute. Still no answer.

"Fudge," Rene said. "Can you see anything through the window?"

I stood on tiptoe and peeked through the small half-moon-shaped window above the door. All I could make out was an empty hallway, punctuated every few seconds by the black and white head of a levitating fur ball.

Rene's luck was no better. "I can't see through the curtains over here. Too bad the deck doesn't extend to the view side." She walked toward the right edge of the deck and pointed to a window above the rose bushes. "That one looks like it might open." She stood on the bottom rail and reached toward the windowsill.

"Rene, what are you doing?"

She glanced around to make sure no one was looking, then leaned over the waist-high railing and craned her neck, trying to peer through the curtains. "I can't quite reach. Kate, grab my feet."

"Grab your what?"

Rene ignored my question and started climbing.

"Get down from there!" I snapped. "Are you nuts? You're pregnant! What if you fall?"

She stood on the top rail for a moment, then snuggled the front of her body against the cabin, placed one hand against the siding for balance, and reached toward the window frame with the other. She glanced down at me.

"Are you going to help or what?"

I gave in and grabbed her ankle.

"Rene, be careful."

"Stop worrying, Mom, I'm almost there. Just a little farther…" She let go of the siding, lifted her left leg, and leaned to the side, balancing only on her right foot. "I knew all those Half Moon Poses were good for something."

Her fingernails tapped against the glass and alerted Bandit to her plan. His yelps faded away from the door, then grew louder as he approached the window.

"I think I might be able to get this window open enough to crawl through." She lowered her left foot until both boots were on the rail again, turned ninety degrees, and placed her hands on the glass. "Hold on tight, Kate."

I had a terrible feeling that this was going to end very badly.

"On three," she mumbled, I assumed to herself. "One … two …"

A thousand things seemed to happen at once. The window opened. Bandit leaped for the void. A surprised-looking Bruce caught him mid-air and yelled, "What the hell?"

Rene gasped in surprise and her feet slipped. I panicked, yanked on her legs—hard—and pulled her back onto the deck, where she landed, flat on her butt.

I bent over her red-faced, prostrate form, reached out my hand, and started to help her up. "Oh no, Rene. I'm so sorry! Are you—"

Bruce interrupted before I could finish my sentence. "Bandit, shut up!"

He flung open the door and hit me from behind.

I fell on top of Rene, who crumbled back to the deck. We both lay tangled together for several seconds, limbs askew, the obvious losers in some demented version of Twister. Bandit crawled all over us, yapping and licking our faces.

"What in the hell are you two doing out here?" Bruce's words slurred, as if his tongue had swollen two sizes too big. "Why were you trying to break into my cabin?"

Rene whispered in my ear, which was conveniently located two inches from her lips. "Let me handle this." She scrambled out from under me, dusted the mud off her pants, and flashed Bruce a bright smile—the kind you see on late-night dentist commercials. "Oh thank goodness, you're here. We were afraid we'd missed you."

While Rene practiced flirting, I watched Bruce. I wouldn't have thought it was possible, but he looked—and smelled—even worse than yesterday. He wore an expression of annoyed exhaustion and the same wrinkled clothes he'd had on the night before. The sweet, vanilla-like smell of bourbon laced his breath. A sharp, musky body odor emanated from everywhere else. Last night I thought he'd aged a decade; today it seemed closer to two.

I picked up Bandit, held him against my chest, and tried to think up a compelling reason for Rene to be jimmying open Bruce's bedroom window. Nothing came, so I blurted out the first words that popped into my head.

"I need more Vicodin."

Bruce's dull eyes widened in astonishment. "So you decided to break into my house to get it? After I told you I'd phone in a prescription?" He stepped back from the door. "I should call the police."

Rene waved him off with a girlish giggle. "Of course we weren't breaking in." She latched on to Bruce's arm and cuddled in close. "Jeez, Kate, the things you say sometimes. You'll have the man thinking we're a couple of criminals!" She flashed another bright smile at Bruce, then gave me a shut-up-and-let-me-handle-this look.

"I hope you don't blame Kate for my little peek-a-boo. She said we should leave when you didn't answer the door, but I've been so curious. I couldn't resist taking a peek."

Bruce narrowed his rheumy, half-focused eyes and extricated his arm. "Curious about what?"

"Why, your cabin, of course. It's one of the refurbished ones, right? I told Kate the next time I come to Elysian Springs, I want to stay in the best." She widened her eyes, feigning innocence. "I didn't think it would hurt anything if I peeked through the window, but it was horribly embarrassing to get caught."

She brushed a loose strand of hair behind her ear. "And besides, we're doing Emmy a favor."

Bruce frowned. "How's that?"

"Kate knows one of the original investors. How can she send back a glowing report if she hasn't seen all of the renovations?"

Rene's voice was so sickeningly sweet, it could have been poured on French toast. How did she get away with this nonsense? If I'd tried to sway Bruce with such obviously fake flirting, he would have laughed me right off the deck and into the back seat of a police car. But not Rene. When it came to men, Rene was—to put it bluntly—a snake charmer.

Especially after they'd had a couple of drinks.

Bruce had obviously indulged in more than a couple, but talking to Rene seemed to reverse their effect. His shoulders unslumped. A smile lifted the corners of his lips. His eyes seemed to brighten.

Rene continued her hypnotizing dance. "I'm sorry if we startled you. We thought nobody was home. We knocked and knocked... Didn't you hear us?"

"I decided to lie down for a minute. I must have fallen asleep."

More like passed out.

"I haven't been able to sleep much since..." His face turned gray. "Well, since, you know."

Remembering his wife's death must have broken Rene's spell. Bruce's shoulders re-slumped. His lips curled downward. The light in his eyes dulled. The three of us stood in silence for several seconds, none of us willing to say the words "Monica's murder." As if by not saying them, we could somehow make them less real.

I spoke first. "I can't even imagine what you're going through."

Bruce sighed. "I suppose you can't. Then again, I don't think anyone can."

Rene lightly touched Bruce's arm, in sympathy this time. I didn't know what to do, so I absently reached up and rubbed my throbbing neck.

"How are you feeling today, Kate?" Bruce asked.

"Like I fell on my head." I smiled. "I'm pretty sore, but otherwise OK. Thanks again for helping me out last night. I didn't need to go to a hospital, but I would have been miserable without that Vicodin."

"You're welcome. I *did* phone in a prescription for you, by the way. You'll need to pick it up at the pharmacy in Eastsound. Let Emmy know if you need anything else. She has my cell number." He extricated Bandit from my arms. "Thanks for grabbing Bandit before he ran off again. Monica was the only one who could ever control this little monster."

Bruce stepped back inside and started closing the door. I wanted to stop him, but I didn't know how.

Luckily, I didn't have to. Rene did it for me.

She shouldered her way inside. "Oh no you don't. I'm not leaving until I get a good look at this cabin." Her eyes grew wide.

"My goodness. This place is lovely. Even better than I thought it would be."

Rene was right. Our cabin was charming, but in a funky, run-down, barely-better-than-a-tent sort of way. Bruce's place was an upscale sanctuary, much like the Retreat House. Its immaculate bamboo floors were accented by bright green Gabbeh rugs. Tall slate fountains decorated the corners and sang soft, gurgling lullabies. The hallway to the right led to multiple bedrooms, including the master bedroom that Rene had unsuccessfully tried to break into. A guest bathroom and a large living room with live plants, ocean view windows, and a new-looking sofa and chair combination sat to the left. The kitchen was straight ahead.

Rene wandered from room to room, filling the silence with mindless patter, like a desperate realtor trying to sell an overpriced condo to a pair of skeptical buyers. Bruce locked Bandit in a room at the end of the hallway, then followed haplessly behind her.

Her first stop was the kitchen.

The kitchen in our cabin boasted mismatched dinnerware, laminate flooring, and cheap Formica countertops. Bruce's kitchen looked like a photo from *House Beautiful.* Stainless steel appliances contrasted nicely with black granite countertops, and a full set of copper-bottomed pans hung from a ceiling rack above the bamboo center island. Huge windows in the dining area provided an unobstructed view of Puget Sound.

Rene opened the cupboards, pulled out dishes, even looked through the contents of the refrigerator—all the while offering her pretend realtor's running commentary.

She opened the cabinet next to the sink. "Look at these dishes, Kate." She pointed to a rainbow assortment of ceramic dishes in bright reds, greens, yellows, and blues. She picked a plate off of the top and looked at its bottom. "These are vintage Fiestaware!"

Bruce stared at her in shocked silence.

She made several positive comments about the Sub-Zero refrigerator, then started opening kitchen drawers and shuffling through their contents, pretending to be interested in the vast array of serving utensils provided by the facility. "We could host a gourmet dinner party here, Kate!"

Rene and I both knew that the only dinners I cooked were the kind you pierced with a fork and tossed in the microwave, but I didn't contradict her.

She abandoned the kitchen and strode purposefully down the hall. "Do you mind if I check out the bedrooms?"

Bruce staggered after her, looking increasingly uncomfortable. "The place is a mess. Why don't I have Emmy show you around after I check out."

"Nonsense." Rene smiled sweetly. "We're here now."

I shrugged my shoulders and mouthed the word "sorry" to Bruce, but I couldn't help but smile inside. No one ever accused Rene of being shy. She walked into the master bedroom and pretended to accidentally shut the door behind her.

Her muffled voice echoed through the wall. "Look at all of this closet space." I heard metallic rattling. "You even have enough hangers!" Bruce put his hand on the doorknob just as Rene opened it and peeked outside. "Hotels never have enough hangers, you know. My clothes always end up a wrinkled mess." She closed the door on Bruce's nose.

I heard her open a drawer and rustle around inside of it. "Are there more towels around here somewhere?" Bruce's eyes got twice their normal size. He threw open the door.

Rene walked through it, carrying a beige bath towel.

"You don't know how good you've got it. Our cabin is a dump compared to this. Even your towels are made of bamboo! Kate, feel this." I reached out my hand, but my fingers barely brushed the uber-soft cloth before Rene snatched it away and thrust it at Bruce.

"Be a sweetheart and write down the information on the tag for me. I *have* to get a set of these for home." Bruce opened his mouth to argue, but Rene didn't give him the chance. She lifted her eyebrows and leveled a stern look at him. "You'll need a pen and paper." She wandered into the next room before he could reply.

"Sorry," I said. "It's easiest to humor her." Bruce's teeth clenched, but he went off in search of a notebook, which gave Rene enough time to look through two more bedrooms. Both appeared to be unused.

Bruce returned and handed Rene a large yellow sticky note.

"Thanks." She tucked the paper in her pocket without looking at it and headed toward the Bandit-incarcerating bedroom. "What's in there?"

Bruce's face turned bright red. He grabbed Rene by the elbow and guided her in the opposite direction.

"I wasn't done yet!"

Bruce pasted on a fake-looking smile. "There's nothing left down there but another empty bedroom, and if you open that door, you'll let the dog out." He walked her back toward the cabin's front entrance, obviously hoping she'd take the hint. "I'm glad you like the space. This and the Retreat House are the center's showplaces. Someday all of the cabins will be like this."

Bruce stopped at the door, but Rene kept walking. Straight to the living room, where she took off her jacket, slipped off her shoes, and curled up on the couch. I took her cue and laid my coat next to hers. She gave Bruce a sweet smile. "I'm parched. Would you mind getting me a glass of ice water?"

Small muscles quivered at the edge of his jaw. "Certainly. I'll be right back." He took two steps away then stopped and looked back over his shoulder. "Wait here."

As soon as he turned on the water, Rene leaned over and whispered in my ear. "I didn't find anything interesting. Check out the guest bathroom. And find some excuse to get in that back bedroom."

Bruce's voice carried from the kitchen. "Emmy wants to create a vacation destination that's heavy on amenities but light on the planet." He returned, carrying two sweat-beaded glasses of ice water—which he handed to Rene and me—and a tumbler of eighty proof amber liquid, which he kept for himself. "She gave her mother and me the best houses—hoping to impress us, I suppose."

"I'm sure Emmy wants to you to be proud of her," I said.

Bruce shrugged. "That was part of it, but certainly not all. Emmy wants me to invest in the center. To tell you the truth, I was considering it, but I don't know any more. I hate to disappoint Emmy, but now that Monica..." Bruce stopped speaking and stared toward the ocean.

I started to reach for his hand but stopped, unsure how he would receive my touch. I clasped my hands together in my lap and leaned forward. "I don't know how else to say this, so I'll just blurt it out. I'm sorry about Monica. But I swear to you, I didn't—"

Bruce raised his hand as if to stop me. "Of course you didn't. I was there. I saw how hard you tried to save her. Besides, what possible reason would you have had to hurt Monica?" He pointed toward the sound of Bandit's scratching and whining. "That stupid dog?"

He took a long drink. "Frankly, this all seems like some kind of crazy nightmare. But no matter how hard I try, I can't seem to wake up."

It wasn't my most compassionate moment, but I saw an opening, and I felt compelled to take it. "Forgive me for asking, Bruce, but who *did* have a reason to hurt Monica?"

He fingered the half-empty glass in his lap. "I keep asking myself that same question. Monica wasn't exactly popular, but hate her enough to kill her?" He shook his head. "No one. It had to be some stranger." His voice cracked. "And it was my fault."

"How?" Rene asked.

"I let her go to that spa alone." His chin quivered. "I sat here in this stupid chair, staring at the ocean, while someone choked the life out of her."

Rene leaned toward him, looking earnest. "You can't blame yourself, Bruce. You couldn't have known."

I didn't join her in comforting him. Bruce seemed genuinely grief-stricken, but for all I knew it was an act. Besides, I was too busy biting back questions to ease anyone's suffering, including my own.

I wanted to ask Bruce about that Vicodin so bad my teeth itched, but I couldn't. Not with Rene present. Bruce was obviously

251

drunk. Maybe even high on drugs. He might be downright unpredictable. I couldn't risk revealing my suspicions about him with Rene in the room.

So I just sat there, resisting an urge to scratch my incisors.

I searched through my list of questions hoping to find something benign, but they all seemed pretty dicey. Stolen any controlled substances lately? Did you know that your lovely deceased wife was cheating? Ever feel an irresistible impulse to strangle a naked, wet woman?

At least I didn't need to ask Bruce his alibi for the time of Monica's murder; he'd already given me that information. If his story was true, Bruce had been in this cabin, sitting on that very chair.

Ultimately, I decided to remain quiet and hope that Bruce would volunteer more information. For awhile, he didn't say anything. When he spoke, his words seemed to come of their own volition, as if Rene and I weren't even in the room.

"It doesn't seem fair, you know. Monica spent her last night sick, and I was so angry with her."

"Angry?"

He glanced up. "Furious, actually. I was mortified about that scene at the restaurant. I didn't even care that she got food poisoning. I told her she deserved it for acting like such a bitch." His eyes turned glassy again. "Our last night together, and I acted like an ass. If I'd only known ..." His voice trailed off.

Rene unfolded her knees, leaned forward, and placed her feet solidly on the floor. "That's odd. I wonder why no one else got sick."

"What do you mean?" Bruce asked. "You felt ill, too."

"Yes, but I had a reason. I'm pregnant, remember?"

Bruce hesitated, as if unsure what to say next.

"It's okay," Rene said. "I told Kate about the baby." She tapped a fingernail against the edge of her glass. "You have to admit, though, it's weird that Monica was the only person who got sick."

Bruce shrugged. "Not really. No one else ate the salmon. Emmy claims she put it in the refrigerator shortly after she bought it, but salmon can go bad pretty quickly."

"What did the medical examiner say?" I asked.

Bruce's jaw tightened, so subtly I almost missed it. "What do you mean?"

"I assume that they tested Monica's stomach contents as part of the autopsy. Did the tests show anything?"

He frowned. "Nobody's telling me anything. All I know is that they shipped Monica's body to Anacortes. They won't even tell me when I can take her home. Besides, what does it matter? Monica didn't die from food poisoning. She was strangled."

"Still," I said, thinking out loud. "It kind of makes you wonder. Maybe I should have Dale call the medical examiner."

Bruce sat up straight, spine rigid. "Enough of this topic. I don't want to talk about Monica's autopsy. It's too upsetting." He drained his glass and stood up. "Ladies, I don't mean to be rude, but I'm exhausted. If you don't mind, I'd like to get some rest."

Rene stood, but instead of turning to leave, she stepped up to Bruce. "I really *am* sorry about your wife. I didn't know Monica well, but I'm married, too. Losing my husband would be, well..." She swallowed hard. "It would be inconceivable."

The moment between them seemed somehow private, so I turned to the side and averted my gaze. When I looked up again, Rene's arms wrapped Bruce in a hug, but her face scowled at me. She gestured with her eyes toward the guest bathroom.

I was admittedly a little slow, but I finally got it.

"We'll leave you to rest, Bruce, but can I use your bathroom first? I think I have a touch of the stomach flu myself."

Bruce's voice sounded resigned. "Go ahead."

I closed the bathroom door and glanced around the small room. I'd have to be quick, but there wasn't much to search anyway. The room's entire contents were a small cabinet, a glass-enclosed shower, and the requisite commode. The cabinet's slate gray countertop was bare, except for a bottle of organic peppermint hand soap.

I forced some urine from my bladder for effect and peeked behind the shower door while the toilet flushed. Nothing but more soap and shampoo. I turned on the water, washed my hands with the candy cane-scented sanitizer, and glanced up at the mirror.

The medicine cabinet.

It couldn't be that easy, could it? I quietly opened the front.

Empty.

Only one more place to look. I opened the cabinet under the sink, where I discovered cleaning supplies, several rolls of recycled toilet paper, and an almost-full garbage can.

Cringing, I dumped out a pile of used Kleenex, discarded dental floss, and few other items I didn't care to identify.

Jackpot!

The bottom of the can contained several prescription vials, including the bottle of Vicodin with Helen's name on it. I set it to the side and examined another: a cylindrical white bottle with a blue and white label. Digoxin.

A knock on the door startled me. "Are you OK in there, Kate?"

"I'm fine, Bruce. I'll be right out!"

I considered pocketing the bottles, but my jacket was still lying on the couch next to Rene, and there was no place to conceal much of anything in my form-fitting yoga clothes. Instead, I shoved the bottles back into the garbage can, covered them up with used tissues, and flushed the toilet a second time for good measure. I cradled my belly in my arm and tried to look nauseated when I returned.

"That stomach flu must be going around," I said. "Thanks again for your help last night. Rene and I will get out of your hair now."

I picked up my coat, grabbed Rene by the hand, and pulled her toward the door. I whispered so Bruce wouldn't overhear. "Let's get out of here." I forced myself not to run all the way back to the cabin.

TWENTY-ONE

"WHAT ARE YOU TWO, idiots?" Michael stomped back and forth across the living room like a frustrated Neanderthal confronted with the first liberated cave woman.

"Michael, keep your voice down. You're overreacting. I'm perfectly capable of—"

He whipped around and held up his palm. A fountain of spittle spewed from his lips. "Don't even start with me on your independent woman spiel. Believe me, Kate, I know. You can survive just fine without me." He pointed at Bella. "I'm sure you think she can, too, for that matter. That's not the point."

I winced. Why bring Bella into this? I had a feeling that Michael was upset about a lot more than Rene's and my visit with Bruce.

Bella whined, clearly uncomfortable with the infighting in her pack. She looked at Michael, then at me, then back at Michael again, as if unsure with whom she should align. I was the Dog Food Provider, but Michael was the Cookie Man, and he had taken her on a hiking adventure. She placed her body between us and tried to diffuse the tension.

I mimicked her actions, hoping that together we'd calm Michael. I licked my lips. I looked down at the floor. I yawned. I considered showing him my belly, but that would have compromised my status as alpha. Besides, I knew it was useless. I'd strained Michael's patience to the breaking point. For now, I'd have to ride out the storm. Michael would calm down with time.

I hoped.

For his part, Sam completely ignored all three of us. He was too busy browbeating Rene.

He threw up his arms, gesticulating wildly. "It all makes perfect sense. One woman has already been murdered on this infernal vacation, why not add two more?"

Bella finally chose sides. She walked purposefully across the room, sat in front of Rene, and glared at Sam. If he wanted to get to Rene, he'd have to go through her first. Evidently I was on my own.

"Now look what you've done," Rene chided. She rubbed Bella's neck and cooed. "It's OK, sweetheart. He's just a big grouch." She looked directly at Sam, then at Michael. "Stop yelling. Both of you. You're upsetting the dog." She patted the cushion next to her. "Come up here, baby."

Bella jumped on the couch and shook her entire body, as if forcing water droplets from her deep black coat. She turned a quick circle and lay down next to Rene.

"Kate and I are both fine," Rene continued. "We were never in any danger." Bella sighed and rested her chin on Rene's lap. "You two have a choice. You can stomp around like a couple of macho cowboy jerks while Kate and I ignore you…"

"You will not—"

Rene's look stopped Sam mid-sentence. "*Or* you can stop lecturing, sit down, and help us figure out what to do next." She paused a moment for effect. "Well, gentlemen, which will it be?"

Sam crossed his arms sullenly but nodded his head yes.

Michael stopped pacing. He barely looked at me when he spoke. "Nothing I say will make any difference, will it?"

A hollow, uneasy sensation fluttered deep in my stomach. Michael wasn't asking about my amateur sleuthing anymore.

I considered several honest responses, none of which would have been adequate. None of which were what he wanted—maybe even needed—to hear.

I could assure Michael that he was important to me, but he already knew that. I could tell him that I loved him, but he already knew that, too. Michael wanted me to promise that someday we would walk together, hand-in-hand, off into the sunset.

Problem was, I couldn't. How could anyone predict the future of a relationship? I was beginning to believe that happily-ever-after only happened in fairy tales.

I took no pleasure in my response, but at least it was honest. "No, Michael, I'm sorry. It won't."

He stared out the window for several seconds, his expression unreadable. When his eyes met mine, they seemed heavy—dulled by a mixture of worry, resignation, and heartbreak.

My heart broke too.

"I can't stand it when you keep me in the dark, Kate. If I help you, will you at least let me know what you're doing?"

"Yes. Of course I will." I joined him at the window and squeezed his hands. He didn't squeeze back, but he didn't move away, either. We stood silently together for several moments. After what felt like an eternity, he sighed, pulled out a chair, and sat down. I sat next to him.

Sam spoke. "All right you two, tell us exactly what happened again, from the beginning."

Rene and I took turns sharing the details of our day's excursions. I finished by describing how I found the bottles of medicine, read the labels, and shoved them back into the bathroom garbage can. "But I don't know if they mean anything."

Michael frowned. "Kate, it's obviously time to call the police."

"And tell them what? That I found some perfectly legal bottles of pills while rummaging through someone else's trash? I don't even know if those drugs have anything to do with Monica's murder. She was strangled, not drugged. Maybe Bruce has a painkiller addiction."

Michael lifted his laptop off of the end table and turned it on. "That would explain the Vicodin, but I'm not sure about other prescriptions. What else did you find?"

"Bruce interrupted me before I got a good look at all of them. I only saw two: the bottle of Vicodin and another labeled digoxin."

"It's a start. Let me see what I can find." He typed for a moment then scanned the screen. "According to this, digoxin is a heart medication." He kept reading. A few clicks later, he looked up. "Nothing I see indicates that digoxin can get you high. It's not even a controlled substance."

"Bruce would have known that," Sam interjected. "He's a doctor. If he's a drug addict, he's not a very smart one."

"Maybe there's some other simple explanation," I replied. "Emmy thinks Helen forgot her prescriptions at home. Maybe Bruce picked up refills for her. Or maybe Helen was at Bruce's cabin for some reason and left them there."

"One prescription maybe, but several?" Sam looked unconvinced. "I doubt it. And in that scenario, how did they end up at the bottom of a garbage can?"

I shrugged. "Someone obviously put them there. If it wasn't Helen, which seems unlikely, then it must have been Bruce."

"Not necessarily," Rene argued. "Monica might have stolen the drugs. She hated Helen. Maybe she thought Helen would get sick without her medicine and have to go home."

I thought for a minute. "That doesn't explain how Bruce ended up with the Vicodin."

"What do you mean?" Michael asked.

"Bruce gave me some of the Vicodin last night. That's what made me suspect him, remember? If Monica took the pills and tossed them into the trash, how did Bruce get them?"

"So we're back to Bruce," Michael replied.

"Maybe." I sighed. "But other than being crazy suspicious, I don't see how the stolen medications can be related to Monica's death."

I looked around the room, but no one seemed to have any answers. Rene absently rubbed Bella's ears. Michael tapped at his keyboard and scanned the monitor. Bella snored.

Sam eventually spoke. "What if the stolen drugs aren't about Monica? What if they're about Helen? Bruce might be planning to kill her, too."

"What would his motive be?" I asked. "Bruce and Helen have been divorced for two years. Besides, Emmy said that Helen always carries extra medication in her purse. Bruce would have known that."

Michael spoke as he scrolled through the site. "From what I can see here, missing a dose or two wouldn't have harmed Helen, anyway. She'd be able to get a replacement prescription long before she was in danger." He frowned. "This is interesting, though."

"What?"

He handed me his laptop and pointed to a page titled "Digoxin Toxicity." "Read this. Does it remind you of anything?"

I read the symptoms out loud. "Nausea, loss of appetite, vomiting, diarrhea…"

My slow-witted mind finally kicked into gear. "Wait a minute. Monica didn't have food poisoning; she had digoxin toxicity!"

Michael agreed. "Bruce tried to poison Monica. When that didn't work, he resorted to something more reliable."

I frowned and read the symptoms again. "Maybe…"

"What is it, Kate?" Rene asked.

"That theory certainly fits, but it doesn't feel right. You saw Bruce today; he seemed truly grief-stricken. And he practically collapsed the morning Monica died." I bit my lower lip. "I could be wrong. Bruce could be the world's best actor. But my gut says he's legit. I don't think he's the killer."

Michael stood up. "Maybe, maybe not. Either way, we need to call the police."

Cold sweat dripped down my back and pooled under my armpits. "I suppose."

"Don't look so glum," Rene said. "The digoxin doesn't prove anything for certain, but it goes a long way toward clearing you."

Michael's face darkened. "Kate, what aren't you saying?"

My mouth felt almost too dry to form words. "I think I screwed up."

"How?"

"I had my hands all over those bottles today. They'll be covered with my fingerprints. And I've been at the Retreat House twice now. How will I ever convince Sergeant Bill that I didn't steal those drugs and plant them in Bruce's cabin myself?"

We all stared at each other in echoing silence. Even Bella woke up from her nap and gazed at me with concern.

Michael picked up his phone. "We'd better call Dale."

———

Dale arrived at the cabin an hour later with a bag of rosemary chèvre muffins, several goat-shaped dog cookies, and a hazy, half-baked idea. The five of us gathered around the kitchen table, discussed options, and formulated a plan.

I didn't like Dale's idea. The risks of collateral damage were too high for my taste. But in the end, I went along with it. Dale made a phone call, then sent Rene, Sam, Michael, and Bella off to Eastsound, convinced that our plan would work better without them. He waited until both cars had driven off before chiding me.

"I swear, Kate, my goats have more common sense than you, and they're only half as stubborn."

I swallowed the last bite of pastry. "I screwed up. I know that. But what are you complaining about? You're the one who told me to get involved."

He crumpled up the now-empty muffin bag and tossed it in the trash. "Talking to a witness or two is one thing. An illegal search is something different entirely." He pulled a glass out of the cupboard and filled it with water. "Did you have to put your hands all over the evidence? Didn't your father teach you anything about crime scene investigation?"

I would have argued that since I was a citizen, not a cop, digging through Bruce's garbage was probably legal, if not exactly neighborly. But I knew what he meant. In hindsight, my whole plan had been pretty foolish. "Honestly, Dale, I have no idea what I was thinking. Would you believe me if I said it seemed like a good idea at the time?"

He smiled. "Unfortunately, yes." He sat back down. "Let's hope our little subterfuge works, or you'll be listening to the prosecuting attorney explain all about fingerprint evidence at your trial."

We sat together for a few quiet moments, while undigested flour and curdling goat cheese congealed in my stomach. "Dale, this waiting is killing me. Distract me. Tell me more about yourself. John wouldn't give me any specifics, but I know something happened. Why did you leave Seattle?"

"We have more important things to worry about right now."

"I'm trusting you with my life, Dale. Humor me."

He sighed. "OK, Kate. You win." He looked off in the distance, as if reciting a memorized story that no longer interested him. "I was quite the idealist when I joined the PD's Office." He shook his head wryly. "Rolled my briefcase to the rescue like I was the Lone Ranger." He took a long drink of water. "Took me ten years to realize that most of my clients were actually guilty."

"Is that when you left?"

"No, not then." He smiled. "Though that would have been smarter. I spent the next five years telling myself that the system wasn't broken, but that it wouldn't work unless everyone—guilty and innocent—had an adequate defense."

"Isn't that true?"

"Actually, it is. But that's a lot easier to accept in the abstract than when you've just helped put a two-time sex offender back on the street."

I saw his point.

"I started having trouble sleeping. Solved that problem with Ambien and alcohol."

I smiled. "I'm guessing that didn't help for long."

He touched his index finger to the tip of his nose. "When that stopped working, I went private. I figured if I was going to sell my soul, I might as well make decent money." He shrugged. "The thing was, most of my clients were still guilty. The last one was the CEO of a hot startup who liked to slap his girlfriend around. By the time she found the courage to report him, she had a broken rib and a dislocated shoulder. I worked it so Mister Hot-Fists got a slap on the wrist and a fine he could pay from the change in his Porsche's ashtray."

Dale paused and looked down at his hands.

"Three days later, he killed her."

I wanted to say something. I wanted to assure him that it wasn't his fault. But only two words came. "I'm sorry."

Dale looked up, no longer wistful. "I'm not. It changed my life. I quit the firm, took all that money I'd made, and bought some land here. I figured if I was going to save someone, they might as well be innocent."

"Hence Dale's Goat Rescue."

"Yep. Those goats never hurt anyone. Humans are the cruel species."

Soft tapping sounded at the door. Dale gave me a stern look. "Remember, be quiet and let me take the lead."

He didn't have to worry. I'd learned my lesson.

Dale opened the door. "Hey there, Emmy." He ushered her inside. "Thanks for coming by. Miss Kate and I here need to talk to you."

I started, surprised. I'd forgotten all about Dale's affected southern twang.

Emmy greeted him with a hug. "I got here as soon as I could, and I didn't tell anyone where I was going, just like you asked." She grinned mischievously. "I feel like a female Double-O-Seven. But why all the secrecy? Did you figure out who killed Monica?"

Dale pointed to a chair. "Maybe you should sit down for this."

Emmy's secretive smiled morphed into a cautious frown. "What's going on? You're starting to scare me."

"Please have a seat."

Emmy sat, but she leaned forward as if she might bolt in an instant.

Dale knelt in front of her and spoke in a soft voice, like a loving uncle comforting a frightened child. "I'm sorry, sweetie. This is going to be hard to hear. We think your daddy killed Monica, and that he might be planning to hurt your momma."

Emmy's cautious worry turned into horrified disbelief—with a touch of anger thrown in for good measure. "You're crazy, Dale." She stood up. "You're *both* crazy. I'm not going to sit here and listen to you slander my father."

Dale grabbed her arm. "Hear me out, Emmy. You don't have to believe us, but at least listen to what we have to say."

Dale described Rene's and my visit with Bruce, though he conveniently left out how most of the evidence pointed right back at me. At first Emmy simply stared at Dale, her face frozen in disbelief. By the time he finished, her body was rigid; her eyes wide; her breath came in short, shallow gasps. Like the doe Bella and I had encountered in the upper field, Emmy desperately wanted to believe that she was among friends, but every instinct primed her to bolt.

Instinct won.

"I need to go talk to Dad." She raced for the door.

Bruce blocked her way. "I can't let you do that, hon. You know I like you. Heck, I wouldn't let just anybody foster Billy and Thunder." I assumed those were two of the center's Nubian goats. "I figured I ought to tell you first, so you could be prepared. But I can't let you talk to your daddy, at least not until after Bill questions him."

"Dale, this is crazy. Dad would never hurt anyone—especially not Mom! I don't know how that medicine ended up in his cabin, but he didn't steal it. Why would he? Even if he *wanted* to kill Mom, missing a dose or two of her heart medicine wouldn't hurt her. He even picked up the replacement prescription for her. There has to be another explanation."

The concern on Dale's face didn't look feigned. "Then this is even more urgent than I thought. For all we know, he tampered with that new medicine. I'm sorry, hon, but we already called Bill. It's only a matter of time before the judge issues a search warrant. Your father will be arrested by nightfall."

Emmy grabbed Dale's arm. "Dale, please. We can't let that happen. Dad's close to a nervous breakdown as it is. Getting arrested might push him right over the edge. You're a defense lawyer for God's sake! Can't you do something?"

Dale stepped back, scratched his head, and pretended to look conflicted. "I'd like to, hon, but I represent Kate here. Talking to your father would be a conflict of interest. I'm only telling you this now because Kate said I could."

That was my cue. I mentally crossed my fingers and hoped Emmy would take the bait. "Dale, maybe Emmy's right. Maybe we *should* give Bruce a chance to explain."

"Please, Dale," Emmy begged. "Let's go talk to Dad. I'm sure he can clear this up."

Dale pursed his lips, pretending to think. After a few silent seconds, he picked up his coat. "All right, ladies. You win. Let's go see what Emmy's daddy has to say for himself."

TWENTY-TWO

Emmy chattered nervously all the way to Bruce's cabin. "You'll see. My dad's a sweet man. He'd never do anything to hurt Mom. I mean, he cheated on her, sure, but he'd never *physically* hurt her." Was she trying to convince Dale, me, or herself? "This is all a big mistake. I'll bet those pill bottles were empty. Maybe they're old. Maybe..."

I tuned her out and continued trudging, step by heavy step.

The ends sometimes justified the means, right? Then why did I feel so guilty? I barely knew Emmy, but my conscience still scolded on hyperdrive—and for good reason. Emmy was sweet. She was trusting. Some might even say naive. And we had lied to her.

Dale hadn't called Sergeant Bill, or anyone else at the police department, for that matter. Before we involved the police, we needed to extricate me from the evidence. As it stood now, even if Sergeant Bill found the prescriptions—assuming that Bruce hadn't already tossed them in the ocean—a jury would be more likely to believe that I had *planted* those bottles in the cabin than found them there.

So Dale came up with a plan: trap Bruce by confronting him with his guilt and his daughter's face at the same time. It was brilliant, of course, but that didn't make it any more palatable.

No tell-tale barks or bouncing fur balls answered Emmy's knock. Just Bruce, who wore a glazed expression and held an almost-empty martini glass. His eyes hovered a few inches in front of our faces, without recognition. Then they locked on Emmy.

"What are you doing here, hon?"

"Dad, are you drinking?"

"Don't worry, Emmy m'dear," Bruce held up the glass in a mock toast. "I'm simply having a couple of Manhattans in Monica's honor." His laugh held no humor. "You know how Monica loved my Manhattans."

Emmy's eyes filled with tears. "Oh Dad, you stopped drinking *years* ago. You promised." She looked at Dale. "Maybe we should come back a little later when Dad's feeling better."

No lilting accent softened Dale's reply. "I'm sorry, Emmy. It has to be now."

Emmy blanched.

"Mr. Crowe, My name is Dale Evans. I'm a friend of Emmy's. I'm helping investigate your wife's murder. May we come in?"

Bruce hesitated. "I'm not in the mood for company right now."

Dale frowned. "I understand." He addressed Emmy with a tone of determined resignation. "Well, we tried."

He placed his palm on my shoulder and guided me toward the stairs. "Kate, come with me. You shouldn't be here when the police arrive."

Emmy visibly panicked. "Dale, wait!" She grabbed Bruce's arm and pleaded with him. "Dad, please. Let them in. They're here to help you. They're my friends."

The word "friend" stabbed like a knife thrust deep into my heart. Emmy trusted me. She believed I wanted to help her father. When she figured out Dale's and my real plan, she might never forgive me.

I almost hoped Bruce would turn us away.

Almost.

Bruce paused for a moment, then acquiesced. "Fine, then. Come in." He staggered away from the door and gestured toward the living room.

I glanced around the empty space. "Where's Bandit?"

"I locked the little vermin in the car." Bruce drained the last drops of amber liquid from his glass. "Never did like that damned mutt, but at least now I don't have to listen to that incessant barking." He paused, then tilted his empty glass toward the light and looked at it quizzically. "How 'bout that? Looks like I need a refill."

Emmy took the glass from his hand and slammed it onto the end table. "You've had quite enough." She led Bruce to the couch and sat beside him. "Pay attention, Dad. You're in trouble. You have to talk to these people. You have to explain that you'd never hurt Mom."

Bruce blinked several times, as if trying to focus. He sat up a little taller. "What are you talking about? Of course I wouldn't hurt your mother." He pointed at Dale, who was still standing. "Who are you again?"

"Who I am doesn't matter, sir. All you need to know is that I'm involved in this case. Ms. Davidson contacted me because she believes your ex-wife may be in danger."

Bruce looked confused. "Helen? In danger? What do you mean?"

"Dad, it has to be some sort of misunderstanding. Kate saw some of Mom's medicine here in the cabin, and she thinks you stole it. I told her there had to be a simple explanation."

I watched Bruce intently, looking for a sign. Some move, some tell that indicated we'd caught him. His body remained stock-still, but his eyes darted back and forth, as if searching for a plausible answer. I could almost hear the sluggish, rusted-out wheels of his brain begin turning.

"Medicine? What medicine?"

Emmy's reply was soft, halting. "Mom's heart medicine. Her digoxin."

Bruce's Adam's apple jumped in his throat. He glanced toward the bathroom.

Gotcha.

"Yes, Bruce, I found the bottles you buried in the trash."

Bruce was caught, and he knew it. His eyes closed; his brow furrowed; his fists clenched. He even stopped breathing.

Emmy saw it, too. Her expression morphed from frustrated, to concerned, to confused, to horrified. "Oh my God. You *did* steal Mom's heart medicine. Why would you want to hurt Mom?"

Bruce leaned toward her beseechingly. "Emmy—you have to know that I'd never hurt your mother. Never. She always has plenty of that medication. And if she didn't, missing a dose or two wouldn't have hurt her anyway."

"Maybe not," Dale replied. "But you picked up her replacement prescription." He towered over Bruce. "What kind of poison did you put in that medicine?"

Bruce visibly started. "What? Nothing! What are you talking about?"

Dale spoke in a low, conspiratorial tone. "I hear killing gets easier after the first time. I'll bet planning Helen's death was a breeze. After all, you'd already murdered Monica."

"Murdered Monica? No way! I didn't put nearly enough digoxin in that Manhattan to—"

A strangled sound came out of Emmy's throat.

Bruce's complexion turned corpse gray.

Dale continued pressing. "I don't understand, though. Why strangle the poor woman when you'd already poisoned her? You couldn't wait a few more hours for her to die?"

Bruce's eyes darted frantically back and forth, searching for an ally. He alternated between trying to convince Dale that he was innocent and begging Emmy for understanding. "No. It wasn't like that. I didn't kill Monica. I just made her sick." He reached for Emmy's hand, but she snatched it out of his grasp. "Honey, I did it for you."

She stumbled away. "For me? How can you say any of this was for me?"

"I only wanted to get Monica out of the way for a couple of days. Maybe get her to go back home. I wanted her to leave you alone." Bruce buried his face in his palms. "It was stupid, I know. But she kept pushing and pushing. I couldn't let her hurt you anymore. I needed a break. We all did."

"But Dad, she thought I'd given her food poisoning. She could have destroyed the resort's reputation. You didn't think *that* would hurt me?"

"I'm a doctor, for God's sake. I thought she'd believe me when I told her it was the flu."

Bruce stood up and lurched toward Emmy.

"Please, Emmy, you have to understand. It was all for you. I loved Monica, but I love you more." He reached for her, but she jerked away, as if scalded by even the possibility of his touch.

Bruce gaped at her for several seconds, then sank to the floor and cradled his head in his arms. "Oh my God, what have I done?"

Dale pulled out his cell phone and dialed.

"Bill? Dale Evans here. I need you to send a couple of officers out to Elysian Springs. And you might want to head on over here yourself."

———

While Dale and Bruce waited for the police to arrive, I called Michael to let him know it was safe to come back to Elysian Springs. Now, almost an hour later, Rene, Sam, Michael, and I all stood together and silently watched the drama come to a close.

The police cars' sirens seemed to have summoned everyone on the property. Strangers from all areas of the resort—employees and guests alike—gathered around us, whispering and shuffling, waiting for Bruce's arrest.

A woman I recognized from the restaurant pointed at me and whispered, "She was in on it. Why isn't she in jail?"

"That was a ruse," her friend replied. "The maid told me she's an undercover police detective."

A student from my yoga class that morning smirked and said, "You're both crazy. She's just the yoga teacher, and she's not even very good at that."

Oh, how I wished it were true. That I were "just the yoga teacher." I'd even settle for being the not very good one, as long as I could be as clueless as the people milling around me. I'd rather be anything. Anything but a core player in this Greek-like tragedy.

Emmy sobbed silently into Josh's arms as the rest of her family milled around them, separate from the rest of us bystanders, yet huddled together for support. I absurdly wanted to join them. I wanted to draw from the group's comforting energy, or better yet, grab Bella and hide behind the bed. But I couldn't do either. All I could do was stand there with the rest of the strangers, focused on the cabin's front door, waiting for Bruce to emerge.

My ears rang. My head pounded. My retinas burned, even in the cool, early evening twilight. I tried closing my eyes and pretending to disappear, but the rude strangers' voices kept yammering. Why wouldn't they stop talking?

The door finally opened. Emmy's sobs grew louder as a deputy led Bruce—now handcuffed—to a patrol car. The deputy placed his hand on top of Bruce's head and eased him into the back seat. Helen whispered something to Emmy, gave her and Josh each a hug, and strode purposefully toward me.

I wasn't sure what to expect, but a "get off this property, you conniving bitch" wasn't out of the question. She stopped a few feet away then paused, frowning, before ultimately deciding to close the gap.

"I suppose I should thank you."

"For what?"

"I was awful to you this morning. But in spite of that, Emmy says you tried to protect me."

I didn't know how to reply, so I remained silent. I didn't deserve Helen's gratitude any more than I had Emmy's trust. I never thought Bruce was planning to hurt Helen; that little untruth was simply part of the deception. The only person I had protected today was myself.

"For the record," she continued, "I was never in any danger. Bruce *did* steal the prescriptions, but not to hurt me. His heart was in the right place. How can I blame him for wanting to protect Emmy?"

"Even by murder?"

She absently rubbed her left ring finger. "I was married to Bruce for twenty-five years. The man I lived with wasn't capable of murder. He must have snapped." She looked at the ground. "Honestly, I feel partially responsible."

"Why?"

"I could see that woman was torturing him—that he was falling apart—but I did nothing to stop it. I even egged her on. Part of me enjoyed watching the show. I was still so angry..." She shook her head. "None of us are innocent in this situation."

The patrol car's engine started. "I'm sorry, but I have to go. I contacted a lawyer, but she won't get to the island for hours. Bruce shouldn't have to face this alone."

Helen said a quick goodbye to Toni. They didn't seem to be fighting anymore, but there was still a distance, even a sadness, between them. They said a few words, then embraced before Helen climbed into her car, alone.

The two-car caravan drove off, police lights dissipating into the pink and purple twilight. I couldn't read Toni's expression, but I wouldn't have been surprised if she were upset. If Michael ditched me to chase after a murdering ex-wife, I certainly wouldn't be happy. But from my guilt-ridden spot on the sidelines, I felt relieved. At least Bruce still had someone on his side.

Michael took my hand. "Not exactly Hollywood's version of riding off into the sunset, is it?"

"No, not exactly."

"At least now we can finally put this behind us." He squeezed my fingers. "We have a lot to talk about."

He was right, of course, so why couldn't I agree?

I was spared answering when Sergeant Bill and Dale emerged from the cabin. Sergeant Bill carried evidence bags filled with the now-infamous prescriptions; Dale carried a dog bed—for Bandit, I assumed. Our eyes met. Dale gave me a smile and a soft nod. Both men walked toward us.

I kissed Michael on the cheek. "We'll talk later, OK?"

By the time Dale reached us, he wore a huge grin. "You done good, kid. Your daddy would have been proud." He winked, redneck facade firmly in place. "Bill here has something to say to you, don't you Bill?"

Sergeant Bill planted his feet wide. "You may have to come back and testify at some point, but for now you're free to go. You are officially no longer a suspect in Monica Crowe's murder."

"Bruce confessed?"

"Yes—at least to dosing Monica with the digoxin. As for the rest, he still doesn't admit to it, but it was him."

"Why would he admit to poisoning her, but not strangling her?"

Sergeant Bill sighed. "Let it go, Miss Davidson. Murderers aren't known for their good common sense. Personally, I think he's setting up an insanity plea."

"Could be," Dale replied. He patted me on the shoulder. "In any case, it doesn't matter. It's not your problem anymore."

I bit my lower lip and stared at the cabin, almost expecting Bruce to reappear. "I still can't believe he did it. I honestly didn't think he was capable of murder. If anything, he seemed self-destructive."

Michael shook his head. "Poor bastard probably snapped. There's only so much a man can take." I suspected he wasn't referring to Bruce anymore.

Dale and Sergeant Bill left a few minutes later. The crowd of onlookers gradually dispersed.

"What do we do now?" Michael asked.

"I'm not sure," I replied. "I need to talk to Emmy, but I suspect she'll tell us to go home. I don't think she's going to care much about yoga, or anything else, for quite some time."

TWENTY-THREE

THE DUSK DEEPENED, AND with it, my resolve. I doubted Emmy cared if the whole center burned down, much less if my yoga classes happened as scheduled, but I planned to teach anyway—at least until she officially fired me. As John O'Connell once told me, a promise is a promise is a promise. I wouldn't let my new students down until given a direct order to do so.

Rene, Bella, and I left our brooding partners at the cabin and aimlessly wandered the grounds. Given a choice, I would have left Rene behind, too. Frankly, I could barely stand to be around myself. But Rene insisted on coming, and I didn't have the energy to fight her.

By seven o'clock the sun had fully set, replacing the purple twilight with deepening darkness. The ozone-like scent of an approaching rainstorm permeated my nostrils. A chilly, moist breeze dampened my skin. I allowed Bella enough leash to enjoy exploring the area around her without endangering any clueless wildlife. After a brief stop to say goodnight to the bunnies, we walked along the perimeter of the garden to take advantage of the illumination of its solar-powered spotlights.

Jennifer—the not-really-grumpy yogini—waved to us from inside the garden. She held gardening shears in one hand and carried a striped harvest basket in the other.

"Hey there, gorgeous." I assumed she was referring to Bella, not me.

Bella let out a soft woof and nuzzled the gate. Jennifer knelt down, took off her flower-printed gardening gloves, and reached through the fence, allowing Bella to sniff her fingers. "Sorry, beautiful. No dogs allowed in here. Those big feet of yours might trample the plants."

Bella whined her disapproval and pawed at the opening.

Jennifer laughed. "Well aren't you the insistent one?" She glanced around to see if anyone was watching. "I suppose as long as you're on leash ..." She opened the gate and let Bella brush past her. Bella flirted, play-bowed, and sniffed Jennifer's basket, before dropping her nose to the ground and ecstatically exploring her new surroundings.

Rene took Bella's lead. "I'll take her for a minute and let the two of you talk. C'mon, girl, let's look around." Bella pulled Rene toward a large pile of what smelled unmistakably like steer manure. "Bella, no! Not over there, that's disgusting. My boots!"

Jennifer cringed. "Sorry about that. I should have warned you about the compost pile."

I smiled and rolled my eyes. "Don't worry about it. I owed her a new pair of shoes anyway."

Jennifer and I ignored Rene's stream of dog-related expletives as we ambled through rows of fragrant rosemary, lavender, oregano,

279

and fennel. "So, how does it feel to officially be a free woman?" she asked.

"Not nearly as good as I thought it would, honestly. I'm not a suspect anymore, but I feel like a traitor. I sort of tricked Emmy."

"I heard that, but I thought it was just a rumor." She clipped a few sprigs of rosemary and dropped them in the basket. "You wouldn't believe some of the crazy things people are saying about you."

Unfortunately, I would. I'd heard them, too.

"I feel terrible. You know Emmy. Do you think she'll ever forgive me?"

Jennifer thought for a moment. "Josh asked everyone to give Emmy some space, so I haven't talked to her yet. But she's a smart woman. She'll eventually realize that you only did what you had to do."

She looked toward the spa area and shuddered. "I still can't believe her father's the killer. I met Bruce a few times when I lived in New York. He seemed really sweet. You can never tell about people, can you?"

I shook my head. "No, I guess you can't."

We walked in silence as Jennifer harvested more fragrant herbs. I nodded at the recently filled sink hole. "Looks like they got the water fixed."

"Yes, but the restaurant's still closed. Between the water problems and all of the drama about Bruce, there wasn't enough time to prepare dinner. Kyle plans to open again tomorrow morning." She set the basket on the ground. "I doubt we'll have much of a crowd, though. Half of the guests checked out the day of the murder. No one left feels much like celebrating." She bent down and clipped several lavender blossoms. "Still, Kyle wants fresh herbs for the breakfast pastries, so here I am."

"I thought you worked the morning shift."

"I do, but Kyle's in an unusually good mood tonight. I sweet-talked him into letting me start at eight-thirty tomorrow, as long as I help him with breakfast prep tonight. I'll get to stay through Savasana tomorrow morning *and* show off my cooking skills." She smiled. "Works for me."

Rene called out. "Oh no, Bella, stop. Kate, help! *Gross!*"

Jennifer and I ran to Rene's aid, but we were too late. By the time we arrived, Bella was already writhing on her back with joyful abandon, waving her legs in the air and wearing a huge doggie smile—right in the middle of the composted cow dung. I grabbed her harness and yanked her out of the muck, though I needn't have bothered. Stinky brown gunk covered Bella from her tail to her eyebrows. She never looked happier.

I cringed and looked at Jennifer. "I'm so sorry. I hope she didn't do any damage."

She laughed. "Believe me, you got the worst end of this deal."

"Maybe, but—"

I stopped, mid sentence, distracted by a tiny object. It sparkled in the garden's floodlights, almost seeming to wink at me.

Rene followed my gaze. "What is that?"

"I'm not sure." I picked it up off the ground and rubbed it against my shirt.

The back of my neck tingled. "It's an earring. A diamond one, I think."

"Let me take a look at it." Rene moved to examine it under the light. "It sure looks like a diamond. A big one. I wonder how it got here?"

My throat felt dry. "You guys, I think it was Monica's."

"Monica's?" Jennifer's voice sounded skeptical.

"Yes, at least I think so. I noticed one of her earrings was missing when I tried to revive her, but with everything that happened, I forgot about it." I glanced around the garden, as if the answer lay buried among the cover crops. "But how did it get here?"

"People lose earrings all the time," Rene replied. "If you look hard enough, you'll probably find one of mine around here somewhere."

"I suppose." That was the obvious answer, but I didn't believe it.

Jennifer frowned. "Are you sure it's even Monica's?"

"No," I replied. "But who else's would it be?"

"Anyone's really. The garden's open to the public. People are in and out of here all of the time."

"Wearing full-carat diamond studs?"

Jennifer shrugged. "For all we know, it's a ten-dollar piece of costume jewelry." She took off her gloves and looked toward Eden. "The light's on in the kitchen. I'd better get this stuff to Kyle before he changes his mind and makes me come in early tomorrow." She looped the basket handle around the crook of her elbow. "Kate, that diamond, or whatever it is, is probably nothing, but if you're worried about it, you should tell the police. They'll know what to do."

She was right. "Good idea. Thanks, I'll do that."

———

"Come on, Rene. Let's head back." I carefully tucked the earring inside of my pocket and started back to the cabin. I was vaguely aware that Rene was chattering beside me, but my mind was too busy sorting through possibilities to listen.

That earring was Monica's. I knew it as clearly as Bella recognized her favorite Teddy bear. The only questions remaining were when it had gotten into the garden and how. The earring might have simply fallen off, but another, more gruesome, possibility seemed more likely: that it had been torn loose as Monica fought for her life.

Dad used to say, "Every contact leaves a trace." He meant that I should always be kind, because my actions had impact, often more than I realized. But he stole that particular life lesson from Locard's Exchange Principle: no one visits a crime scene without taking something with him and leaving something behind.

Was that something, in this case, Monica's earring?

I mentally listed everyone who could have come into contact with the orphaned piece of jewelry. The easy answers were Monica, the murderer, and me, but we were far from the only possibilities. The police, the EMTs the hot tub maintenance guy—anyone who came to the spa after Monica's death could have accidentally picked up that diamond.

The list of people who might have dropped it in the garden was smaller. Monica could have lost the earring any time between the night before her death—when I saw her wearing it at the Retreat House—and her last ill-fated spa visit. I supposed Monica could have spent part of that time at the garden, but she didn't strike me as the wandering-close-to-the-manure-pile type.

The murderer was the next logical choice. Bruce had ample opportunity to kill Monica that morning, but enough time—or reason, for that matter—to stroll through the herb garden? That seemed unlikely.

Maybe Jennifer was right. Maybe the earring wasn't Monica's at all. Maybe it had been left in the garden weeks ago. Maybe—

"Earth to Kate, are you there?"

I started at the sound of Rene's voice. "Huh?"

"Have you been listening to me?"

I cringed. "No, sorry. I was thinking. What did you say?"

"That I need your help. I've decided to tell Sam about the baby tonight."

I smiled at her. "Oh, honey, I'm so glad. It's about time. I'll get Michael and Bella out of the cabin, so you two can have some privacy."

Rene held up her hands, alarmed. "Oh no, you can't do that! You have to be there!"

She couldn't be serious.

"I mean it, Kate, I can't tell him without you." She shook her head. "I just can't. Sam won't throw a fit if you're there. And if he *does* get mad and storm out the door, well, then I'll need you even more." She touched her palms together in the Anjali Mudra, the prayer-like gesture used when saying Namaste. "Please?"

Her request surprised me. Rene typically strutted through life wearing a facade of confident self-reliance. But not tonight. Tonight, my friend didn't hide her vulnerability. As I looked into Rene's unshielded eyes, she allowed me to see the truth. If Sam left her, Rene's heart wouldn't be the only thing broken. His leaving might shatter her soul.

How could I say no?

"OK. Let me talk to Michael and figure out a plan. Maybe he and I can hang around outside while you and Sam talk. If I hear even the slightest peep from Sam, I'll break down the door and come to your rescue."

Rene adamantly shook her head left and right. "Michael can't be there. You'll have to find some excuse to get rid of him."

"Why do I have to exclude Michael?"

"Seriously, I love Michael and all, but you're family. He's not. Sam will understand why I told you, but he'll never forgive me if Michael knows about the baby before he does."

Her eyes grew earnest. "I know you two are having troubles too, and that I'm asking a lot, but please?"

Michael would forgive me when he found out the truth, right?

"OK. Give me a couple of hours. I'll think of something."

TWENTY-FOUR

THE FIRST THING I did when I got back to the cabin was give Bella a bath. Then I called Dale and left a message about Monica's earring. I probably should have called the police, but given my history, I figured it couldn't hurt to consult with an attorney. Those two tasks accomplished, I devised a brilliant strategy to occupy Michael while Rene and Sam had their talk.

Michael crossed his arms and glowered at me through wrinkled eyebrows. "You have *got* to be kidding me."

I thrust the leash at him. "She needs a walk." I pointed at Bella, who was lying flat on her side, twitching and snoring.

"But you already walked her, and she's still tired from her bath. Look at her—she's sleeping!"

"For now, maybe. But mark my words, she'll be wound up and driving us nuts by bedtime. She hasn't had nearly enough exercise today. I'd take her myself, but my neck is killing me." I rubbed my shoulders for emphasis. "So it will have to be you."

Michael's face seemed to morph into an odd-looking caricature of itself. His lips puckered together and turned down. A deep vertical line creased the center of his forehead. "I hoped you and I could finally spend some time together. This vacation hasn't exactly been romantic so far."

He grumpily snatched the leash from my hand and marched toward Bella. I said a quick prayer of thanks to the universe, grateful that for once my plan had worked. And it almost did. Michael was leaning down to clip the leash onto Bella's collar when he froze.

"Wait a minute..." He stood up and peered at me through suspicious eyes. "You're trying to get rid of me, aren't you?"

I should have denied it. I should have assured Michael that I wanted nothing more than to spend the rest of the evening with him. Barring that, I should have avoided the question entirely. Instead, I opened my mouth and said something stupid. "I'll make it up to you, I promise. But would you please take Bella and go? I need some alone time."

"Alone time?" He glanced toward Sam and Rene, who were both relaxing in the living room.

"Well, yes. At least alone with them."

Wrong answer.

Michael's teeth clenched. His face turned bright red. His chin started trembling. He lifted the fist that held Bella's leash and opened it. The leash clanked to the floor.

"I am not your errand boy."

I closed my eyes, torn between competing loyalties—to Michael and Rene—and practically beaten to the ground by a very real, relentlessly pounding headache. My patience shattered.

"Michael, stop arguing with me and just do it, would you?"

Michael's chin stopped trembling. He glared at me defiantly. "No, as a matter of fact, I won't. I'm done." He threw open the door and stormed through it.

I followed, waving Bella's leash like a battle flag. "Done with what? Get back here!"

Michael whipped around. The porch light illuminated his blood-red face. A small vein throbbed high up on his forehead. "Get back here? You just ordered me to leave!" I'd never seen him so angry. Even his nostrils quivered. "You've been avoiding me this whole trip, and you know it. If you're going to break up, do it already!"

He stomped away from the cabin, swearing.

"Michael, wait!" I'd gone too far, even for me. I ran to catch up with him and grabbed his arm, but he yanked it away. He stomped backwards, still yelling.

"I've had enough of your crap, Kate. Now *I* need some alone time. Walk your own damned dog." He paused long enough to pick up a rock and throw it. He turned his back to me and continued marching.

Every muscle in my body ached, especially my heart. I wanted to follow Michael. I wanted to explain. I wanted to apologize, not only for tonight, but for my erratic behavior the entire trip. But how could I? I didn't know what was wrong with me, either. I promised Michael six months ago that I'd never shut him out again. What if that was a promise I wasn't capable of keeping?

Rene met me outside the cabin. "Kate, I'm sorry. I had no idea he'd get that angry. Go after him. I'll be fine."

I closed my eyes, rubbed the center of my forehead, and sighed. "It's OK. We'll work it out later."

At least I hoped so.

I flashed her an anemic smile. "Come on. Let's go back inside. It's time." I led Rene to the living room.

"You ready?"

She nodded her head yes, but I could tell from her trembling lips that she was lying. I wrapped my arms around her shoulders, gave her a hug, and whispered the words she'd used to encourage me so many times before: "You know I love you. You'll be fine."

She left my side and tentatively approached the couch. "Sam, we need to talk."

Sam laid down the magazine he'd been pretending to read. He looked from Rene to me and back again. We all knew this was it: the conversation we'd been simultaneously anticipating and dreading the past three days. What we didn't know was how it would end.

"I'll give you two some privacy." I patted my leg. "Come on girl." Bella stood up and padded softly behind me. "I'll be in the bedroom if you need me."

Rene's soft voice faded to silence as I closed the bedroom door. Bella leaped on the mattress, turned a quick circle, then lay down and rested her chin on her paws. I tried to distract myself by meditating, but my mind refused to focus on anything other than the conversation happening two rooms away.

I considered doing some yoga poses, but my neck vetoed that idea, so I killed time by straightening up after Michael. I felt around under the bed, where I found two mismatched socks and a single filthy tennis shoe—men's size ten. I tossed the shoe next to its twin in the closet and wandered around the room gathering the assortment of shirts, socks, pants, and skivvies that Michael had dropped on the floor. I folded them carefully, stacked them neatly on the dresser, and looked around the newly cleared space. Without Michael's clutter, I felt even more isolated.

I crumpled everything up in a ball and threw it back on the floor.

What was going on out there?

Couldn't they talk a little louder? All I could hear was Rene's unintelligible mumbling. At least no one was yelling—so far. I paced back and forth, desperately wanting to hear their conversation. I picked up the "Vegans Do It For Love" coffee mug on the nightstand, drained the water inside it, and tilted it up to the ceiling, much like Bruce had done with his empty martini glass.

"What do you think, Bella? Will this work?"

Bella flopped on her side and groaned.

"Might as well give it a try." I shook out the remaining water droplets and quietly placed the mug's rim against the door. I was about to press my ear against the bottom, when Sam yelled. "Oh my God, are you serious?"

He didn't sound angry, but how could I tell? Bella jumped off the bed and stood at the door, ears pricked forward. She pushed her nose against the impenetrable slab of wood, as if willing it to open.

"I know, baby, I want to go out there, too."

What if Rene needed my help? But then again, what if I barged in at exactly the wrong moment? I knelt next to Bella and rested my hand on her back. "What do you think?" I sat there, hemming and hawing, indecisively holding that ridiculous coffee cup for at least twenty seconds.

Rene screamed.

That was my cue.

I dropped the mug to the floor, grabbed Bella's collar, and threw open the door. Bella and I charged through the kitchen but skidded to a stop before entering the living room. Rene wasn't wailing in agony or crying out in fear; she was screaming like a kid on a carnival ride. Sam twirled her in the air, grinning.

"We're going to have a baby!" He stopped spinning and set Rene on the ground, almost tenderly.

Rene's lips trembled. "You're not mad?"

I knew I should sneak back into the bedroom to give them some privacy, but I couldn't. I needed to be part of the moment, even if only as an impolite spectator. Besides, I couldn't have dragged Bella away if I tried. I crouched on the floor and eavesdropped, hoping they wouldn't notice.

Sam reached up and touched Rene's face. "Honey, how could I be mad?"

"You told me you'd never have kids—no exceptions. You said nothing would change your mind." Her voice was barely above a whisper. "I thought you might leave me." Tears streamed down her face. Something far less attractive dripped from her nose, but Sam didn't seem to notice.

"I was an idiot." He gripped her shoulders tightly. "And so were you. How could you not tell me?"

"I was too afraid."

He gave her a stern look. "Did you even listen to those wedding vows we made? We're partners. We stick together, no matter what."

Rene placed her hand on her belly. "Even if I get fat?"

"You can't possibly believe that I would care about that." He held Rene at arm's length and looked from her head to her toes.

His gaze landed back on her eyes. "Besides, you are going to look *so sexy* pregnant."

Sam lowered his arms and looked away. "Rene honey, this past week … with all of the secrecy … I thought I was losing you."

Rene didn't reply.

"I love you. I will always love you. But you have to be honest with me. You owe me that much."

"I do, it's just—"

He didn't let her finish. "No justs. Prove it. Don't ever keep something like this from me again."

Rene only flinched a little. "I won't. I promise."

Sam looked toward the kitchen. "I know you're hiding there, Kate. Come join us."

He beamed at me as I walked into the living room. "We're going to have a baby!"

"No kidding. Really?" My lame attempt at sarcasm was foiled by the tears in my eyes. I gave them both a hug. "I'm really, really happy for you guys." Even Bella wagged her tail and looked at Sam, if not with unbridled adoration, then at least without malice. I scratched her ears. "Good girl, Bella."

Rene's expression changed from contrite to mischievous in two seconds flat. She waited until Sam and I were both watching, then made eye contact with Bella and lifted her lip. Bella showed her teeth in return.

"Rene!" I scolded. "It was you this whole time!"

Rene laughed. "I can't believe you two never figured it out. I spent hours teaching Bella that trick. I bought a dog training book and everything." She winked at Sam. "Don't get me wrong, I still don't think Bella likes you all that much. But she shows her teeth strictly for cookies." She smiled coquettishly. "You're not mad at me, are you?"

Sam frowned, but I could tell he didn't mean it. "You're a jerk, Rene." He grinned at me. "This baby had better be a boy, or I am *totally* screwed."

I stood there and watched my two foolish friends, feeling vindicated. As usual, I was right. I *told* Rene not to keep secrets from Sam. For that matter, I told Sam to confront Rene. They didn't listen to me. Instead, they wallowed in their own fears and assumptions about each other. And you know what happens when you assume. It makes an ass out of u and—

Me.

Rene and Sam weren't the only fools in the room. I'd been making plenty of assumptions myself. I assumed Michael wanted more from our relationship than I could give. I assumed that once we talked, I'd either have to leave Michael or watch him leave me. I assumed that avoiding the conversation was the only solution.

What if I assumed wrong?

I didn't know what Michael's and my future held, but I owed him more than I had given him these past few days. I owed him the truth.

Rene read the look on my face. "Go after him, Kate."

I turned to grab Bella's leash.

"Go," she said. "We'll watch Bella."

Sam added, "And thank you."

TWENTY-FIVE

I GRABBED A FLASHLIGHT off the table, slipped on my jacket, and rushed out the door. I didn't exactly forget about the earring in my pocket; it simply didn't seem all that important. Any murderers still at large would be too busy celebrating Bruce's arrest to worry about love-sick yoga teachers. I only knew one person at Elysian Springs who was probably plotting my demise—and his name was Michael.

I intended to find him.

I started by scanning the area immediately around the cabin. Michael's car was still parked next to Sam's, so he couldn't have gone far. But where was he hiding? Michael didn't often sulk, but when he did, he liked company. He probably wasn't alone.

I headed off toward the more public areas of the center. As I hiked the main path to the office, I mentally berated myself. Who could blame Michael for being angry? I'd treated him like a bad case of chickenpox—itchy, unsightly, and highly contagious. And for what? I knew Michael was building up to something, but I didn't know what. It could be anything. It could be—

Oh, who was I kidding? Of course I knew what he was building up to.

He wanted to take our relationship to the next level. The kind that involved long white dresses, deep black tuxedos, and floral bouquets tossed at mortified singles. But I was afraid of change, even more than stagnation. If our relationship didn't move forward, I might lose Michael. If it did, I might lose myself. So, like an anxious racehorse afraid of the whip, I put on my blinders and ran full speed ahead, assuring myself that as long as I avoided the conversation, I could proclaim ignorance. And as everyone knows, ignorance is bliss.

Until it isn't.

It certainly wasn't bliss now. Right now, ignorance was wandering alone, in the dark, not knowing what I wanted, much less where to find it.

I headed across the foot bridge toward the main parking lot. A crisp breeze stung my cheeks; dark clouds obscured the stars; the electric smell of an impending storm filled the air.

The parking lot seemed eerily deserted—morbidly quiet. It wasn't surprising. Half of the guests had hightailed it out of Elysian Springs the day of the murder. The rest only stayed for the wedding. From the whispered words I'd overheard before Bruce's arrest, the only *retreat* anyone wanted was the hell off this island. Most of the guests were probably firmly hunkered down in their cabins, packing for the early morning ferry.

I looked for Michael everywhere I could think of, to no avail. First, I tried the spa. Completely empty. Not a single bather, naked or otherwise. I walked the perimeter of the garden, and trudged down to the main lawn. A "closed" sign decorated the office. The lending library housed nothing but books. I even stopped by Eden in case Michael was inside drinking away his frustrations. A sign on the door confirmed what Jennifer had said earlier: the restaurant was closed until breakfast the following morning.

My exhausted brain finally kicked into gear. *Call him, dummy.* I pulled the Yoga Chick out of my pocket and pushed the power button. She powered up briefly, then died.

Her feathered face seemed to scold me. *You know you're supposed to charge me, right?*

I sighed, frustrated, and shoved the phone back inside my pocket. I might as well give up and head back to the cabin. With any luck, Michael was already there, waiting to continue our fight.

I plodded along the trail, shining the flashlight ahead of me. A few steps away from the cabin, the beam illuminated a pair of red, glowing, wolf-like eyes. The coal-black creature behind them leaned forward and intently watched me, as if ready to pounce.

"What are you doing in Sam's car?" Bella pressed her nose through the half-opened window and answered by licking my fingers. "This is their idea of taking care of you?" I reached through the window, unlocked the door, and grabbed Bella's leash, which was still attached to her collar. Bella, now rescued from her stint in solitary confinement, happily pulled me toward the cabin. "Some parents they'll be," I grumbled as I stomped toward the door. "They could have at least rolled the windows up higher and taken off your leash. Anyone could have come by and stolen you!"

I knew one thing: two irresponsible pet sitters were about to receive a stern lecture from an angry pet parent. I reached for the door knob, fully prepared to start my tantrum—and froze.

What on earth was that sound? No need to press my ear against the door this time. The groaning reverberating through those walls was loud enough to be heard back in Seattle.

I wasn't exactly innocent. By the age of thirty-two, I'd had a few heated liaisons of my own. My subconscious mind *must* have known what was happening, but my conscious mind refused to believe. I peeked through the curtains...

And instantly regretted it.

Gross!

I rubbed my eyes, trying to erase the image now permanently scalded on my retinas. Suffice it to say that I'd just witnessed Sam's naked rear bouncing sunny side up. Rene was buried somewhere beneath him.

I flew away from the window, trying not to gag. "That's it, Bella. From now on everybody gets their own room." Bella, for her part, seemed unconcerned. She sat patiently on the doorstep, head cocked to the side, waiting to be let in. I scratched her ears. "It could be awhile, honey." I giggled. "At least Rene got over her morning sickness."

What should Bella and I do now?

Obviously, we couldn't enter the cabin. I considered hanging out in the car, but that didn't sound like much fun, either.

"Well, girl," I said to Bella. "Michael's obviously not here. Looks like you're going to get that walk after all. Want to see if he went to the beach?"

At the sound of the b-word, Bella jumped off the deck and dragged me in the direction of the water. We walked along the lighted main pathway for a couple of minutes, then veered off on the smaller, unlit path that led to the beach.

The night was completely black, almost obsidian; its darkness, impenetrable. A carpet of moldy leaves and fragrant pine needles crunched under my shoes. Bella and I passed several empty campgrounds, a few fallen trees, and a pair of beady red eyes that *didn't* belong to a German shepherd. I played the flashlight in front of me, grateful for its tepid illumination. With it, I could see the broken branches that were strewn haphazardly across the path. Without it, I'd be blind.

A sharp sound cracked behind me. Bella stopped, sniffed the air and looked over her shoulder. The hair on the back of my arms tingled.

"Hello, is anyone there?"

No one answered.

My internal critic chided me. *Come on, Kate, you're being silly. It's probably another deer.* I still couldn't turn my head to the left, so I pulled Bella in closer and slowly rotated my entire body in a full circle, shining the flashlight all around us. Nothing but plant life. I placed my hand on top of Bella's shoulders and whispered, mainly to assure myself. "It's OK, girl. Nobody's there."

My words weren't convincing. The tingling sensation in my arms spread to the back of my neck. Something—or someone—was watching us.

A single, giant raindrop fell on my forehead. Then a second. Then a third. Bella jumped at a distant roll of thunder. I zipped up my jacket and turned back toward the cabin. "That's it, Bella, we're out of here."

As if on cue, a million more raindrops joined the party, soaking our bodies in icy wetness.

"Bella, quick!" I yelled.

I ran back toward the cabin, barely even looking at the ground. A flash of light lit up the night, followed by another roll of thunder. Bella jumped to the left and yanked on her leash; a familiar, electric pain shot down my arm. The flashlight flew though the air, clattered to the earth, and turned off.

"Damn it!" I crawled on the ground and groped through the muck, desperately searching for that beacon of light. Cold, slimy mud oozed through my clothes and squished through my fingers. My hands found rocks, sticks, and clumps of rotting leaves. My fingers plunged into something furry, cold, and squishy, with a wretched, sulfur-like stench.

Don't think about it, just keep looking. My hand finally wrapped around the flashlight's metal cylinder. "Found it!" A few solid smacks against the palm of my hand, and it turned back on. I yelled a victorious "Yes!" out to the universe.

A heart-stopping boom and a blinding white light hit at the same time. A fir tree crashed across the trail, split in half by lightning.

Bella reacted with pure, unstoppable instinct. She bolted, like a deer running away from a cougar. The leash slipped through my fingers and she crashed through the brush, off into the darkness.

"Bella, come!" I yelled. Bella and I had practiced this recall hundreds of times. In fact, that simple, two-word sentence had already saved her life once. But this time, I might as well have been yelling obscenities in Sanskrit. Bella was too terrified to do anything but run. I tore after her, screaming the useless phrase over and over. I had to find her before she got lost—or worse.

Frenzied heartbeats pummeled my chest. I considered going back to the cabin, but by the time I got help, it might be too late. Bella could be permanently lost. The leash she dragged behind her gave me no comfort. She could easily get it caught on a fallen branch and choke. Why, oh why, hadn't I left her in Sam's car?

Rain dripped off my nose and ran down my chin. Icy cold water poured down the back of my shirt. But I barely noticed. My entire body was energized by numb, adrenaline-fueled fear. I stumbled along the trail, calling Bella's name. I tripped over a branch and fell again, face-first into the brush. Rough bark cut into my palms; jarring pain jolted up my right knee. I lay there for a moment and sobbed.

Pull yourself together, Kate. This is no time for self-pity.

The cuts on my hands, the stabbing pain in my neck, the torn pants covering my bloody knees—none of it mattered. All that mattered was finding Bella.

A snapping branch cracked to my left. I jumped up and whipped around, hoping—praying—to see Bella, but my flashlight illuminated a hooded form. His dirty brown work gloves reached for me, and I panicked. I screamed and tried to scramble away, only to slip and fall again. My shoulder twisted painfully as he grabbed my arm and roughly yanked me upright.

He pointed a flashlight in my eyes, blinding me.

"Kate, is that you? Calm down! What are you doing out here?"

Relief replaced panic, at least momentarily. I recognized his voice.

"Kyle," I sobbed. "You have to help me. I can't find Bella. She's lost. We have to—"

He grabbed my shoulders. "Hold on, Kate. Slow down. I can't understand you. Who's lost?"

"My dog, Bella" I cried. "She must be terrified!"

"That huge German shepherd?"

I gulped back more tears and shook my head yes.

"I saw her a few seconds ago. I thought it was a deer, but—"

I cut him off. "Which way did she go?"

He pointed toward the water. "She was running up the hill toward Suicide Bluff."

The full meaning of the words hit us both at the same time. The sign near the edge of the cliff taunted my memory: "Danger. Cliffs are unstable. Walking prohibited less than three feet from edge." Bella didn't understand the risk. She wouldn't shy away from the unstable edge. In her panic, she might even run toward it—and its fifty-foot drop.

Kyle grabbed my arm. "Come on. We'll find her."

"We should split up. One of us can go get help."

"There's no time. If she slips and falls ..."

He didn't need to say more. "Let's go!" I ran toward the trail.

He pulled me the opposite direction. "No, Kate. She went this way."

We slipped, we slid, we stumbled, we crawled. Blinded by darkness, the rest of my senses became hyperalert. My skin quivered with the icy stab of each raindrop. The smell of wet, rotting decay assaulted my nostrils. The sour taste of fear burned my tongue.

We skidded to a stop at the end of the trail, in front of that ominous danger sign.

"Bella, come!" I yelled for the millionth time. Nothing.

Kyle pulled back the hood of his raincoat, exposing his striped cotton hat. He swept his flashlight across the horizon.

"Do you see her?" I knew the answer was no, but my grasping mind had to ask.

"Stay here," Kyle ordered. "Don't move."

He carefully made his way toward the cliff, playing his flashlight along the sharp rock outcroppings. Less than two feet from the drop-off, he knelt down and continued forward, crawling carefully on hands and knees. When he arrived at the edge, he pointed the flashlight's beam toward the rocky beach over fifty feet below.

His voice cracked. "I'm sorry, Kate. You need to come here."

Warm tears dripped down my cheeks. "Oh, no," I whispered. "Please, God, no."

Kyle remained silent.

My mind clawed against knowing, clinging to denial. I couldn't bear to look. If I didn't look, it wouldn't be real. I would go back to the cabin, lie down, and go to sleep. When I awoke in the morning, I'd realize that tonight had been nothing but a horrible nightmare. Michael would laugh at me. Rene would harass me. Bella would make me feel better with warm, wet German shepherd kisses.

But only if I didn't look.

When I spoke, my voice sounded flat, as if I'd lost the ability to convey human emotion. "Kyle, tell me. What do you see?"

"I need you to come here. Now." His voice was filled with regret.

I slowly, hesitantly moved forward, step by agonizing step. The dark cliff beckoned me, even as my heart resisted. Once I looked over that edge, there would be no going back. Once I saw her, it would be real. I sank to my knees and crawled next to Kyle.

"Over there." He sounded resigned. As if every word—every action—had been scripted by a force bigger and more powerful than him. I took a deep breath, leaned over, and followed the light, expecting to see Bella's broken body.

I saw rocks.

Nothing but rocks.

I backed away from the edge. Hopeful confusion supplanted my dread. "Kyle, what is it that you want me to see?"

The next seconds seemed to pass in slow motion. Kyle's gloved fingers grabbed my shoulder and I gasped, breathing in the unmistakable smell of wet compost. The smell evoked sudden jolts of memory, like images seen through a child's View Master.

I flashed on Bella's soiled coat; then the pile of compost; then Monica's earring; then Kyle's brown-stained gloves.

Kyle.

Kyle was in the garden the day Monica died—that's where he was when he heard the sirens.

Minutes after the earring was torn from Monica's body.

I looked into his deadened eyes, and I knew. Monica *had* found Kyle that morning, after all.

Kyle was the killer.

I flinched before I could stop myself.

I tried to pull away, but he held me in a vice-like grip.

"What's the matter, Kate?" His voice held no inflection.

"Nothing. Let me go." I kept my facial expression neutral, but I couldn't hide the tremor in my voice.

Kyle slowly closed his eyes, then opened them again. He sighed. "Ah, Kate, we both know I can't do that." He shook his head. "I so hoped it wouldn't come to this."

I tried to play dumb. "Come to what?"

He spoke as if he were in a trance. "I fooled myself, you know. When Bruce got arrested today, I thought everything would be OK. I was relieved—giddy even. I truly thought that this nightmare was finally over.

"But then I talked to that stupid hostess. She told me you found an earring in the garden and linked it to Monica. She said you were going to call the police." He kept talking, as if I weren't even there. "I didn't even realize that awful woman had lost an earring. It must have gotten caught in my clothes during the struggle. Then when I went back to get my stuff from the garden..." His voice trailed off for a moment. He looked back, as if suddenly remembering my presence.

"I knew it was only a matter of time before you remembered that I was in the garden shortly after Monica was killed." His jaw muscles twitched. "Why did you have to go and find that earring? Everything was going to be fine. Now I have to get rid of you, too."

I had to keep him talking, at least until I could find some way to escape. "How did you know where to find me?"

"I didn't. You came to me. You stopped by Eden right after the hostess left."

"I was looking for Michael."

He gripped my arm tighter and shook his head, as if trying to convince himself. "No, it was fate. The universe brought you to me. It was showing me a way out."

"The universe told you to kill me?" I couldn't keep the incredulousness out of my voice.

"Yes, but I didn't get it, at least not at first. I didn't know what to do, so I followed you back to your cabin, hoping to see a sign." He lifted his lips in an insane-looking grimace. "And the universe intervened again. You went to the door, but you didn't go inside. You grabbed the dog and kept walking."

I wanted to back away from him, but I couldn't. There was nothing behind me but air. So I kept listening.

"I was still following you when the dog bolted. That's when it occurred to me. This trail is dangerous. Searching for your lost dog, alone, at night? You could easily fall to your death. An accident would be so much more compelling than another murder."

My body flashed cold. Bella. What had he done to Bella? "Kyle, please. Tell me. Where is Bella?" My voice cracked. "Did you hurt my dog?"

He stiffened, clearly offended. "What kind of monster do you think I am? I'd never harm an innocent animal!" He nodded away from the water. "Your dog ran back toward the cabins."

The words tumbled out before I could stop them. "You'd never hurt an animal, but you'd kill two women?"

He leaned forward earnestly. "Please understand, Kate. I don't *want* to kill you. You've left me no choice."

"What about Monica?"

He shook his head, as if still trying to believe it himself. "I was already upset about that idiot hostess when Monica found me in the garden and accused me of food poisoning." He shrugged. "How was I supposed to know that Bruce had drugged her? I never cook flesh. I thought she was right. I thought I had accidentally poisoned her.

"I followed her to the spa and tried to reason with her, but she wouldn't listen." He looked at me beseechingly, as if asking for forgiveness. "You have to understand. She was going to sue me. I would have lost everything."

I kept my senses on high alert, searching for some way—any way—out of this. All I needed was one instant of distraction.

"Wouldn't your insurance have covered a lawsuit?"

He laughed, but without humor. "I cancelled my liability insurance three weeks ago. I put every penny I had into the restaurant, and then some. I maxed out my credit. My suppliers were about to cut me off, so I had to cut costs somewhere. I only needed a couple of weeks to drum up some cash. I figured I'd be OK in the meantime. A vegan café—how risky could it be?" He smiled sardonically.

"And here I thought *Emmy* had no business sense. Turns out I'm the stupid one." He shuddered. "That dog of Monica's kept yapping and yapping and yapping. She told me to untie him and leave her alone. That she'd see me in court. When I unhooked the leash, it felt so strong in my hands…" He stared off into the distance. When he looked back, his eyes were wet. "She was evil, Kate. She made me go against everything I believed in, but that wasn't enough for her. She was going to take away my livelihood, too. She deserved to die."

Bella's deep barking sounded in the distance. Kyle yanked me closer and my foot slipped, sending a cascade of loose dirt over the void. Adrenaline shot though my body, but somehow I kept my voice calm.

"Kyle, I'm not like Monica; I've never intentionally hurt anyone."

I might have imagined it, but I would have sworn that his energy shifted. I sensed hesitation—indecision. Maybe I still had a chance.

I made eye contact and placed my free hand lightly against his arm. "You don't need to hurt me. You *can't* hurt me. You're not a killer—not really. If you let me go, I'll help you figure a way out of this."

"Don't you see, Kate? There *is* no way out. Not anymore."

I heard Michael's shout. "Kate! Where are you?"

"My friends are coming. It's time to end this."

He leaned over the edge.

"Kyle, please!"

Kyle didn't look at me. He didn't speak. He barely even breathed. He slowly opened his hand and released my shoulder. His arm floated down to his side.

That was my chance, and I took it. Like Bella careening away from a lightning bolt, I acted on instinct. I didn't think about Kyle. I didn't think at all. I scrambled away from the edge, screaming at the top of my lungs. "Michael, help! I'm over here!"

I doubt Michael heard me. I barely heard myself. My voice was obliterated by an avalanche of rocks and the gut-piercing echo of Kyle's scream.

I whipped toward the sound, ready to fend off another attack.

The ledge was empty.

At first I stood there, shocked, and stared at the void. My mind refused to accept what had happened.

How could he be gone?

It all happened so fast. In the snap of a finger—a split second in time. One instant Kyle stood there, holding my arm and threatening to push me over the edge.

The next, he was gone.

When the truth hit, it felt like a freight train. I sagged to my knees. "No, no, no, no, no, no."

I sobbed the words over and over and over again, but they made no difference. No amount of denial, no measure of remorse—nothing would make him reappear.

Michael crashed through the trees, propelled by a fierce-looking Bella. He ran to my side, reached down, and pulled me into his arms. Bella crawled on top of us both, whining and licking the side of my face.

Michael's words came out in barely intelligible, panicked fragments. "Oh my God, Kate ... thought I lost you. Bella came back ... couldn't find you. I heard screaming."

My unrelated responses were wrapped in choked sobs. "I'm so sorry. I've been a complete jerk. Please don't leave me. I love you!"

"Of course not." Michael's voice grew firm. "I'm not going anywhere." He hugged me close and rocked me back and forth. When he pulled back, his face held a mixture of worry, relief, and confusion. "Kate, what happened? Are you hurt? Why did you scream?"

"I'm fine." I pointed at the edge. "The screaming. It wasn't me." I looked down at the ground. "It was Kyle."

Michael's face turned grim. He handed me Bella's leash. "Stay here."

I didn't argue. I never wanted to go near that ledge again.

Michael crawled to the edge and pointed his flashlight down at the shore below.

I buried my face in Bella's wet fur and waited for him to say the words I never wanted to hear.

"I'm sorry, Kate. He's dead."

TWENTY-SIX

I SPENT THE REST of the night besieged by a nightmarish army of ambulances, patrol cars, paramedics, and police officers. I wanted to retreat to my cabin. I wanted to sleep. I wanted to wrap my arms around Bella and never let go. But Sergeant Bill had questions, and I supposedly had the answers. So I huddled in Emmy's office, wrapped in a blanket, teeth chattering. I told Sergeant everything I remembered—and plenty I wished I could forget.

Everyone treated me kindly during those two hours of interminable questions. Emmy brought chamomile tea; Jennifer, fresh pastries. Michael whispered sweet words while Rene held my hand. I should have felt happy, or at least lucky. I was alive, Bella was safe, and all of my loved ones surrounded me. But guilt permeated deep into the marrow of my bones. Had I caused Kyle's death? Had my actions somehow compelled him to jump? Our last moments would haunt my nightmares for a very long time.

Dale came to the center to make sure my rights were protected, but he needn't have worried. I was the only person who blamed me for Kyle's death. Sergeant Bill might have been skeptical at first, but the facts supported my statement. He already knew that Monica thought she'd been poisoned by food. Jennifer added that Kyle got surprisingly upset when she told him about Monica's earring. When an officer searched through the restaurant's files and found the cancelled insurance policy, well, no one doubted my story.

Sergeant Bill stopped by two days later to check on me and tell me what his investigation had concluded: that Kyle's death was likely an accident. He even took me back to the cliffs and showed me a recently collapsed area of rock where Kyle had been standing. The only surprising thing, he assured me, was that Kyle and I hadn't *both* fallen to our deaths.

I hoped he was right. I desperately wanted to believe that Kyle hadn't jumped—that his confrontation with me hadn't caused him to take his own life. But in spite of Sergeant Bill's assurances, no one *really* knew what Kyle did in those final moments. Not for sure. I'd have to learn to live with that.

Emmy forgave me for tricking her, but she still fired me. She said that after two deaths on the property in three days, she needed to give everyone a few days off to grieve. She even postponed her wedding a week.

She did, however, invite Michael, Sam, Rene, and me to stay at Elysian Springs until the wedding, as long as we were willing to cook our own food and forgo maid service. Kyle had passed on, of course, so there would be no meals at Eden for the foreseeable future. And the staff was short one additional maid. At

Helen's urging, Emmy searched Maidzilla's cabin, where she found the missing cleaning supplies, several bottles of the restaurant's wine, and a surprisingly large stash of stolen herbal tea. Emmy immediately fired Maidzilla, but planned to wait until after the wedding to hire a replacement.

I surprised everyone—myself, included—by saying yes to Emmy's offer. I wasn't ready to go home. I barely had the energy to keep *myself* upright, much less support my students. Before I could pay attention to anyone else, I needed to refill my own well.

Sam and Michael went back to Seattle for the first few days. Sam, to put in some work hours, Michael to give Tiffany a few days off and make sure that Pete's Pets was still standing. When they returned, they brought a fifteen-pound bag of Bella's dog food, all of her medications, and my industrial strength kibble grinder. Bella's crate was securely tied to the top of Michael's Explorer, and a cell phone I actually knew how to use—Old Reliable—was in the glove box. Michael made sure that my old phone was fully charged; he even added a thousand extra minutes. He told me that he never wanted to take chances with Bella's or my safety again.

Sam and Rene moved two cabins down, where they could celebrate their expanding family in their very own, much more private, bedroom. Michael stayed in the cabin with Bella and me, but he gave me plenty of space and didn't press my fragile psyche. We both knew I needed time to heal.

When I called Mandy and told her that I'd be staying on Orcas a few extra days, she responded with two nonnegotiable words.

"I quit."

I groveled until I got the other teachers to cover my classes and asked the Power Yoga instructor to manage Serenity Yoga until I returned. At the time, she was grateful. The work gave her some much needed income while her back healed. Less than forty-eight hours later, she sounded significantly less enthusiastic. By day five, she asserted that starving would have been preferable.

If her daily, panicked phone calls were any indication, the studio was still in an uproar, but I'd sort everything out when I got home. If I'd learned one thing from my experience with Kyle, it was this: a business—yoga studio, restaurant, or upscale retreat center—was just a place. Friends, loved ones, family. They were important. Not places. Not things.

Now, twelve days after Kyle's death, Sam, Rene, Michael and I shared a table at Emmy's wedding reception. My neck hadn't bothered me for three days in a row. The seemingly interminable rain had abated. The sun beamed through the Retreat House's windows, warming my shoulders and turning the sky above Elysian Springs a brilliant, cerulean blue. Cat Stevens crooned "Morning Has Broken," promising the hope of a new day. Sam squeezed Rene's fingers with one hand and wiped dribbles of tomato sauce off her chin with the other. She barely noticed. She was too busy guzzling sparkling cider and shoveling down huge forkfuls of pasta.

For the first time since Kyle let go of my arm, I smiled.

I rested my head on Michael's shoulder and watched Emmy and Josh sway softly together in their first dance as husband and wife. Josh wore an obviously rented tuxedo paired with black Birkenstocks. Yellow daisies adorned Emmy's hair; a simple, white satin dress swished above her knees. The tiny diamond on her finger couldn't compete with the sparkle of her smile. They looked right together; so right that I didn't even feel nauseated when Josh's beard brushed her cheek. I'd never seen a more beautiful couple.

I looked around the room and took stock of my new friends, just like I'd done that first evening at Eden. So much had changed since that night only two weeks ago.

Helen and Toni sat next to each other at the head table, whispering and smiling. The distance between them seemed to have evaporated. I met Helen's gaze and smiled. She nodded, then reached under the table and took Toni's hand. I had a feeling that their relationship wouldn't stay quiet much longer. That was a *good* thing.

Bruce sat nearby, sipping from a water glass and gazing affectionately at his daughter. I assumed he'd return to New York after the wedding, though he'd have to come back to Orcas eventually. He wasn't a suspect in Monica's murder anymore, but he still faced assault charges for drugging her.

At Emmy's request, I officially fired Dale so he could consult with Bruce's legal team. Bruce's Seattle-based attorneys had plenty of experience, but they lacked Dale's particular brand of homespun charm. Dale didn't want to take on another criminal case at first, but I eventually got him to agree: Bruce had suffered enough. Living with, loving, and losing Monica was ample punishment for three lifetimes. And I knew from experience: no one advocated for his charges—human or animal—quite like Dale.

Dale assured me that although Bruce might face some jail time, he would probably get off with a fine and probation, given the circumstances. The coroner's tox screen proved that Bruce had been telling the truth: he'd given Monica too little digoxin to cause her any long-term harm.

Cat Stevens gave way to "The Macarena," and guests flooded the makeshift dance floor, laughing and dancing in line. Dale sat on the sidelines, drinking champagne and tapping his toe to the music. Bandit lay on leash next to him, wiggling and obviously itching to cause trouble. Every time he stood to bark, Dale gave him a stern look and he dropped back to the ground. If anyone could train that little monster, it was Dale.

When Dale agreed to help Bruce, he demanded Bandit and a "big-assed donation" to Dale's Goat Rescue as payment. Dale claimed that he'd always wanted a Jack Russell terrier, but I suspected Bandit was simply another one of his rescues. Whatever the reason, I was glad. No one should have to live where they aren't wanted. As for my legal bills, Dale decided that I owed him free yoga for life. I sincerely hoped that he'd move back to Seattle some day and collect.

Jennifer walked up to the table, interrupting my visual eavesdropping.

"Are you guys having a good time?"

"Absolutely," Rene replied between mouthfuls. "I hope you don't like living here."

Jennifer looked confused. "Why not?"

Rene grinned. "Because I'm taking you back to Seattle. You'll be my personal chef." She pointed to her almost-empty plate. "The risotto was yummy. The spring rolls were even better. But I *cannot live* without this tomato gnocchi." She gazed longingly at the food table. "Is it true that everything's vegan?"

"Yes. Emmy insisted. It's her tribute to Kyle."

"Well," Rene said, "it's good anyway. I might have to go back for seconds."

"That would be thirds, Rene," I said dryly.

"Whatever." She waved her hand. "I'm eating for two, you know."

"You really *did* do a fantastic job making all of this food," I said to Jennifer. "You have a gift."

"Thanks." She leaned down and whispered. "You can't tell anyone, because Emmy and I are still working out the details. But she's going to open the restaurant again in a couple of weeks. She's making me head chef."

"That's wonderful!" I paused, confused. "But I thought Kyle owned Eden. What happens now that he's, you know, gone."

"Ownership reverts back to Emmy and Josh." Jennifer stood taller. She looked almost confident. "Now that I'm going to be part of the business, Emmy's been teaching me all about it. She's a heck of a lot smarter than people think. When she and Josh sold the restaurant to Kyle, she made sure that if anything happened to him, they would get it back."

I paused. "I've been afraid to ask Emmy this. Do you think the resort will survive?"

Jennifer nibbled at her lower lip. "You know, I do." She looked off to the side, as if trying to remember the details. "The original investors insisted that Emmy buy something called a 'key person' insurance policy. It covered Josh, Kyle, and Emmy. Since the police ruled Kyle's death an accident, it looks like it will pay out."

"Will it be enough?" I asked.

"Enough for now. They'll be able to fix the plumbing, at least. They won't be able to renovate any of the other buildings for awhile, but that's OK. I kind of like our funky cabins."

I smiled. "Me too."

Jennifer walked away, looking nothing like the grumpy yogini who had skulked in and out of my yoga classes. Her energy seemed lighter, as if her heart were more open. Her feet skipped lightly along the ground. She seemed … happy.

Emmy and Josh pressed a long-bladed knife through another of Jennifer's creations: a three-tiered coconut whipped cream cake covered in dusty pink rose petals.

Michael took my hand. "They look pretty good up there, don't they?"

I smiled. "Perfect."

He hesitated, seeming uncharacteristically timid. "Kate, I've been meaning to ask you something."

"Yes?"

"Well…" He cleared his throat, then quickly looked down at the ground.

He only paused for a few seconds. Not nearly enough time to process the thousands of thoughts, images, and emotions that coursed through me. I knew what Michael was about to ask; I'd known it for two weeks. I sat next to him, feeling like I might be sick.

Was marrying Michael the right choice?

How could anyone know what was "right" for the rest of her life, really?

I wanted a crystal ball. I wanted to look into the future and know, with absolute certainty, how my life would unfold. This grasping, this burning fear of uncertainty, tortured me.

Then I remembered the teachings.

According to yoga, each of us has infinite choices, countless possible pathways in life. The exact road we wander is largely irrelevant. How we relate to those choices; how we travel those pathways—that's what matters.

Sam and Rene held hands and giggled about babies. Emmy smeared petal-infused frosting across Josh's face. The four of them looked blissfully happy.

I, on the other hand, had been suffering for days. Suffering—like all forms of emotional decay—flourished only in darkness. In ignorance, ego, aversion, and fear.

It was time to find the light.

I still had major control issues, that much was certain. But if Bella could be trained to get over her fears, so could I. We'd call it the Kate Desensitization Project. Michael and I would start out slow and grow together. I'd give him some closet space, maybe his very own drawer. Given enough time, I might even get used to his toothpaste-encrusted toothbrush. We'd take a few more family vacations and figure out how to cohabit in peace. We wouldn't actually have to combine households until after the wedding.

The nausea in my belly morphed into bubbles of hope. This could work! People had long engagements all the time. Michael and I could wait years before we tied the knot. Plenty of time for me to overcome my neuroses. Plenty of time, for that matter, for Michael to develop better housekeeping skills.

I finally had my answer, and with surprising certainty. I wanted a future with Michael. I wanted to marry him. I squeezed his hand and smiled. Butterflies banged at the edges of my stomach.

Michael cleared his throat.

"Kate?" He paused again.

Yes?

"I think we should move in together."

My shocked mouth flew open. Then I closed it again.

Michael stared at me, his expression an irreconcilable fusion of hope and dread.

It's how we travel the pathways that matters, right?

I closed my eyes and took a deep breath. When I exhaled, I felt the butterflies flutter out of my stomach. I opened my mouth and sent my answer with them, before I had time to change my mind.

"OK, Michael, yes. We'll move in together. But I grew up in my house. It would break my heart to sell it."

Michael's entire body broke out in a smile. "I wouldn't want us to live anywhere else."

"And if this is going to work, you have to help do the dishes, whether you cook or not."

"Deal."

I flashed on that disgusting, flattened toothbrush, and shuddered. "And I don't care if it bankrupts us. We're adding another bathroom."

Michael's eyes sparkled; the creases surrounding them deepened. "Agreed." He reached out his hand. "Shake on it?"

I have a feeling my eyes sparkled, too. I grasped the front of his shirt, pulled him in close, and covered his lips with my own. Michael and I might not be getting married—yet—but no mere handshake would do. A deal this important should be sealed with a kiss.

THE END

© Jason Meert

ABOUT THE AUTHOR

Tracy Weber is a certified yoga teacher and the founder of Whole Life Yoga, an award-winning yoga studio in Seattle, where she currently lives with her husband, Marc, and German shepherd, Tasha. She loves sharing her passion for yoga and animals in any form possible. Tracy is a member of the Pacific Northwest Writers Association, Dog Writers Association of America, and Sisters in Crime. When she's not writing, she spends her time teaching yoga, walking Tasha, and sipping Blackthorn cider at her favorite ale house.

For more information, visit Tracy online at TracyWeberAuthor.com and WholeLifeYoga.com.

WWW.MIDNIGHTINKBOOKS.COM

From the gritty streets of New York City to sacred tombs in the Middle East, it's always midnight somewhere. Join us online at any hour for fresh new voices in mystery fiction.

At midnightinkbooks.com you'll also find our author blog, new and upcoming books, events, book club questions, excerpts, mystery resources, and more.

MIDNIGHT INK ORDERING INFORMATION

Order Online:

• Visit our website www.midnightinkbooks.com, select your books, and order them on our secure server.

Order by Phone:

• Call toll-free within the U.S. and Canada at
1-888-NITE-INK (1-888-648-3465)
• We accept VISA, MasterCard, and American Express

Order by Mail:

Send the full price of your order (MN residents add 6.875% sales tax) in U.S. funds, plus postage & handling to:

Midnight Ink
2143 Wooddale Drive
Woodbury, MN 55125-2989

Postage & Handling:

Standard (U.S. & Canada). If your order is:
$25.00 and under, add $4.00
$25.01 and over, FREE STANDARD SHIPPING

AK, HI, PR: $16.00 for one book plus $2.00 for each additional book.

International Orders (airmail only):
$16.00 for one book plus $3.00 for each additional book

Orders are processed within 12 business days. Please allow for normal shipping time.
Postage and handling rates subject to change.

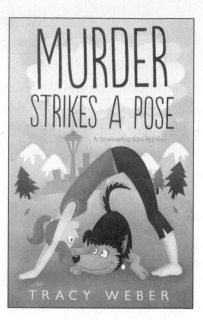

Murder Strikes a Pose
Tracy Weber

Yoga instructor Kate Davidson tries to live up to yoga's Zen-like expectations, but it's not easy while struggling to keep her small business afloat or dodging her best friend's matchmaking efforts.

When George, a homeless alcoholic, and his loud, horse-sized German shepherd, Bella, start hawking newspapers outside her studio, Kate attempts to convince them to leave. Instead, the three strike up an unlikely friendship.

Then Kate finds George's dead body. The police dismiss it as a drug-related street crime, but Kate knows he was no drug dealer. Now she must solve George's murder and find someone willing to adopt his intimidating companion before Bella is sent to the big dog park in the sky. With the murderer on her trail, Kate has to work fast or her next Corpse Pose may be for real.

978-0-7387-3968-7 $14.99